MIXTAPE 1986

EDITED BY

ALIN WALKER
MONICA LOUZON

Copyright © 2022 by The Dread Machine

Authors retain the rights to their contributions. No part of this anthology may be reproduced in any form without written permission from the author, except by reviewers, who may quote brief passages in a review. To request permission, please contact the publisher at info@thedreadmachine.com.

ISBN 978-0-9909100-2-2 (Hardback)

ISBN 978-0-9909100-4-6 (Paperback)

ISBN 978-0-9909100-3-9 (Epub)

Edited by Alin Walker & Monica Louzon

Cover by Luis Carlos Barragán

Interior by Martin Shannon

Published by The Dread Machine

43 Lexington Rd.

Avon, CT 06001

https://www.thedreadmachine.com

Printed and bound in the United States of America.

First printing March 2022.

*For our subscribers, Kickstarter backers, friends, and family.
We wouldn't be here without you.*

Content warnings can be found at the back of this book.

CONTENTS

INTRODUCTION
ALIN WALKER

I'll be honest—I didn't put a ton of strategic thought into this anthology's theme. I'm an '80s kid who, in the midst of the most terrifying year of my life, longed to return to a world I recognized. I needed to remember the way it felt to hop on my bike and go on adventures with my friends, to step into a neon-lit arcade with my pockets heavy with quarters, and to stay up all night playing Nintendo games on a tube TV in a shag-carpeted basement.

I needed to go home—just for a little while.

This anthology was my escape hatch. It pulled me through 2020, and I managed to acquire a co-editor and close friend along the way. While the stories in this book aren't meant to be comforting, we hope they provide you with a brief reprieve from the noise and chaos of the post-Internet, pandemic-stricken world.

All of the dread-filled tales in *Mixtape: 1986* were selected from a call for submissions we held from late 2020 through early 2021, and they each brought us back to the '80s in different ways.

Jonathan Duckworth's **"One of Those Nice Guys"** introduces us to a trucker just trying to do the right thing by helping out a vulnerable-looking girl he meets in a diner.

"Working the Graveyard Shift" by Eli Jones harkens back to Cold War paranoia. His story about a botched burglary is as riveting as it is humorous and unexpectedly heartwarming.

Ali Seay's **"Just Elaine"** perfectly captures '80s-era Ocean City (my co-editor Monica was *way* excited about this) and puts a new spin on family drama.

Edith Lockwood made us both cry with her story **"Derailed,"** which gives you an authentic taste of teenage love and retro amusement parks.

"The Neon Knight" by Andrew Punzo presents readers with the nerve-wracking anticipation that struck every arcade wizard when they encountered a brand new machine.

Amanda Cecelia Lang's **"Latchkey"** introduces us to a boy trying to navigate his new reality as a latchkey kid—and survive The Bad Things that pursue him at sunset.

"Dots and Dashes" by Shenoa Carroll-Bradd was the one exception to our "no time-travel" rule because it's too riveting to put down. (The second-person perspective provides a bit of *Choose Your Own Adventure* nostalgia, too!)

Keily Blair wowed us with **"The Day Caroline Bloomed,"** We love their portrayal of a trophy wife who's trying to reclaim agency over her future.

Speaking of regaining agency over one's future, **"Designs on Redemption"** by Chris DeStefano introduces us to a flawed fashion designer attending a coke-fueled yacht party during the days when the U.S. Flammable Fabrics Act was still a recent memory.

Kids on bikes facing grotesque monsters were very much a 1980s trope, and they feature prominently in **"Welcome to Camp Klehani"** by Caleb Stephens and in Brent Larson's **"The Angler."** Both stories contain truly unforgettable creatures and characters.

Would this even be an '80s collection without a demonic toy of some sort? Fret not: **"Jaws"** by Christopher O'Halloran checks that box. You'll never look at teddy bears the same way again.

Anyone who grew up in the '80s knows that bullying wasn't

taken very seriously, and kids were often expected to fend for themselves. Mark Towse reminds us in **"Brian"** that some victims aren't as vulnerable as they may look.

But not all bullies were found in schoolyards, were they? During the HIV/AIDS epidemic, families and entire towns turned against their own. **"And the Universe Went On"** by Jason Burnham is a remarkable story about estrangement and forgiveness that broke our hearts (in a good way).

"Every Day's a Party (With You)" by Christi Nogle explores what it means to be a mother, a daughter, a friend, and an individual. Who are we, really?

Throughout **"When the Streetlights Go Off,"** P.A. Cornell reminds readers that it's *never* a good idea to get drunk and explore an abandoned house.

We also made a *Mixtape*-themed mixtape! If you'd like some tunes to go along with your reading, check out our *Mixtape: 1986* Spotify playlist at https://www.thedreadmachine.com/playlists.

You never know what dreadful things are gonna happen next. So, buckle up (or don't—we're going back to a time before seatbelt laws), and let *The Dread Machine*'s first anthology distract you from the craziness of our real world with some things that will Definitely Not Happen To You!

Thank you so much for supporting writers, artists, and indie publishers!

ONE OF THOSE NICE GUYS
JONATHAN DUCKWORTH

K arl is finishing his chili when he notices the girl—ninety pounds of skin, bones, and dirty-blonde split ends in a grimy pink crop-top—trying to talk up the pair of bikers at the diner's counter.

"We ain't interested," one of the bikers says.

"Dumb skank must think we're congressmen or something," the other guffaws.

They laugh. The girl watches them mutely for a few seconds before turning away and shuffling down the counter to an empty stool. She's barefoot, her pink shirt pilled and grease-stained, her denim cutoffs faded almost white. Underneath the hem of her crop top, her ribs show like piano keys. This is a little truck stop in the long stretch of nothing—the Llano Estacado—that comes after Lubbock, Texas. She had to have hitchhiked here.

She's sixteen, maybe seventeen. The age Zadie would be now.

The waitress, a stocky woman built like a beetle, approaches her. "Babydoll, you need me to call somebody for you?"

The stare the girl turns on the waitress is so strange and impassive that the older woman—twice her size, easy—flinches back. "No," the girl says. She's got a scratchy voice, a smoker's voice.

The waitress doesn't press the issue and seems relieved when the girl turns from her.

But now the girl is looking at Karl, and Karl's eyes meet hers. Before he can even think of looking away, the girl is walking on her bare feet toward his booth.

"Hi," she says, sitting across from him.

"Hi," he says back. He reaches for his coffee mug, and even

though it's empty, he still tries for a sip, just so he's doing something.

"I need a ride."

She needs more than a ride. She needs shoes, a shower, a good meal. Well, he can give her one of those things.

"You hungry, kid?" Karl asks.

She smiles. For how dirty her face and hair are, her teeth are like brushed porcelain. "Sure, Mister, I could eat," she says. The way she trills the *Mister* makes Karl's skin crawl.

Karl orders her the same bowl of chili he just had and a small cup of coffee. As they wait for the order, the girl stares at Karl, not quite smiling, not quite making any expression, really. If he had to put an adjective to what her face is doing, it'd be *patient.*

One of the bikers points to Karl, and the two of them start sniggering. "You like your jailbait lean, huh, buddy?"

Karl doesn't say anything. He just fixes the biker with a withering stare. For maybe half a second, the two jokers eye him, size him up, but Karl's a big guy, and since he hasn't said anything, they turn back to whatever their own business is.

"What's jailbait, Mister?"

She asks it so innocently. How do you answer a question like that?

"What's your name, kid?"

"You can call me Liz."

You on any milk cartons, Liz?

"Short for Elizabeth?"

"No."

Silence.

There's that patient look again.

For the first time since noticing her, Karl starts to feel a glimmer of trepidation. Maybe it's the optics of a trucker sitting in a booth with a scrawny blonde teen. Maybe it's how quiet she is.

Or maybe it's how her baby-blue eyes don't reflect any light.

When the waitress arrives with the chili and cola for Liz and a coffee for Karl, he's relieved.

Liz doesn't touch the soda, but she sniffs the chili, her nose wrinkling like she's inhaled pure vinegar. Without even a glance at her silverware, Liz reaches her fingers into the steaming chili and plucks out a cube of chuck dripping with sauce. She brings it to her lips and pushes it past her teeth, her fingers and thumb disappearing behind her lips before reemerging. She swallows; no chewing. She repeats this with two more pieces before pushing the bowl away.

Skinny as she is, Karl would have figured she'd be hungrier. Unless she's on the rock—the sunken eyes, the slightly jaundiced skin, the avian slenderness of her frame all hint toward her being a junkie. Or unless she's sick with the virus.

"Too spicy?" he asks.

"Too tough," she says, crossing her arms over her chest. "And it's been dead too long. So how about that ride, Mister?"

"Where are your people, Liz?"

"All around, if you know where to look. Now, how about that ride?"

He should tell her no. Instead he asks, "Where are you headed?"

"Anyplace you're headed is fine."

A runaway for sure. Maybe he'll drop her off at the highway patrol station in Plains near the New Mexico state line. Not that he trusts highway cops to do right by a lost girl. Perverts, most of them.

Karl pays his check and then uses the toilet. She's waiting for him when he gets out—that is, she's standing right outside the bathroom door. When he leaves the diner, she follows him closely, never allowing more than a foot between them.

"You must be one of those nice guys I've heard about," Liz says.

He's got his misgivings, but what can he do? Leaving her in the diner would be worse than whatever risk he's taking by giving her a lift.

He'll take her to the next town before he gets onto 380. To Brownfield. Less than a half hour's drive, and then she'll be someone else's problem. Even that bothers him; a person shouldn't be thought of that way—as a problem. She's someone's daughter, or at least she was at some point.

Liz climbs into the passenger seat and buckles up. She looks tiny, like a bug in the seat's leather cushions. After pulling out from the diner and onto the road, the next few minutes are quiet, just the steady grumble of Karl's rig. It should be peaceful.

He can feel Liz watching him.

"How about some music?" Karl suggests. He puts in a tape before she can say anything.

The soothing warmth of Vivaldi's Spring plays through the speakers for only a few seconds before Liz jabs the eject button and yanks out the tape.

"Not a Vivaldi fan?" Karl forces a smile.

"It's unbearable. Just like every sound up here."

He decides not to ask; decides to let sleeping dogs lie and accept the uncomfortable silence.

Brownfield can't come soon enough.

A few minutes pass with Liz's watchful eyes never straying from Karl. Is it wariness? No, can't be that. Whatever Liz's deal is, she's definitely not afraid of him.

"So, uhh, where are you from?"

"Someplace you've never heard of."

"Small town?"

She doesn't answer. When Karl glances over at her, he notices something that makes his guts twist. Two huge lumps on either side of her throat, just below her jaw, are swelling. The sight pains him, sends him back to the hospital visits when Zadie was still fighting her losing fight, when Karl had a full head of hair, and when he and Mia still had every reason to be together.

Those last days were the worst. He still keeps the last crayon drawing Zadie made for him in the glovebox—Zadie as a monarch butterfly. On the reverse side of the drawing, in yellow crayon—so hard to read, in more ways than one—are Zadie's mathematical musings: *"Daddy told me 100 butterflies together weigh 1 ounce, and there's 16 ounces in a pound, and I'm 42 pounds, so I weigh the same as 67,200 butterflies! That's a lot of butterfly!"*

Just thinking about it brings tears to his eyes, but Karl doesn't cry. He can't bear to look at Liz right now. As bad as it was for Zadie, at least she had parents who held her hands until the end.

What does this poor kid have?

He wants to ask what's killing her, but he knows that's the last conversation a sick kid wants to have, so he lets the silence be.

Liz starts talking. "I love the fields of dry grass here, and the cracked earth warmed by a full day. This place used to be beautiful, before the roads, before the electric wires and their horrible hissing. Once, I could hear deep music from the cracks in the world, but not anymore. Now your wires run everywhere."

Karl looks at her. The swollen nodes in her throat are the size of plums. Her eyes are somehow more sunken and her lips pale, almost translucent. For the first time, he notices a scar running along her cheek from the corner of her lip—a hair-thin line.

"There's still beauty," she says, looking out the window at a skeletal row of cottonwoods and the big, star-dusted sky above them. "There's still so much beauty up here, but the music is gone. Even down below, it's gone. I'd need to go deeper than anything living ever has, deeper even than the great worms who thresh the crust and slumber in the lungs of the earth, to find it again."

Karl feels himself on the verge of tears. He doesn't understand what she's saying, but there's something in her voice—a haunted longing for what can't be. It hurts him, plucks a chord inside him whose tone he knows all too well.

"Why haven't you stopped the truck yet, Mister?" Liz's voice is sharp and scratchy again, the wistfulness gone.

Before he can answer, Liz's hand settles on his thigh. He almost starts out of surprise but manages to keep his hands steady on the wheel.

"Hey, kid, mind taking your hand off me?"

"Usually, by this point, they pull off to the side," Liz says.

He looks at her again. This kid who's flashing her strange perfect teeth at him, who's got her little hand on his jeans. All the pity he was feeling turns to something else, something he can't quite reckon.

"Usually, they'd have at least touched me by now. Brushed my wrist, pushed my hair away from my eyes, something like that."

Karl feels sick. He shakes his head, fighting off the revolting images her words conjure. "Kid, I don't know what kind of fucked up bastards have picked you up before, but I'm not—"

"You don't seem to want me," Liz says, tilting her head. "Not even a little. But you're not telling me anything either, so you must want to fuck me. It's always one way or the other with you truckers. Except when it's both."

"What are you talking about?"

He tries to push her hand away, but she manages to keep a hold of him—hell, her grip tightens, and he feels her fingertips pressing into the muscle and fat of his thigh.

"Some of them, they cry to me. They pick me up because they need someone to talk to about how shitty their lives are. It's pathetic. You people have no idea how much your tears *reek*. And self-pity ruins your flavor; it's like if you cured meat with alum."

"Kid—"

Her fingers dig deeper, and Karl almost drives the rig off the shoulder. The truck judders and rattles and bounces but he manages to get it back onto the lane, wincing.

"And then there's the ones who think they're heroes for picking up a little lost girl. They always leave me with the cops, always want to call my parents, and it's always an absolute fucking mess to get myself out of those revolting stations with their noisy ceiling lights and all the smells. I kill those ones as soon as I figure them out."

Karl's heart jackhammers against his ribcage. His lungs are burning. His gut knots. He wants to be somewhere else—anywhere else.

"Most of them just want to fuck me. I like those ones. They're simple, easy. They do most of my work for me. They take the truck off the road, drive it somewhere dark where no one will interrupt us. Sometimes they want me to suck their cock, and that's always fun. Hilarious, really, when they find out their mistake." She laughs, and there's a wet sloshing sound in her throat from where the nodes have expanded. She almost looks like a frog, a bubble in her throat as big as an orange.

"I don't, I don't want to—"

"I know you don't," Liz says. "I knew from the start. But you didn't start crying either, and I don't think you consider yourself as some kind of white knight. So what is it? Why'd you pick me up?"

"I—"

"Let me guess; you pitied me because I remind you of someone. Is that it?"

Karl keeps his eyes on the road—the strobing white lines are the only thing grounding him now, the only thing keeping him from shaking apart entirely—and watches Liz with his peripheral vision.

She doesn't look like Zadie. Not even a little bit. As far as personality goes, there's nothing in this strange, hellish teen that could ever imitate his sweet baby girl.

She digs her fingers into him again, and this time he knows she's broken not only the fabric of his jeans but also through his skin. "Tell me what it is."

"You looked like—" he starts but then whimpers from the pain.

Liz relaxes her grip. "Yes?"

"You looked like someone who hadn't been treated nice in a long time."

Liz lifts her hand from his jeans. He doesn't look down, but he feels blood pooling where her sharp nails cut him. "You're lying. What do you want from me? Everyone wants something—it's what gives you people your flavor."

He forces his eyes from the road, from the soothing, hypnotic lines illuminated by his headlights, and takes in her anger, her hunger, and emotions he knows he can't begin to comprehend.

"I don't want anything," he says. "I just want to get to the next truck stop, that's all. I swear on my daughter's soul."

Liz's expression cycles through a progression of moods—shock, then anger again, then a flat look of frustration—before she looks away as if she can't stand the sight of him.

"Pull over."

He hesitates.

Liz clamps her hand—her claw—on his knee. "I said pull over."

His arms are flabby, his legs two soggy noodles held together only by his jeans. Somehow, he manages to turn the wheel and pump the brakes. The rig rumbles off the asphalt and onto the uneven terrain of the Llano Estacado.

As the truck grinds to a halt, its headlights illuminate a swath of tall grass and scrub brush.

Karl expects Liz to order him out of the car, but instead, she flings her door open and almost tumbles headfirst onto the ground. She shambles, then trips, falling into the patch of dirt lit by the headlights. The engine is still on. She's in the truck's path.

He could run her over.

Instead, Karl watches as the bulge in her throat swells to obscene dimensions. Liz heaves and retches, and then—

The jet that sprays from her mouth is bright and yellow, almost neon. It sizzles and fizzes as it strikes the earth, the grass, and the greasewood shrubs. It withers and blackens what it touches. Stalks and branches shrivel, then dissolve entirely.

The way Liz buckles afterward and almost falls on her face invokes a powerful instinct in Karl, and before he knows what he's doing, he's out of the truck and limping toward her.

He's halfway to her when she throws her head up and hisses. Karl recoils, expecting to be sprayed with the same liquid that melted the greasewood shrub, but there's nothing but a blast of rotten meat breath. For an instant, her skin breaks along the scar, along its seams, and Karl glimpses her true face, the leathery dark scales and rows of teeth beneath her soft human veneer.

But then it's gone, and the same tired, sickly girl he first saw at the diner is looking up at him.

"Get back in your truck and get out of here," Liz growls. "Only a fool picks up strangers."

Karl obeys. He drives away, and it's only ten minutes later—after he's blasted past a weigh-in station and has the strobing lights of a highway patrolman on his tail—that he realizes he's been pushing his rig over 95 miles per hour.

Karl never picks up a stranger again, but he does watch them. He knows what to look for now.

In South Carolina, he notices another barefoot girl like Liz at a gas station, watching him and the other truckers filling up. In Arizona, it's a college-aged guy in a Sun Devils shirt who stinks of skunky weed and claims his car broke down, but Karl spots the narrow seam around the corners of his lips. In a diner in Pennsylvania—and this is the one that really keeps him up some nights—he sees a pair of highway patrolmen eating raw hamburger with their fingers, carefully stowing pinches of meat past their false teeth, into their true mouths.

ABOUT JONATHAN DUCKWORTH

Jonathan Louis Duckworth is a completely normal, entirely human person with the right number of heads and everything. He received his MFA from Florida International University. His work appears in *Pseudopod*, *Beneath Ceaseless Skies*, *Southwest Review*, *Tales to Terrify*, *Flash Fiction Online*, and elsewhere. He is a PhD student at University of North Texas.

WORKING THE GRAVEYARD SHIFT
ELI JONES

Meyer snubbed out his last cigarette, watching the house across the street. There wasn't another person or occupied car on the block, only a handful of porch lights reflecting off his rented Scout. Town was too small to bother with streetlights beyond those shining on the highway bypass. The neighbors were all asleep; the windows went dark half a pack ago. Meyer waited, fingers drumming arrhythmically on the steering wheel. Nothing seemed right with this job.

All of Central Oregon was on edge from arson threats and food poisonings—literal poison—springing up from that goddamn Bhagwan and his nut jobs out in Rajneeshpuram. Half the state troopers in Jefferson and Wasco counties were headed there tonight, some big dust-up. All part of the plan, Leyla'd said when she hired him.

Still. Should be some city police, neighborhood watch—something. He'd been sitting outside this house, watching, since sundown. Nearly midnight now and not one peep from a neighbor or concerned citizen; hell, not even a hassle from bored teenagers.

"You'll land in Redmond. We'll have a car waiting for you. Head north on the 97, take the bypass. You're looking for a total hickville place named Town." Leyla had run through her brief as if it were a boring part she was stuck playing in community theater. "The bypass cuts straight through Town, so don't worry about missing it. Can't miss the house either, big goddamn yellow monstrosity. Left at the stoplight—yeah, it's one stoplight—up the hill, the place'll jump out at you. You take the computer. Take any disk and tapes you find. Don't turn it on, and don't load any disks. You'll drive up the 97 and east on the 84, then fly out from Kennewick. Leave the computer in the car; I'll take it from there. Five thousand now, another ten upon delivery." The lack of specifics had bothered Meyer, that assumption of no issues with the police, with the residents of Town, with the homeowners.

The look the pockmarked kid at the rental agency had given him bothered him, too. "You're the fourth guy this month to fly in, pick up this here Scout, and say you'll drop it off in Kennewick," he told Meyer. "Fourth. It's like they got you all lined up, working in shifts. And every time, the Scout shows back up with maybe sixty miles on it—not a word from Kennewick." The kid shot him a look, one of those over-the-glasses, you-should-know-better looks.

"Yeah? I don't care." Meyer lit a cigarette then flicked the match, striking the kid's nametag. "Which means *you* don't care either, got it?"

Meyer did care. The whole thing ate at him on the drive up and through the hours of waiting.

The entire night was tense. He could feel it, smell it—like a big thunderstorm. Lightning, brush fires, flash floods—the air was thick with tragedy.

Time to move.

Gloves, black stocking cap, penlight, baton. Brown work pants, grey nylon windbreaker, and his black work boots. Of the whole outfit, they were the only things that belonged to Meyer, the only things not out of Goodwill, not disposable. His ex-wife had bought him the boots when he got the Hardaway Technologies night watchman job, back when Ford was getting sworn in and pardoning Nixon. He'd lost that job before Carter took the oath. Reagan sworn in twice, and still no gainful employment for Meyer—no wife, no house, no family. Just random stands with Leyla and the odd breaking and entering gig, some minor incarceration.

The driver's side door creaked when he opened it, a high-pitched, rusty whine. Still no lights.

The yellow house looked out of place, two stories with a high-peaked roof, four columns on the front porch, a front yard of large stones, pea gravel, cactus. This wasn't a poor neighborhood, but every other home on the street was single-story, ranch-style, with carports rather than garages and irrigation ditches cutting through the front lawns.

He ran across the street, quick and low, past the empty driveway, the two-car garage, and the carved wooden sign affixed to the wall next to the front door proclaiming the home the residence of Theodore and Cricket Hardaway.

Theodore Hardaway had been a figure at Hardaway Technologies back when Meyer worked security at the Hillsboro location. The head of Research & Development, a medical technologist with ideas for more compact artificial hearts, better prosthetic limbs, military man amplifiers. Now Hardaway was the bigwig in charge of the Bend plant, living in the ugliest house Meyer had ever seen in the armpit of the High Desert even though Hardaway Tech probably held nothing near the number of military contracts they'd had during Vietnam.

Slipping between the house and garage, Meyer vaulted over the wooden gate in a smooth arc, then went around the back, creeping close to the house until he came upon the basement window. Cardboard and cling wrap clutched the frame where someone had temporarily patched a broken pane.

Meyer hesitated. The first low rumble of thunder hammered through the silence. "You're the fourth one," the kid had said.

It was a short drop from the window to the enameled utility sink, with stairs off to his right. On the left stood a tall shelf laden with boxes of junk and old computer hardware. The place was huge, a cluttered mess. Maybe another time, Meyer would have riffled through the stacks to find something worth pawning, but tonight he didn't want to spend any more time in this house than he had to.

As he turned to move up the stairs, an electrical panel caught his eye. Then a second, then a third. Lots of juice for a family home.

Using his penlight, Meyer picked his way through the utility room to the kitchen, then the dining room. He paused again in the foyer. Carpeted stairs reached upward, probably to all the bedrooms.

Pictures lined the foyer wall: baby photos of young Teddy, school photos of the two girls, and graduation portrait for the eldest daughter, Justine. She stood a foot and a half from her father in cap and gown, the plastic smile on her face matching his. *Ricky would be around her age.*

Meyer hadn't spoken to his son in nearly a year, since his last three-month stint for breaking and entering. The kid said he didn't want to hear from him anymore. His ex picked up the money orders Meyer sent but never the phone. Meyer kept sending money but stopped calling. His son was probably better off without an absentee workaholic turned absentee jailbird. He didn't know whether Ricky graduated or dropped out. There were three thousand miles between them now, Ricky living with his mother in Fort Lauderdale.

Abandoning the foyer, Meyer turned down the hallway and passed the living room to slide open the faux-wood grain double doors into the office. Burnt orange carpet climbed halfway up the walls where it met dark wood paneling. Two bookcases on the side walls housed technical journals, Leon Uris, and vertically stacked photo albums. A large rolltop desk sat on the back wall, left open, beside a plain, extended workbench that took up the rest of the wall.

Meyer's penlight played over the desks. Computers and disk caddies covered the workbench—how helpful, when Leyla told him to take *the* computer. There were some odd stains on their wood surfaces, maybe some type of oil. Blood? Hard to tell with just a penlight.

Another computer, a VIC-20, sat inside the rolltop. Meyer quickly estimated the machine's weight versus that of the others on the workbench, then started unplugging the VIC-20's cables.

At first, it sounded like a car driving past the house; then he saw the lights cut through the windows, the unmistakable grating rattle of a garage door. *Shit.* He killed the penlight, tucking it into his waistband, drew the expandable baton. He didn't have a mask. *Have to count on looking generic enough—just another unemployed bum robbing to make ends meet.*

Three steps and he was at the doors to the office, sliding them almost shut, leaving a half-inch gap. He fought to keep his breathing steady, his pulse from racing, his head clear. Maybe it was just Theodore. That'd be easy enough. He'd talked his way out of crazier situations. But if it was the entire family? Hysteric children could spiral everything out of control. Meyer didn't want to use the baton. *Sometimes you need to have something in your hand to look intimidating.*

"Come on! I'm just gonna take a piss, alright? Jesus! You didn't stop the whole way here; I'm gonna burst." A young man's voice, whiny with the twang of an upper-middle-class dufus.

Meyer grimaced. Just the type to play hero; he'd probably have to use the baton after all.

"*Christ.* Fine. Just hurry, Carlo! No snooping around! I need your eyes on the basement door." It was a young woman, who muttered to herself as she approached the office. "Hell of a lookout."

Meyer pressed himself against the wall as she threw open the doors and marched straight to the workbench. She was tall, wearing running shoes and a sweatsuit, her hair tucked into a dark baseball cap, flashlight in hand. As she hunched over, flicking through the disks in one caddy, Meyer stepped away from the wall and slid the doors closed. No time to look for a latch.

"Hey," he said, not a whisper, but just loud enough to get her attention.

The woman spun, flashlight arcing up to shine in Meyer's direction. Her free hand streaked to her waistband, coming up with a chrome-plated, snub-nosed revolver. *Wonderful.*

"Jesus Goddamn Christ!" she yelled. Meyer dropped his baton. Not such an intimidating item now. "Who the hell are you?"

"Looks like I'm here for the same thing you are," he said, trying to keep his tone friendly. "I was first, though."

"Yeah, well, I live here, asshole," she said. "And you're more like the fourth. I shoulda guessed someone'd be in here after I saw that shitty Scout outside. You commies never learn."

"Oh, I'm no commie." Meyer kept his hands up, fingers splayed, projecting calm. His willingness to talk rather than shoot, hit, or restrain had gotten him bounced from his Hardaway Technology job, but here, it might keep him alive. "I'm a red-blooded American businessman, enjoying the fruits of Reaganomics."

She snorted. "Pretty glib for a thief."

"Pretty sneaky for someone who lives here, Justine."

"Okay. I used to." Holding the flashlight and revolver steady, she glanced over at the rolltop. Meyer kept his hands up. "You were taking the Vic?"

"Computers are hot commodities, now. Soon, everybody'll have one." He lowered his hands. "You taking some disks? Mad at your father?"

"Stepfather. Nothing concerning you." Not just estrangement, palpable hatred colored her words. *Christ, does Ricky sound like that when talking about me? Does he think about me at all?*

Justine exhaled. The flashlight stayed put, but the revolver dropped to her side. "So, you're really not with the others? Just who the hell are you, then?"

"I'm just here to take a computer—not to get shot, not to hurt anyone."

"But the Scout—"

"What about it? I take things. You wanna think it's part of a conspiracy of commie thieves, fine. I see a four-by-four with the keys in, I take it. Don't mean anything."

Uncocking the hammer, Justine tucked the revolver back into her waistband. "You know what? Fine." She stepped to the side, over by the workbench, and hefted a disk caddy under one arm. "Go ahead. The Vic's all yours."

Meyer reached behind his back, slid the office doors open. "Thanks, but I—" He stopped, noticing the light flooding to the office from the hallway as a door opened and closed. "Friends of yours?"

Justine cursed and dropped the caddy back on the workbench. As she sprinted to the door, Meyer stepped to the side, slid down the wall, and finished unplugging the Vic. On a whim, he flipped open the dropped caddy on the workbench and shoveled disks into the pockets of his windbreaker.

"Carlo!" Justine whisper-shouted into the hallway. "Goddamn it, stop snooping around." A series of footsteps echoed, coming up from the basement, then a choked cry followed by loud thump, a wet squelch, and a low, synthesized growl. "Carlo?"

Meyer lunged toward the office doors, grabbing Justine by the shoulders and pulling her back. He slammed them closed and thumbed the catch, latching the two doors together. "Just what the hell was that?"

The revolver was back in Justine's hand, trembling this time. "I told you not to snoop. I told you to stay in the car. Damn it, Carlo. I warned him."

"Hey," Meyer said, his tone sharp. "Either get it together or put down the gun. And maybe tell me what's going on?".

Justine took three deep breaths, closed her eyes. "Theodore's pet project—man amplification, only without the man. It was some idea for the Army. 'Just need a body,' he said. 'Can't defeat what you can't kill.'"

"What, like zombies?"

"Remote-controlled zombies. It started with the dogs. The neighbors' dogs kept going missing. I was home for the holidays for that first break-in. Theodore surprised the guy, hit him over the head." She paused, shivering. "He said it didn't concern the police—that he could make security guards for the house. The first zombie stopped the second and third attempts."

"How clever are they?" Meyer said. 'Attack on sight' didn't seem safe in a house filled with family, although Theodore seemed uninterested in familial well-being. A thought poked Meyer's brain. "Is Theodore here? Are they controlled locally?"

"It's all automated," Justine said. "He's got some computers set up in the house, running the code for a patrol. It's a wireless system, Mom said. Something Hardaway Technologies worked up with the military. Like a radio." She shrugged. "Probably hasn't looked at them in a week. 'Set it and forget it' is Theodore's parental style."

"You sure seem to know a lot about this."

Justine's left hand clenched, unclenched. "It's what I got from Mom. She's useless, won't tell anyone else. I tried to tell the police, but the ones in this stupid hick town are on Hardaway payroll. I've got to go to the media. It's the only way."

Slow, heavy footsteps thumped down the hall. More than a single set. One sounded like they were heading upstairs. "Well, we need to get out of here. Get your friend, too. Anyone else you know in the house?"

Justine shook her head. "No. We have to get Carlo to the car in the garage. They shouldn't follow us out there."

"Yeah," Meyer said. "Shouldn't." He pulled out his baton, for all the good it would do against the dead. One pair of footsteps shuffled by just outside the door. "How decent a shot are you?"

She stopped shaking, flashed a grin, looking every inch a kid. "High score on *Hogan's Alley* down at Rudolpho's good enough?"

Meyer unlatched the door. "I have no idea what that means," he said. "Start blasting." He threw the doors open, immediately pressing up against the wall.

The form in the doorway was man-shaped, six-foot if an inch, with a panel of lights and a camera lens on the chest. Wires embedded in the skin traveled up and down the arms, in the neck, into the scalp. The skin hung limp, grey, the eye sockets empty. Two bullets rocked the head backward, snapping the neck. The thing's head lolled to one side, but the zombie kept moving. Two more shots staggered the monster until the fifth and final bullet penetrated the panel of lights. Arcs of electricity crackled up and over the wires, and the smell of burning, rotten flesh filled Meyer's nose. He fought the urge to vomit.

Justine wrapped her arm around her face, her cheeks green, her voice muffled. "One shot left."

Meyer looked out the doorway. Nothing else in the hallway. He stepped out, clean air filling his lungs. Not that it would be clean for long with the body still smoldering in the office. "Alright, at least one more is upstairs. Let's grab your friend and go."

Justine moved out of the office, closed the door, then coughed twice. "Check the living room," she ordered. "I'll look in the kitchen."

The living room was clear, with two couches and a TV cabinet, its hi-fi in a wall unit. Meyer noticed a liquor cabinet and considered taking a shot—or more—from the whiskey bottle.

Zombies. Soldiers who could be hot-wired after getting chewed up and spit out, who could fight battles until the end of time. An endless army. The madness of it. The inhumanity.

Meyer ducked out of the living room and walked to the kitchen. Justine knelt on the tile, cradling the head of an unconscious young man, his breath ragged. "He's alive," she said, "but I think his skull is fractured. Shit, there's so much blood."

Meyer threw open drawers until he found some kitchen towels and handed them to Justine. "Hold this to his head. You think his neck's okay? Let's get him to the car."

This was survival mode thinking: work together, get out alive. Leyla could piss up a rope regarding this job. Meyer took a deep breath and reset his grip on Carlo's knees, tucking the young man's ankles under Meyer's own armpits. He didn't realize how out of shape he'd become. Probably just nerves—jacked the heart rate, made it hard to breathe properly.

They were just in the garage, Meyer stepping down to the concrete floor, when he felt a clammy hand grab the back of his neck and yank. He dropped Carlo's legs, more out of surprise than any instinct. Justine stumbled backward, falling to a sitting position, her back slamming the front bumper of the car—hard. Her body protected Carlo's head from another impact, but his dead weight pinned her down.

"You asshole," she yelled, then froze as she saw what gripped Meyer.

Meyer wriggled out of the monster's grasp but stumbled over Carlo's legs. The second zombie, as tall as the first but sporting wires wrapped around exposed bone, snatched Meyer's left leg and pulled him across the floor. Meyer's hands slapped uselessly against the cement. He screamed as the walking corpse hoisted him over its head.

Meyer scrabbled at the top of the door frame, wriggling his body, trying to unbalance his attacker and escape its iron grip. He heard wood crack, the whine of the nails coming loose, then the ringing report of a gunshot reverberating in the garage and out into the night air.

The zombie staggered, sparks flying from the control box penetrated by Justine's final round. Meyer released the door frame and dropped onto the monster, sending both of them to the ground. There was a searing, sharp pain in his right side—a flash of intense heat as his torso hit the control box. He rolled off the zombie before his windbreaker could catch fire. Green smoke filled the air, the rancid odor again, but worse because of this creature's more decayed state.

"*Hogan's Alley?*" Meyer asked. It hurt to breathe, hurt to move, hurt to lie still. He'd need a hospital bed next to Carlo at this point.

"I put a semester's tuition into that machine," Justine said. "Glad to see it paid off."

Meyer rolled to a seated position. He put his hand in the windbreaker's pocket, touched the mangled disks inside. Not that he counted on Leyla coming through this time. She'd sent three other men to a premature death and unnatural afterlife. At least he had the five grand initial payment.

"These freaks were in the basement?" he said after a moment, nodding at the smoking corpse.

Justine nodded. "Yeah. There's a secured door. Theodore's little workshop. He usually keeps them there, but he must have some system set up to release them when the alarm is triggered. Now, grab Carlo's legs. We can get him in the car and get both of you to the hospital. Your color's not so good."

Grabbing the doorknob, Meyer pulled himself up. "This has to be stopped, you know. That workshop is probably where he keeps the disks you and I were after." He groaned, staggering into the house. "I think I wanna smash it all."

"Wait, dammit, help me with—shit!" Justine roared, struggling to wriggle out from under Carlo's unconscious body as Meyer ducked back inside.

Stumbling down the last of the steps, Meyer looked into the workshop through the open door. He saw more of the room from this angle than he had when he first entered. A tall shelf divided the room in half. Tucked behind the shelf, a door stood open, revealing another room lit in dim green hues. *Theodore's little workshop.*

Meyer slipped into the room. Four computer displays took up most of a desk on the other side—one running code Meyer didn't understand, two showing static, and the last one a blurry, jerking feed moving around the kitchen—the third zombie's chest camera.

On the table next to the displays, Meyer saw three piles of stacked bills, identical to the five stacks he'd received from Leyla. One pile of twenty thousand, one of fifteen, one of ten. Forty-five thousand dollars—the initial payment the three dead bastards had received. His five thousand felt paltry. Left over. The sum you'd pay a slob like Meyer when the money started running out.

"Screw you, Leyla," Meyer muttered as he shoved the bills into an empty box. Fifty thousand seemed right to him.

"Hey, jerk-off. Thanks for the help." He looked up when he heard Justine's voice on the stairway, then glanced at the third zombie's video feed. Still blurry, it showed the basement stairway—and the back of a young woman, running shoes, sweatsuit, hair tucked into a baseball cap, now-empty gun in her waistband.

"Behind you, Justine!" Meyer shouted. There was a solid *thwack* and Justine tumbled down the stairs.

The zombie was quick, dropping to the basement floor before Meyer could get halfway across the room. He watched Justine suck in a breath, try to get up, make it to her knees. This zombie must have been Leyla's first man, Theodore's prototype. It had an exposed skull and thin strips of ligaments and muscles visible under paper-thin skin. The control box was larger, cruder than the others, with more wires jabbing into the creature's body.

Meyer scanned the room, looking for anything he could use to delay the oncoming horror. The three electrical panels caught his eye. *Lots of juice for a family home.*

It was a longshot. His only shot.

Meyer rushed past the zombie to the panels, flinging them open and tripping the breakers in a barely-controlled panic. The zombie turned and lurched toward him.

"No!" Justine shouted, launching herself onto the thing's back. Meyer hesitated as the monster swung one of its long arms, twisted its body, sent her flying into the tall shelf. It crashed to the floor in a deafening racket. The zombie turned back to Justine.

"I'm fine!" Justine yelled, raising a hand above the pile of tools, cords, circuit boards, and other junk she was buried under.

Meyer went back to flipping breakers like a madman. The basement went dark halfway down the second panel, but Meyer continued until he reached the last breaker on the third box.

The zombie twitched, spasms turning it around, its control box buzzing. Cut off from the computers, it walked forward aimlessly, banging into the utility sink over and over. Moonlight streamed in through the paneless window. The monster looked pathetic now, stuck in a looped command.

Meyer smashed the back of its head in with his baton until its brains spilled out into the massive sink. He continued to strike, busting the chestplate on the enameled edge. *What kind of monster turns this thing on his kid?* He flipped the whole putrid mass into the basin and turned the taps. The electronic components sparked and shorted as the spigot spat out rust-colored water. The lights on the zombie's control panel flickered and died.

They ransacked the workshop, moving fast. What equipment Meyer couldn't destroy, they loaded into the passenger seat of Justine's car. Stacks of disks piled on the floorboards. Carlo awake in the backseat but in need of some stitches.

Meyer handed Justine a stack of bills—ten thousand dollars. No reason to be greedy. Forty thousand was just fine.

"What's this?" she said.

"Reward." Meyer shrugged. "More quarters. Dirty commie money. Tuition."

Justine smiled. "Pretty generous for a thief."

"Pretty brave for a kid who just blew up her inheritance."

"Theodore's gonna leave everything to Hardaway Tech anyway." The smile shrank. "Truth is, we didn't have a father. Not really."

"Maybe it's better that way," Meyer said. "Maybe you're better off."

"A shit dad who tries is better than nothing. We needed him, and now...I think he needed us, too."

"Can we *go*?" Carlo whined.

"Good luck with everything, kid," Meyer said. He turned to leave.

"You know," Justine said, opening her driver's side door. "I still don't know who you are."

"Don't care," Meyer said, jogging to the Scout. Faint sirens were in the wind, getting closer. "Which means *you* don't care, got it?"

Both cars were on the bypass before the flashing police lights splashed against the house.

It was still early morning when Meyer returned the Scout to the rental agency in Redmond.

"Thought this was going to Kennewick," the clerk said, an older woman.

"Change of plans," Meyer said. "I need another vehicle—better gas mileage, that kind of thing. Long road trip."

"I see," the clerk said, paging through a stack of forms. "And where are you planning to drop the vehicle off?"

"Fort Lauderdale."

ABOUT ELI JONES

Eli Jones is a data analyst and speculative fiction writer. When he's not writing, you can find him shouting at computers, filling 10×10 rooms with orcs and pie, and wondering what being old feels like. He lives in the Cascadia Bioregion with his wife and two children.

JUST ELAINE
ALI SEAY

"Go on," my mother says. She has a beer in one hand and a cigarette in the other. I know my parents are dying for me to go off down the boardwalk—which I've never been allowed to do before—so they can screw.

She gives me little playful flips of the hand as if to shoo me away.

"But—"

She looks momentarily sympathetic. "Elaine, I know it will be weird without..."

"Bevvie," I say. I won't let her trail off.

"I know it will be weird. It's usually the two of you."

The two of us. Side by side. Always together. And now I'm supposed to go into the yawning purple night alone, crushed in by the roar of the ocean, blinded by the bright flashing lights, my ears ringing with the distant sound of games in the arcade.

The boardwalk.

Alone.

At night.

I've never done this before, and I mostly don't want to.

My mother shakes her head. She fishes in her jean pocket and pulls out a handful of silver. Quarters. She puts them into my hand forcefully. "You can have fun," she says. "Maybe you'll meet some kids."

My limbs are heavy with weariness. I just want to go into my room and read a book. Be alone. I'll put my Walkman on, turn up Bon Jovi. They can screw; I don't care. I just don't want to leave.

"It's important for you to learn to be on your own, Elaine."

I scratch the itch beneath my arm and swallow hard to push back tears. "Okay." My words are lost under the sound of the ocean outside our rented condo, but she must sense my defeat. "When can I come back?" What a stupid thing to have to ask. How embarrassing.

"Not for two hours. I want you to try." She bends over then, hands on my shoulders, and says, "I know this is hard. It's our first vacation without her, and I know you miss her being with you all the time. I know you miss talking to her, but your sister is always with you in spirit. You know that."

I look away. Now I'm dying to go because I don't want to have this conversation. They ruined my life, her and Dad did. Because of them, I lost Bevvie. "I'll be back," I say. I hurry off into the night.

It's only dark for about a block, until the rental condos give way to the eateries and shops along the boardwalk. "I wish you were holding my hand," I say aloud. "I wish we were running together."

I wander up to the pizza place and order a slice of cheese.

"I'd peg you for a pepperoni girl," the guy behind the counter says, being friendly.

"That was my sister. She liked pepperoni."

"Was?"

He's an older man with a big beer belly, five o'clock shadow, a friendly smile. I recognize him. We've been vacationing here for as long as I can remember. I wonder if *Sal's* is his place or if he just works here.

"Yes. She's not here," I say, bowing my head. I don't want to talk about it.

"Soda?" he asks.

"Coke."

I feel him studying me, like he's trying to place me, as he draws my drink from the fountain machine. I pay him, grab my greasy paper plate and waxed cup, and scurry to a vacant bench outside before anyone else can take it.

I watch the people.

That was our favorite thing to do together at the ocean. Watch the characters go by. Couples, kids, teenagers acting up. Bevvie and

I knew what it was like to be watched, and we liked to take our turn.

A kid flies by on his skateboard. He's got a huge boombox on his shoulder, blasting The Beastie Boys. I sing along in my head for a moment. If my parents knew I even knew who The Beastie Boys were, they'd have a cow.

Everything used to make our parents have a cow.

A woman passes in front of me, way too close. She's sucking on what looks like a cocktail straw on fire, but then I realize it's one of those thin cigarettes. I've seen billboards for them. Marketed to women. Weird.

When she passes along with her whining brood of children, I see him. My heart does a little kick in my chest.

He's perched on the boardwalk railing at the top of the steps leading down to the beach. His arms are crossed over his Vans t-shirt, and his hair is buzzed close on the sides. The front is longer, blond, and falls across his brow.

My heart kicks again.

He's watching me. Still.

I wolf down the last half of my slice. Nerves. But also, part of me thinks if I eat as if he isn't watching, the boy will be disgusted and turn away from me. That he'll wander off into the night to find a normal girl. A pretty girl.

When I look up, he's still watching. I'm still nervous.

Whistles, bells, melodies, and cheers—the sounds and flashing lights of the arcade call to me. I get up, dump my trash, and dust my hands on my jeans before ducking into the glowing womb of game-play. I leave the boy out there to realize there are more appealing fish in the sea.

I feed quarters into the Skee-Ball machine. There's a loud clunk, and the wooden balls roll down into the dispenser. I concentrate on each shot, hitting 20, 40, 100. No one pays attention to me.

I score 100 again on my final ball. I want to turn to my sister and cheer. I want her to squeeze my hand. Instead, I look around and see all the people there with someone else—families, groups of friends, a few couples taking their eyes off one another just long enough to play *Pac-Man* or *Donkey Kong*.

I feel a burning along my skin, along my rib cage—an ache. I ignore it.

I feed more quarters into the machine and watch the reddish-brown balls come rolling down the chute to me. Skee-Ball has always been my favorite. Bevvie favored The Claw Machine. She liked to watch as I piloted the claw to all the colorful prizes. We had a special shelf for my few winnings at home.

My neck tingles, and I know I'm being watched. I turn around fast and nearly collide with him—the Vans t-shirt boy. He gives me a crooked smile that makes me think of the sappy teen movies all about discovering who you are, being true to yourself, and finding that first passionate love.

I love those movies, but I hate them too. I'll never have a reddish-blond bob, a crooked smile, a dorky but fun admirer, or the rich boy who's willing to go against it all to be with me.

I'm just Elaine.

No longer even Elaine and Beverly. Just Elaine.

"You're really good, you know?" he says, shoving his hands into the pockets of his Jams. They have random geometric shapes on them. The hair on the back of his forearms is so pale it's like corn silk. He's tan. He smells like coconuts.

I have no idea how to talk to boys. No boy has ever talked to me. "Thanks," I blurt.

I turn fast to get a ball, breaking the spell the fairy tale prince pretty boy has on me. I wince when a lancet of pain sears my torso.

"Can you teach me?"

I laugh. "No."

"Why not?" He leans closer and I get the scent of dryer sheets and cologne. Is he my age? Older? I'd guess sixteen.

I want him to come closer and I want him to leave. He touches my arm and I jump. He raises his hands like he's under arrest. "Sorry."

I shake my head. This is a bad thing. A very bad thing. He should leave me alone. I should be alone.

I toss another ball. It hops into the 100 circle.

He laughs. "Look at you go!"

Nerves have gotten the better of me, so I focus as hard as I can, let the ball roll off my fingertips, up the incline, rumbling noisily and then pop!—into the 100 circle again.

"Wow!"

I shake my head, scratch my side, sigh.

"I'm Rick. And you are?"

I want to say "busy" or "taken" or "not interested" glibly—any of the things the heroines of those sappy movies would say—but I'm not glib or clever or pert. I'm just me.

"Elaine," I say.

"Alone?"

I think about saying no, but I don't. "Yes. Just playing for a bit. Then I'm going home."

"Oh, come on," he says, giving me that half-smile. It makes my stomach tingle, and I feel like I'm falling though I'm not.

I don't say anything, so he keeps going. "It's Friday night! In Ocean City! You're out on the boardwalk alone. And you met me. You don't want to go home."

I look at him—really look at him. What does he want with me?

I want to be excited and tingly and giddy. Instead, I feel a sense of plodding dread. He should go. I should go.

Someone should go.

I can smell fried dough and popcorn and the sweet reek of cotton candy. My stomach turns, and my skin burns. I scratch it and try to move past him.

He grabs my arm.

I freeze.

He isn't hurting me, just holding me, and it dawns on me that besides Mom and Dad and Beverly—and doctors, of course—not many people touch me. He's the first stranger to do so in a very long time.

I feel his touch like it curls through me. Down into my center. Like a fire warming me, a lightning strike. I catch my breath and try to block out the fear.

"Come with me," he says.

"Where?"

He grins. He's pleased. I can tell that getting me to go somewhere with him makes him happy. It makes me feel something, too. A new sensation.

Power.

"Just off the boardwalk, they have an oddities tent."

"Oddities?"

"Freaks. Geeks. Weirdos. Gross stuff. Most of it's probably fake, but—" he shrugs. "Ya never know."

"Sure." I feel sick. Gawking at people who are less fortunate? Different? Even if most of it is fake, what about the ones who aren't? "I don't think—"

He raises a hand to silence me—to plead his case—and I let him interrupt.

"If they are real freaks, then this is the only job they can really get, you know?" He rushes on, seeing he has my attention. "And you'll actually be supporting freaks. Where else could they work? But in this environment, they have family, and they get money."

I stare at him, unsure of what to say. Finally, my mouth decides. "How old are you?"

"Seventeen. Why?"

"I'm fourteen," I say. I go back to the Skee-Ball, proud of myself that I found an out. He won't want me. I'm too young.

He's not leaving. He's standing there, smiling at me. "So?"

"So, what?"

"Exactly."

I toss the ball and hit a 40. The ball jumped at the last minute. "Bogus," I mutter.

He takes the last ball from my hand, tosses it, and it gutters. No points.

I sigh.

He sighs too, but then he laughs and takes my hand. "Come with me. Let's go."

"Go?"

"To see if the rumors are true."

A whisper creeps up my spine, tickling the fine hairs inside my ear. *Go. Go. Fuck it. Go and do it...*

I try to ignore it, but his thick fingers curl around my wrist. I feel a flare of desire. A thick cloud of teen lust engulfs the rational part of my brain.

"Why me?" I blurt.

"Why not you?"

I stare at him. Confused.

"You're pretty," he finally says. So softly that over the bells and whistles and growing throng of kids in the arcade, I almost can't hear him.

But I do, and my mind is made up.

"Let's go."

———

It's strange stepping down out of the bright cacophony of the boardwalk. If you exit to the beach, the transition is gradual. Smooth. The lights and sounds fade as you distance yourself. But when you exit the boardwalk to the street on the opposite side, the world quickly goes quiet, dark, and strange.

We head toward the residential section instead of toward the hot spots.

Have I made a mistake? Is he luring me away? Should I be afraid of him?

Of course not.

The world was better with my sister by my side. Safer. Saner. I was the follower; she was the leader. My mother always laughed when I said that. "How could Bevvie possibly be the leader?"

He tugs me gently down a street. The sign hangs askew. I can't read it in the darkness.

There are pine trees, towering and whispering above trailers. This is the place my folks have joked about—the people who have "summer homes" here. Instead of having the money to rent a condo, they keep a trailer.

Tin cans in the trees, my father jokes. I don't think it's funny. I think it's mean.

Be brave, Elaine.

I squeeze his hand. He squeezes back.

There's that rush of power again.

There's a light ahead. It's a double-wide, and someone has hung a sign out front.

FREAKS

GEEKS

SEVEN DAYS A WEEK

Somewhere in the trailer park, someone is blaring "Don't Dream It's Over," and I start to hum, feeling very much like I'm in a dream myself. Alone—or as alone as I can get, I guess—with a boy. Off the boardwalk. At a place I should never be, not in a million years.

There's a bald woman smoking a cigar sitting on a folding chair at the entrance. In the soft light shining from the doorway, I see her tattoos—demons and devils, mermaids, UFOs, something that looks a bit like a spider and a bear had a baby. She squints against her smoke and says, "Two bucks."

I pat my pocket, feeling the dull clinking heft of quarters, but Rick plunges a hand into his board shorts and comes out with two crumpled bills. He thrusts them at the gatekeeper and puts a hand on my lower back.

I am suddenly hungry. From head to toe. Hungry for what exactly, I don't know, but it's there—a throbbing, desperate hunger.

We step inside the double-wide, and dead ahead is a neon sign. *ESP Psychic Readings.* I have an urge to flee, but Rick ushers me into a room to the left. Lava lamps illuminate the room, painting the wood-paneled walls with ambient colors—glowing blobs of green and blue, hot pink and molten yellow. I squint into the gloom and see a woman.

She licks her lips. Her tongue lengthens until it practically touches her eyeballs, and I flinch.

Behind me, Rick chuckles.

"Behold," the barker crows, seeming to materialize from a dark corner of the room. "The Lizard Woman. She's nimble, she's quick, she's a reptilian lunatic!" He cackles as if he's just made up the most delicious rhyme.

I cringe.

The Lizard Woman looks bored and put upon. Her skin looks like it's a mottled grayish-green. The colored lights don't help. She looks like she's got scales in places and makeup to accent them. Her eyes bulge a bit, and her tongue darts out again. It's forked and looks dry. I bet if I touched it, it would feel like sandpaper.

She licks her eyelid again, and when I gape, she grins at me.

"Move along, move along," urges the barker. "The tallest man in the world awaits you in the next room!"

I doubt he's the tallest man in the world, but the "tallest man" is pretty damn tall. Next to me, hand on my waist now, Rick gives a low whistle. "He is a big one, isn't he?"

"Yes," I whisper.

The man's face is gaunt, and he also looks bored. He's in short pants. Probably because he's too tall for regular clothes, but maybe so the customer can confirm that his legs are actually his.

I want to say, "I'm sorry," to this man. I'm sorry you're here. I'm sorry you're bored. I'm sorry you look sad. I'm sorry you're too tall for normal pants.

I'm sorry we paid money to stare at you.

"Brandy and Candy are in the next room," the tallest man in the world says, his voice deep. It rumbles up out of him, startling me. "Two tighter sisters, you'll never see!"

Rick takes the opportunity to put his whole arm around my waist.

My stomach drops. I let Rick lead me, though. I can't just stand here forever, staring at this giant man.

The sisters sit on a loveseat together, wearing matching dresses —or should I say *dress*. Someone had to modify it to fit their torso, and make the skirt wide enough for their four legs. They only have two arms, though. Their heads don't quite line up. The girl on the right, whose neck is twisted, looks a bit dimmer in the eyes than her sister, who stares at me.

What is it my mother has been muttering my whole life? *There but for the grace of God go I...*

I don't believe in God. Especially not after the way I lost Bevvie. If you saw Brandy and Candy, you wouldn't believe in God either—not unless He's a cruel and inhuman Creator.

"Hi there," the sister on the left says. "I'm Brandy and this is Candy, and it's not nearly as bad as it looks."

"Jesus," Rick says. "This is fucking weird. Gross."

They're people. They are humans. I want to punch him. Instead, I nod and say to Brandy, "I'm sure."

She cocks her head, which tugs on Candy. She seems confused that I've addressed her. Do people just file through? Stare? Make them feel like shit? Is it worth whatever their cut of the dollar admission fee is?

Probably.

People don't realize how much their intrusive gaze can penetrate and wound already tender flesh.

"Nice to meet you," I manage.

Rick is staring at me. "You're talking to it?"

I glare at him, but Brandy just laughs. "It's nice to meet you, too, dear. Most people think I feed my sister dead fish and rotten meat." Her clever eyes dart to Rick and then dance back to me. "But we're not monsters. We eat just like everyone else. Some of Candy's diet is a little different. She needs more protein. More iron."

Candy offers me a slobbery smile, and I smile back. Like her sister, she offers me a playful wink.

Rick groans and says, "This is weird. Let's just go. Can we leave now?"

"You'll do just fine," Brandy says, looking me in the eye. Candy grunts in agreement.

I nod. I feel warmed by this. Comforted. Understood. "Good luck."

"You, too, darling."

Rick and I file out of the room. I don't want to be with him anymore. I don't want to be here anymore, either. I push past the other rooms to the exit. He follows.

Outside in the dark, salt-tinged night, I bend over, hands on knees, and catch my breath. I turn and head toward the boardwalk. I'm crying. When did that happen?

"Hey!" Rick shouts. "Where are you going?" He's running to catch up with me.

I shove my hands in my pockets to keep myself in check. I can hear the music from the boardwalk. Peter Gabriel is belting out "Sledgehammer." I'm pissed. Furious.

Rick grabs my arm, and all my hopes of calming down flee.

"Hey, I'm talking to you," he snaps. "You're just gonna leave?"

"Yeah," I say.

"Who said you could do that?"

"I did," I snarl. My temper. There it is.

He laughs. He thinks I'm being funny.

"I thought we'd take a walk on the beach. Be romantic." He grins at me, turning the charm back on. "Maybe more."

I stare at him, dumbstruck. "No."

"No?" He laughs again and grabs my wrist.

I dart away.

"What the fuck?" he says.

"That's what I want to know," I say. I turn and start walking, but he's right behind me, so I break into a run, racing toward the boardwalk with him on my tail. I'm almost to the ramp leading to the back of the fry shack. I'm so close when I trip on a random piece of lumber and go down. Hard. The knees of my jeans blow out instantly. I can feel blood and gravel, sand and wetness on my knees.

He's laughing again.

"Poor damsel in distress." He walks up and offers me a hand. "Come on. Don't be that way. Come back with me. I'll be nice if you be nice."

More protein. More iron. A different diet. Brandy's words slip through my mind.

He tugs me. I don't move. "Jesus," he says under his breath. "Bitch."

My fist clenches around the board and my arm rockets up before I realize what I'm doing. The itch under my arm is driving me insane. My shirt feels wet there, too.

The board hits the side of his head with a loud crack. I feel Rick's neck snap when it connects. I hit him again and he buckles completely.

My heart is pounding. My head aches. I look around, terrified someone will see what I've done. There's a trash bin on wheels by the dumpster from one of the eateries. It's empty.

I flip it on its side and wrestle him in, then pull as hard as I can to right it again. He tumbles to the bottom with a thud.

I wheel him back across the street into the darkness of the field bordering the residential area. There's a stand of towering pines. I muscle the bin into their covert embrace.

My shirt is soaked, and the itch is so intense that it burns. I dump the trash bin on its side and his body rolls out.

"You're supposed to be gone," I whisper.

She can't hear me. She doesn't have ears. But she knows I'm

talking to her. They tried to get rid of her, but they only made her hungrier. Stranger. Stronger. I giggle from the anxiety coursing through me. The doctors severed my sister's vestigial body from mine months ago, but they couldn't excise her face, her eye, her mouth, her brain. Not in the same surgery. She's too close to my organs. Too close to what I need to live. Insurance won't cover the expensive procedures to remove those tissues, since they're "cosmetic," and my parents can't afford it on their own. Instead, they inserted a probe where they thought whatever acted as Bevvie's brain was, to zap her, to kill her.

The truth is, no one else really knows what's her, what's me, or how we function together. No one knows, and I don't care.

I have to walk around without her little body there to comfort me, but I still have the rest of her. My parents would want to start all over again if they knew. A future surgery may erase her face, but I don't think they can erase her forever.

I whip my shirt off—I'm still getting used to shirts off the rack.

Bevvy's eye opens a few inches beneath my armpit, just above the curve of my bra band. She blinks at me. Her mouth curls up on one side, smiling. She can smell him.

"I got you something for you, but if anyone finds out, we're in big trouble."

We. I miss saying that.

He groans, and I realize he's not dead—just paralyzed. I must have hit the right thing at the right angle. Blind luck.

I find a rock in the darkness. Bevvy's drool runs down my ribs.

I push Rick onto his back with the toe of my sneaker. He stares at me with wild, confused eyes. I smile down at him. I'm the freak. I'm gross. I'm an "it." I take off my bra.

He sees Bevvie and his eyes get even wider.

"What did you say to me?" I whisper. "'I'll be nice if you be nice?'"

He tries to move away and when he can't, he panics. I only watch for a moment, just to be sure my sister sees. Then I hit him with the rock over and over again, until there's a crunching sound, and he stops twitching like a broken toy.

I sit on the soft pine needle carpet and pull him to me, bringing the soft part of his neck to my chest. To Bevvie's mouth. Like a mother feeding her infant.

Bevvie's diet is a little different. She needs more protein. More iron.

For the first time since we started this terrible vacation, I don't feel like an oddity or a freak. I don't feel alone anymore.

ABOUT ALI SEAY

For the last fifteen plus years, Ali Seay has written professionally under a pen name. Now she's running amok and writing as herself in the genre she's always loved the most. Her debut horror novella Go Down Hard came out in 2020 from Grindhouse Press. She lives in Baltimore with her family. Her greatest desire is to own a vintage Airstream and hit the road.

DERAILED

EDITH LOCKWOOD

Everybody screams at the carnival. It's how you have a good time. After a while it fades into the background, with the slide-whistles, clattering roller coaster wheels, and the *chunk-chunk* of the chain lift grabbing the first car.

Marcy's easy to pick out, sitting up front, blonde hair in a high ponytail with a pink scrunchie, looking fly as hell. She waves at me and my chest tightens. Later, I'll pull the scrunchie from her hair and slide it around my wrist while I kiss her. It feels dirtier than wearing her underwear.

I wore my best Levi jeans and varsity jacket tonight—the same jacket I slipped around her shoulders on our first date because it was cold. And because I was too chicken to put any other moves on her.

Tonight, I'm going to tell her I love her. Maybe even go all the way. We've been talking about it. She bought condoms, as a joke. Put one on me, as a joke. Then she said cool beans and asked me to drive her home. My balls were blue for a week.

But at this moment, my girl wants cotton candy. And she will have it. I told her to get on the coaster while there's no line. I can miss one ride with her.

Just one, though.

She screams as the roller coaster drops. I can't see her anymore, but I know it's her scream. She's always jonesing for roller coasters, psyched about even this podunk carnival with one rickety wooden coaster with one drop.

I think the town looks the other way on this carnival because the owner is a Vietnam vet, and everybody feels bad about calling them baby-killers. Marcy said the rides look fine and points out all the "inspected by" stickers. I think the rides look grody. She said you look like a pussy. Yeah, my girl called me a pussy. Isn't she righteous?

"What do you want?" says the girl at the booth. She snaps her gum, pissed I've made her wait two seconds.

"Uh, cotton candy."

"No doy! But like, how much?"

"One, airhead."

"Bite me." She sneers and hands me a sugary fluff ball wrapped around paper cones.

The smell of nearby corndogs—meat bubbling in oil—turns my stomach. The cotton candy doesn't help. Marcy never wears sugary perfume shit like that, just plain deodorant that smells like soap.

I wind my way through the Friday night carnival crowd: major hot college chicks, obnoxious little ten-year-old dweebs, and moms in their mom-jeans that zip up to their belly buttons, hanging on the arms of dads in denim jackets. Marcy and I will be like that. I kid you not. Here's my five-year plan: she'll go to college, because she's a total nerd. I'll get a job at the manufacturing plant or something. I've got my eye on a split-level on Maple Street. We're gonna have three kids and a station wagon.

Everybody is still screaming. Lots of screaming. Must be the last turn on the coaster. Shouldn't it be done by now? This carnival is totally lame, and the coaster is tiny.

I slip between tents to get back to Marcy faster, running between two canyon walls of dirty, colored fabric.

The Tilt-A-Whirl finishes "Running with the Devil" and slows down, switching to "Time After Time." Our song. It was on the radio the first time we made out. She asked is this our song now? I said I guess so. She said I love this song, and I thought *I love you*, but I was too chicken to say it.

People are still screaming. The ride has to be over by now. Why are they still screaming?

"Marcy!" I shove through the line for the Tilt-A-Whirl, knocking kids out of the way, booking it toward the coaster.

"Chill out, dude!" says a kid in an Iron Maiden t-shirt.

"Marcy!" I ditch the cotton candy in the trash.

A chick's funnel cake goes flying in the air, raining powdered sugar. "Are you totally mental?" she shouts.

A crowd gathers around the roller coaster. Not one person has a high blonde ponytail with a pink scrunchie. Where's Marcy? Where the fuck is Marcy?

"Marcy!"

"Son, don't." Some dad in aviator glasses tries to hold me back. I shove him away.

My brain doesn't realize what I'm looking at. Not at first. Then I see it, just before the station, underneath the overturned roller coaster cars, leaking onto the tracks. The pink scrunchie, tied around matted blonde hair dyed red, spotted with white flecks. Teeth. Those are teeth. Fucking shit, it's what's left of her face. That should be her face. Where is her face?

The medic on-site bends over and blows chunks. A second later, I do the same, barfing up my mom's shepherd's pie until only little drops of acid dribble out.

I sit in the grass. It smells like meat, like corn dogs cooking in oil, except it's Marcy. What's left of Marcy.

I'm just sitting here waiting for Marcy. She'll get off the coaster any second. She probably hopped on the swings because I was taking so long. She'll meet me back here any minute. I scan the crowd for her high ponytail and pink scrunchie, so I can stop her before she sees this fucked up shit. After all, she almost dumped me after I took her to see *Re-Animator*.

I sit there until the cops show up and start shouting at everyone. One of them cuffs me in the back of the head when I lunge forward to grab her scrunchie, but he gets too close to the smell and ends up barfing on himself. Last thing, before they drag me away: I throw my jacket on her. It's getting cold out.

————

They call it an accident. Marcy is dead and they call it an accident. The carnival owner never gets run out of town or pays a dime. They interview him after "the accident," and he hobbles around with a cane and cries a sob story about being drafted in Vietnam, people spitting on him when he came home, and how this carnival is the only thing he's got left after shrapnel ruined his leg.

Just an accident, but too gruesome to put on the evening news. They call my angel crushed under a roller coaster—her skull smashed until her brains leak out—an accident. A statistic.

Marcy is not a statistic. She is a mad-smart girl, outrageously pretty, and we're going to get married and have three kids and buy a station wagon.

She is not an accident.

———

The night after the DA decides not to press charges, I steal my parents' Panasonic camcorder. It barely fits in my backpack. I buy a ticket and walk the midway until my legs ache, then hang out inside the Tunnel of Love until the carnival closes down around midnight. Empty popcorn containers litter the ground, along with gnawed corn dog sticks and empty soda cups.

I heft the camcorder onto my shoulder, feeling like Tom-fucking-Brokaw. It doesn't have a light, so I have to hold a flashlight in my left hand. The cassette whirrs next to my ear.

A light flicks on in the trailer where the owner lives. Fucking piece of shit. I turn off the camera and flashlight and hide inside the milk bottle stand. Stuffed animals hang from hooks above me, grinning into the darkness. Silence blankets the carnival. No one's screaming now.

The light flicks off again.

After another five minutes, I turn the camcorder back on. Christ, this thing is heavy. Why was Dad too cheap for the Handycam?

I get all the grody stuff on tape. Grime and dirt cake the joints of the Tilt-a-Whirl. Proof. Rust flakes off the Ferris wheel when I blow on it. Proof. Thirteen bolts come loose on the pirate ship when I test them with my bare fingers, and one is missing on the Rocket Roller Coaster that killed Marcy. Proof.

Caution tape wraps the roller coaster station like a straight jacket. Brown fluid stains the tracks, the cars, the grass. It's just oil. Not Marcy.

I put the cap over the camcorder lens and carefully lay it in the grass before I sit down. Dad will kill me if it gets broken.

I can't breathe. I can't see through all the tears. I haven't cried this much since my dog Buster died when I was seven.

The light flicks on in the trailer. Go to sleep, you fucking geezer.

It flicks off again.

I wipe my cheeks. My jaw aches from clenching it. Time to get out of here and get the tape to the cops.

"Tommy?"

I look up. Marcy sits in a car at the station, her eyes wide.

"Marcy!" I'm over the gate in a flash, pounding up the steps, climbing into the car with her. "You're alive. I knew it!"

She's wearing the same outfit—purple and green leggings with leg warmers bunched around her ankles and a long sweater with sleeves draped over her hands. She always looks choice like that.

But the pink scrunchie perched on top of her head matches the one around my wrist.

"Tommy, you have to get out of here. Before the ride starts again."

I don't know what she's talking about, but I don't need to. My hands reach for her and pass through her chest. Cold air creeps from her like an open freezer. I automatically take off my jacket—my Members Only jacket she doesn't like—and wrap it around her shoulders. It falls into a pile on the seat.

"Babe, hurry!" she says. Her hand passes through my arm. It burns.

"I'm gonna get you out of here. Just sit tight."

"You can't do anything. I'm non-corporeal. A specter. An apparition."

"Babe, English, please."

"I'm dead, you dip! There's nothing you can do." She slaps my shoulder and I flinch away. Even though her hand passes through me, it stings.

I snap my fingers. "Like that episode of *The Twilight Zone*. You have unfinished business. I'm gonna avenge your death, and then you can move on. You can go to Heaven." I jump onto the platform and look down at her in the car. "Come on, let's go."

"I don't know if there is a Heaven," she says.

"If there is, you'll go for sure. You're an angel. We didn't even..."

"Do it?" She tilts her head and smiles. It's a secret smile, just for me, revealing the braces she won't show anyone else. But why is it so sad? "You're so dumb, but I love you."

"Really?"

"Tommy, look out!"

Something slams into my knee. I fall back into the roller coaster car with Marcy. I try to stand up but I can't. My leg won't work.

"Who are you?" says the owner. He smells of cigarettes and cheap beer. "You're trespassing."

"Son of a bitch!" I try to stand up, but the pain is too fucking much. My knee must be broken.

"Are you one of those fucking reporters?" he says, words slurring together.

"Yeah, that's right. I'm Tommy Brokaw. Everybody's gonna know about this death trap." I pull myself up using the lap bar.

"I knew it!" says the old man. "Damned nosy reporters. Always making up lies. Told them I killed babies. I didn't kill any babies. I wasn't a baby-killer."

"You killed Marcy! It's your fault she's dead!" I yell.

"Tommy—" says Marcy, like she's trying to warn me.

"I'll come back—every night. Everyone will see what a dump this place is," I say.

"Tommy," says Marcy. "Stop.

"I won't stop until you're in jail. The electric chair. They'll fry your eyeballs."

"Tommy, shut up!" says Marcy.

"No. No, no, no," says the old man. "I won't let you."

"What are you going to do about it?" Even with my knee broken, I can still take this guy. I'm no Chuck Norris but I'm not a wet noodle, either. I grab the front of his shirt, and he shoots me.

I didn't even see the revolver in his hand. Wet warmth soaks the front of my shirt.

"You—you can't do that," I say. Marcy is right; I am a dumbass. "The cops..."

He jabs his cane into my stomach. I tumble back into the car. "Dumb little shit. Tried to ride the coaster when it was shut down. Very stupid. Can't blame me. Not my fault. Coaster was shut down. Rode it anyway." He hits the control panel with his cane, and the chain lift picks up the cart.

"Tommy, get up!" says Marcy. Her hands pass through my shoulders.

"Non...corporeal," I say. See? I'm not a total lost cause. I can learn things.

The wheels clunk and clack as the cart rises into the air. Slick blood coats the floor and I can't seem to get my legs under me. Cheerful music blares from tinny speakers.

"Tommy." Marcy surrounds me, tears in her eyes, kneeling on the floor with me.

"It's okay, babe. Don't cry."

"Hold on. You have to hold on."

I manage to hold on until the third turn, when I'm thrown out, and my neck snaps.

———

The rest of the story comes to me in bits and pieces. The cops come out in the morning, and the old man shows them my body. The coaster broke my neck, but the old man ran my body through the track a few times to hide the gunshot wound. The cops buy it until Marcy follows one of them around, freezing his ass off, and gets him to step on the camcorder in the grass. The tape plays the old man murdering me in mono sound because I'm a dumbass who only put on the lens cap and didn't shut the camcorder off. The old man's slated for the electric chair, and I hope they zap him so long his eyeballs run down his cheeks.

The carnival folds. They wrap caution tape around the entrance and throw up plywood. My mom comes by sometimes with flowers and I scare up butterflies. She seems to like that. On Friday nights, kids sneak in and tell each other to listen for the chain lift, and then the screaming.

I put my jacket around Marcy's shoulders. She's real, warm, and I don't pass through her. I tug the scrunchie from her hair, slip it on my wrist, and bury my hand in her permanently permed hair. The roller coaster isn't exactly three kids and a split-level and a station wagon. Okay, my five-year plan went a little off-track.

"Love you, babe."

She smiles at me—her secret smile—just before the roller coaster drops, and we scream together.

ABOUT EDITH LOCKWOOD

Edith Lockwood is a harmless little old lady who enjoys baking, quilting, and poisoning her wealthy husbands shortly after her marriages are consummated. Her dislikes include cold weather, prenuptial agreements, and nosy snoops who ask too many questions. She doesn't Tweet. #snitchesgetstitches

THE NEON KNIGHT
ANDREW PUZO

If asked about a boy named Herbert Leavenworth Painter, ninetenths of the town of Valeville, Illinois would say they'd never heard of him. The rest would agree that he was as forgettable as your father's accountant. His father, an accountant, often said the same, and if it was after five his words would be slurred so that "disappointment" would sound like "dizzapoinet," and his pointed breath would mist his glasses so heavy with condensate that Tanqueray could rebottle the stuff straight.

Herbert's mother loved him from a distance but found the child uninspired. With his face like a potato cut in half and features pulled from his biology textbook's description of modern man (...*attributes of Homo sapiens that distinguish him from Homo neanderthalensis include his chinned mandible, flat forehead, and small teeth...*), Herbert's mother was dissatisfied with his yearbook pictures year in and year out and never purchased proofs for friends or family.

But to Herbert, this was largely unimportant. Because at the Kastle Arkade, seven blocks from the middle school, Herbert Leavenworth Painter was much more than a small, unremarkable boy. He was a God.

From *Dig Dug* to *Donkey Kong*, *Space Invaders* to *Pac-Man*, the initials HLP burned bright atop each screen announcing "High Scores" or "Best Players" or "Hall of Fame." Erected there in pixelated block font, they laughed in the face of every kid in town who got sore thumbs and cramped hands trying to bring down the godhead. HLP was the envy and admiration of all who frequented the Arkade, and it was here—in this small space of dark room lit by the glow of dozens of machines, filled with the noise of bangling quarters and a faint smell like birch beer gone flat—that Herbert was known, and at home.

Herbert stood under the hood of the *Asteroids* machine, encircled by a crowd of boys whose pale faces alternated between delight and desire. He maneuvered his triangular chalk-line spacecraft, playing the Thrust/Fire buttons like piano keys. With the dexterity of a pianist, he would lift his hand at just the right moment to push his rimless glasses back up his nose, the screen thick with darting asteroids and hostile flying saucers.

"Wait for it. Just wait," said one of the awestruck faces hovering over Herbert's shoulder.

His spacecraft spun madly, *pew-pewing* everything in sight.

"Oh! Now! No, no. Sorry. Wait for it..."

A tiny rocket of an asteroid blazed up from the lower right quadrant of deep space. A hornet, they called them. Herbert whirled and fired. The asteroid exploded into space dust, but the second hornet it overlaid kept coming, even as Herbert turned to face new threats.

A collective inhale. One boy yelled, "Hey wa—"

Herbert hit Hyperspace with whiplash reflex. His spacecraft reappeared in the only square inch of screen not crowded with danger.

Pewpewpewpewpewpewpew.

A cheer went up, smothering the few groans of unfulfilled schadenfreude. Hyperspace was the last resort when the fracas got too heavy—the "break glass in case of emergency" option. It deposited the player in a random spot on the screen, usually right in the path of an oncoming asteroid, but it never seemed to play out that way for HLP.

The noise startled Otto Kastelmann, the Kastle Arkade's aging proprietor, who was sleeping on his stool behind the counter where he made quarters and sold snacks. His fingers dove for the weighted sap he kept tucked beside the cash register, but when he saw the children, he smiled, withdrew his hand, and let his lids droop again.

A half-hour later, after the crowd moved on to other adventures,

Herbert sat at a table in the small anteroom of the Arkade, eating cheese puffs with a tall, wiry boy just beginning to grow into his unconventional good looks.

"That was great! I mean, *really* great! The way you dodged that hornet..." He shook his head. "Legends, Herb. The stuff of legends."

"Thanks, Tommy." Herbert pushed his glasses up his nose and left a neon orange smudge of cheese dust. "It wasn't all that special."

"Yes, it was! And it isn't just luck, Herb. Luck doesn't account for things like that. And if it does, then nobody is lucky like you."

Herbert started to think about this but only got so far; a mutual friend of theirs came sprinting around the corner and down the street. As he ripped by the Arkade's plate-glass storefront, he caught sight of Herbert and Tommy, skidded to a stop ten feet past the door, and reversed course to get inside.

"Except for this cat," Tommy said. "What's the good wo—"

"Shh!" The newcomer put a finger to his lips, his eyes alight with a devilish gleam. He lifted the domed lid atop the garbage can near the door and, with an artful flourish and a pinch of his nostrils, dropped into it like a free diver, landing with a rattling clink in a sea of soda bottles. His fingers broke the surface to reaffix the lid, and he peeked out from behind the hinged push-plate.

Three athletic-looking boys in blue spandex wrestling singlets came clopping down the blacktop like raging, red-faced bulls. The butt cheeks of their uniforms were cut out. The word "Loverboy" was scrawled in white fabric paint across their torsos.

Tommy spit out his drink, and Herbert laughed so hard he nearly fell backward in his chair.

Geoffrey Zapada, the great and terrible, stepped out of the garbage can and joined them at the table. "You were asking me what the good word was?"

Tommy nodded.

"The good word of the day today, children, is *Loverboy*." He made a scissoring motion with his fingers and struck a mocking macho man pose. "I made some modifications to their uniforms—improvements, really—while they were showering. What's new with you two?"

"Herbert nearly popped his high score on Asteroids," Tommy said. "Dodged a double-decker hornet too. It was unbelievable."

"Really?"

Herbert grinned.

"You know, your lack of grace when not flying around space or getting chased through a maze never fails to astonish me." Geoffrey wiped a napkin on the condensation building on Tommy's soda bottle and handed it to Herbert. "Off with the warpaint, Rambo."

"Thanks," he said, scrubbing the orange smudge from his nose.

"Do you think you'll top it next time?" Tommy asked.

"I'm not sure," said Herbert, turning to Tommy. "I've probably had my best days on all these games. I'm top score on every one, state record on six, and as close as I'll ever be to ranking nationally. Maybe I should try my hand at something else."

"Then what do you propose we do after school tomorrow? Or the day after that? Or over this weekend?" Geoff asked.

"Well, I have my date," Tommy replied.

"I was asking Herb, Tom-Tom," Geoff said. "And that's only going to be a one-night affair, anyway."

"How do you know?"

"Because no girl wants to make it with the lead puppet from a Disney movie."

Herbert stopped laughing when he saw the look fall over Tommy's face, which did, in fact, bear a strong resemblance to Pinnochio—dark hair, rosebloom cheeks, and a jutting, downturned nose that a small but fanatical sect of girls at Valeville Middle thought was his best feature. He looked every inch of his personality. Tender-hearted and excitable, Tommy was an earnest friend, always cheering Herbert on and shouting directions or warnings when he played.

"Why don't you jump back in the trash with the rest of the rodents, rat-face?" Tommy muttered to Geoff.

"That a boy, Tommy. You tell him," Herbert said.

Suddenly inspired, Geoff scrunched up his narrow features in an expression of vicious joy and, with his cheese-colored teeth bared, started hissing and twitching his nose. He ate a cheese puff off the table and then crawled beneath and started pawing at Tommy's legs.

"Aw, jeez! C'mon, Geoff! Knock it off!" Tommy shouted. His knees bumped the underside of the table while Geoffrey Z. shrieked with glee. Herbert groaned. He knew they would have continued like that for another ten minutes if the Arkade door hadn't been kicked open by two men in brown uniforms, cursing and hollering directions at each other around a ponderous wooden crate on a hand truck.

Otto jolted awake. When he saw the men, he brightened. "Good! Good!" He clapped his hands and went to help.

Everyone in the Kastle Arkade stopped what they were doing and stared at the box with the same imbecilic expression. Herbert's heart broke into an irregular gallop, and his breath threatened to fog his glasses. A new game. A new conquest. HLP flashed through his mind and onto a leaderboard.

The men and Otto rolled the crate toward a space in the back between two other games. On one side sat a wildly unpopular machine where you played cheap rehashes of other games to recover instruments stolen from the rock group Journey while listening to 8-bit versions of their songs. On the other, a *Black Knight* pinball machine that was all the rage for its Magna-Save feature, its upper deck with independent flippers, and the grave, robotic oath of the Black Knight himself, who declared to his challengers, "I will slay you, my enemy."

The grunting, swearing threesome maneuvered the crate into place, leaving enough room on all sides for Otto to pry it open. They wriggled the hand truck free and went to the counter to handle the paperwork.

Herbert pushed his way through the crowd forming around the wooden monolith. In the pale glow cast by nearby headboards and screens, he saw foreign words stenciled over the rough surface in block letters. Herbert couldn't understand them, but they looked harsh and guttural, seeming to advertise danger within. The largest words read *DIESES ENDE OBEN* beneath an arrow pointing upward.

The unintelligible words reminded Herbert of the last Painter family vacation, six years ago, when he was eight. They went to Beijing after his father had been promoted to partner. In the Beijing Zoo—one of their first stops—Herbert wandered off alone to see the tigers.

The signs on the bars of the enclosure were mostly in Mandarin, but he got the message. Prowling shapes lurked beyond, melding with the shadows. Glowing eyes. Gleams of fang. *Danger within. Stay out.*

Still, Herbert had pushed as close as the bars would allow, rapt, until one of those serpent-like, slinking silhouettes locked onto him with round, phosphorescent orbs of yellow-green pricked with black. They seemed to float there, in the darkness of the jungle, as his excitement plummeted into full-bladder panic.

In a blink, those eyes halved the distance to the bars. Herbert had tried to back away, but the crowd swelled and pressed around him, readying cameras and jockeying for a look. With an earsplitting roar, shouts from the spectators, and the flash of a dozen pictures, the eyes were there before him, and a neon orange face, shot through with black ribbons, yawned out a pink tongue and yellowing fangs.

He'd screamed when the tiger bumped into the plexiglass barrier just past the bars while the crowd cheered and took more photos. Security found him, alone and afraid, because no one stepped forward to comfort the crying boy in their midst.

Herbert felt that way now, and the memory came on so quick that it made him queasy. This close to the new machine's crate, he could smell the raw, sweet odor of the wood—but beneath it, something heavy and indomitable. Grease and fire, like a locomotive engine.

Herbert pressed his hand against it to steady himself. A faint thrumming vibrated beneath his fingertips. The idling of a doom machine. The purring of a jungle cat.

Otto worked his way through the gathered children, crowbar in hand. "Look out! Give room!" he shouted in his heavy German accent. "You're in for a treat if you would just give room!"

Herbert started to back away. The crowd pressed against him.

"Aich! Give room!"

Herbert reeled, trying to turn around, but the mass surged, clenched, held him fast.

Otto burst through the sea of small bodies and stood before Herbert in chiaroscuro relief, looking grim and depraved in the dim light as he wedged the end of the crowbar under a corner and started to pry. Nails creaked.

"LOOK OUT!" Otto shouted. He wormed the crowbar in deeper and leaned his weight into it.

Herbert managed to twist himself away, but the bobbing heads were a vast ocean between him and the door. He heard a roar behind him. The crowd gave and fell back in a massive swell.

"AICH! LOOK OUT!"

The tiger.

Herbert turned to see Otto toss remove the top of the crate and step back. The four walls fell to the threadbare carpet with a collective WHUMP!

The new machine, deep black with arcing laces of obscenely bright lightning crisscrossing its surface—lime green, hot pink, urine yellow, electric blue—towered above the others. The fathomless, blank tube screen was as wide as one of the children stretched head to toe. The headboard bore a legend in blacked-out font, lighter than the machine's body by only a shade: *DER NEONRITTER*.

The crowd fell silent. Herbert's fear dissipated. The machine was unlike anything he'd ever seen.

"*The Neon Knight*," said Otto, breathless.

And it was Herbert's to beat.

As Otto struggled to push the machine against the wall and boot it up, Herbert, Tommy, and Geoff stepped back into the anteroom, followed by several others.

"Whattaya say, Herb? Whattaya think?" asked Tommy.

"I think we've figured out what to do with the rest of today, at least," said Herbert, fervently polishing his glasses. His jittering fingernails made small tapping sounds against the glass.

"Ease up before you bust your specs," said Geoff, his own eager expression barely constrained.

"Do you think it takes American quarters, Herb?" Tommy asked.

"How would he know? The thing isn't even in English."

"Probably," Herbert said. He fished out one of the dozen or so quarters in his pocket and looked at it. Washington on one side, the War Bird on the other. Shiny and freshly minted in 1986. "Der Neonritter," he said slowly. The words felt heavy and obtuse in his mouth, like machine parts. He wanted to spit them out.

"So whattaya think, Herb. What's the plan?"

Before Herbert could answer—or tell Tommy to stop asking questions—they heard a collective "Ahhhhh" from the crowd surrounding Otto and the machine.

The kids in the anteroom parted, leaving a broad, unbroken stretch of ragged carpet between the boys and *The Neon Knight*. Herbert started down it, striding past monuments and memories of bygone victories at the control boards of the games on either side. Tommy and Geoff fell in behind him. The crowd at the end of the Arkade made way, pressing their backs up against the machines. Otto leaned against the *Black Knight* pinball game, facing Herbert.

This was not done by charity or custom but in recognition of an earned right and a plain fact. Simply, the right of the best to go first, and that the best was Herbert Leavenworth Painter.

Herbert approached the strange machine, sizing up his opponent. A solitary, dim orange 25¢ coin return button told him the game was single-player and, despite Tommy's fears, outfitted to accept American quarters. The control board had the standard configuration: a joystick slotted with the four points of the compass to occupy his left hand and four black buttons—engraved *Schwert, Schild, Licht*, and *Lauf* in white, medieval lettering—for his right.

The black screen now displayed neon letters that matched the machine's multi-colored casing: *DER NEONRITTER*. Below that, in much smaller letters, *Beginn*. Herbert was underwhelmed. The dark legend across the headboard hadn't even lit up.

"I will slay you, my enemy!"

Herbert flinched at the voice booming from the *Black Knight* pinball machine. The cruel knight on his rearing steed looked down at him with red eyes. Otto searched the machine for where he might have hit a button with his elbow, shrugged, and then pointed at the right-hand buttons in front of Herbert. "Sword, Shield, Light, and Run," he rattled off as he indicated each one.

"Where'd you get this, Otto?"

"*Der Neonritter*, young Herbert, is a very old, old game I only heard of back home. A friend of a friend over the Wall knew a man who knew a man selling it. It's an East German relic. The only one in the United States, of this I am sure."

"Which means . . ."

"You could set a national record, young Herbert, if you can beat whatever scores are on there already."

The crowd rustled. Mentions of the Wall and East Germany titillated them, but the promise of a national victory was the closest thing to an orgasm most of them had experienced.

"You could do it! You could do it *right now*, Herb!" Tommy said. Geoff nodded and, for once, didn't open his mouth.

"How do I beat it?" asked Herbert.

Otto shrugged. "This I cannot say. I know only what I've told you. If you need help translating the Deutsch—"

The door banged open, and one of the deliverymen came in, holding up a sheet of paper that Otto forgot to sign and looking mighty pissed about it.

"—let me know." With that, Otto left.

Herbert deposited his new quarter into the slot. It clinked down into the guts of the machine, and, as the boys around him inhaled in excitement, he saw the neon colors flash just a bit brighter and heard the faint thrumming edge just a gear higher.

The sense of standing too close to the cage of a dangerous animal returned to him.

"Well, whaddaya waiting for?" said Geoff.

Herbert, in startled reflex, hit *Beginn.*

The screen washed crossways in a ripple of pixelated neon rainbow and unveiled a scene reminiscent of *Asteroids*—crude geometric shapes drawn in white lines, the empty spaces within and without them filled with darkness. A pair of gauntleted hands outstretched before him, sword and shield held in a slack, half-ready position. He pressed *Schild,* and the shield raised, partially obscuring his view.

Herbert lowered it and examined his surroundings. A few thick sets of parallel lines that rose straight up from the ground and canted at sharp, unnatural angles appeared to be trees. Some of them ended in a splay of frenzied branches before the uppermost level of the screen; others continued ad infinitum. Herbert couldn't see beyond his immediate area.

"The light, Herb," said Tommy.

Herbert pressed *Licht.* The hand holding the sword made a sheathing sound and produced a torch. It cast a thin glow, exposing an endless forest of trees like pale bones.

"Can you move around?" asked Tommy.

Herb pushed the joystick to the eastward slot, turning ninety degrees. The torchlight illuminated more of the two-dimensional woods. The boys murmured in muted amazement. They had never seen a game allowing full range of motion in a world not predefined by levels or paths.

Herbert made three more turns, coming back around to the north and seeing nothing but more woods. His light dwindled at two-second intervals. He pressed the sword button, and the torch extinguished with a snuffing sound.

Herbert sucked in his lips. He didn't know what to do.

This was an unusual situation for him, but the game itself was unusual—no clear instructions, just a forest for him to wander in until he... What exactly? Herbert felt dozens of eyes pressing into the back of his neck.

He pushed the joystick forward. There was a loud tearing sound, like fabric ripping, and then he was falling, falling . . .

The boys gasped. A cut and zoom-out showed his character impaled on iron spikes driven into the bottom of a pit. Herbert could see now that his character was a questing knight, albeit a dead one, dotted and dripping pixelated blots of raw red across the screen.

It had all happened so fast that he didn't have time to think. A part of him blocked out the surrounding crowd's visceral reaction. But it had happened. And everyone saw it. In the first few seconds of the first level of a new game, HLP lost.

Heads shook and mouths whispered. Tommy cast a fearful glance at Geoff, who stared at Herbert grimly.

The word *Tot* materialized above his knight in gore-splattered neon letters. Herbert didn't need Otto's translation to know what it meant. Below it appeared a question: *Spiel Nochmal?*

Herbert pushed another quarter into the slot. Another rainbow wave rolled across the screen, and his knight stood at the ready once more.

Herbert lifted his light and spun in a full circle. He saw the rough edge of the pit he had fallen into before and the remnants of the crude, triangular leaves used to conceal it. The trap seemed designed to prevent him from getting somewhere he was supposed to go, so he skirted its edge and continued in that direction.

He used the torch to look for more piles of leaves and some signal of his objective. A distant circle appeared, breaking the monotony and the geometry of the trees. Herbert raised the torch and peered. The circle remained, unmoving, at the threshold of the darkness. Herbert could see a humanoid outline below it.

He heard noise to his immediate right—like a side of beef hit with a baseball bat—and once more, the screen zoomed out to show the German words that could only mean *Dead* and *Play again?*

Beneath the words, another humanoid—white and skinny like a walking corpse—danced over his fallen knight, brandishing a club.

Two of the spectators broke away from the crowd and left the Kastle Arkade, slipping past Otto and the deliveryman and walking out into the deepening, cooling sun of that autumn afternoon turning autumn evening with a quickness of step that suggested the outside world was a place they would rather be after all. Herbert produced another quarter.

In this manner, the godhead fell.

An unseen pit. A blunt club. Mired down in mud and sucked into quicksand. Hope sparked in the eyes of the remaining few when Herbert discovered the flagstone path, but when he chose left instead of right and was trampled into a puddle of bones, blood, and broken armor by a monstrous half-goat creature, the crowd dwindled like the stash of quarters he fed the machine. These deaths were senseless and sporadic, at once both numbing and painful. But what hurt the most was seeing the once-great HLP reduced, block by block, piece by piece, down into what he was, which is what all of them were. Ordinary, forgettable, unremarkable little boys. It reminded them that he was no different than they and that whatever deific qualities they endowed him with were an illusion and a lie. Nearly two hours after he started, only Tommy and Geoff remained.

"Herb?" Tommy said.

"What."

"Don't you think it's time?"

"Time for what?" The images on the screen reflected in Herbert's glasses. His voice was as flat as the forest he wandered through. He found the flagstone path again and went right instead of left, saw a tunnel ahead in the distance.

Tommy looked out to the darkening sky. "Time to, you know, call it, maybe."

"You mean give up."

Tommy looked to Geoff.

Geoff said, "He isn't saying that, Herb, he's—"

"Saying I'm not good enough to win."

"I never said that! I'm saying you'd do better tomorrow after some rest, is all."

Herbert didn't respond. The only sound was the mechanical clicks of buttons and a joystick.

"I'm just saying—"

"Shut up, Tom," Herbert said.

Tommy flinched. Geoff's face darkened.

"I'm sorry, Herb," Tommy said. "I didn't mean—"

"No, he *did* mean it, you jerk!" Geoff yanked Tommy's shirttail. "Since when do you think you can talk to your friends like that?"

Herbert said nothing.

"Too good for us, huh?" Geoff shouted. "What gave you that idea, champ? The national bigtime you're so close to cinching?"

"GET OUT!" Herbert screamed.

Geoff stomped toward the exit, leading Tommy by the arm. Otto shifted and mumbled on his stool and fell back into slumber when the door slammed shut.

One of the large flagstones Herbert stepped on depressed and shot skyward, mashing him into the ceiling of the tunnel.

"HRRRRRGHHHHH!"

A visceral expression of raw frustration, anger, and self-destruction. Herbert knew he was shooting himself in the foot and his friends in the heart, but he couldn't stop himself. If he didn't have this, he didn't have anything.

He looked at his reflection—small and obscure—in the convex picture tube. Seeing what others saw, what everyone saw. Now even here, at the Kastle Arkade. But it was here that Herbert had the power to be seen as something more. He had done it before. He could do it again. He *had* to do it again.

His last quarter shone bright and fresh, another born in '86. He squeezed it for luck so hard that Washington's bust imprinted on his palm, then dropped it into the machine.

This time, Herbert tried to take it all in. To make himself *see*. He didn't move or spin his knight. Instead, he let the entirety of the screen fill his eyes. He remained like that for almost two minutes. With everyone gone, he could clear his mind and think.

He took a single step forward.

This game, Herbert thought. *Not a game. No directions. No lights. No music. Not a game. Can't win because you're playing it wrong. You're playing a game. Not a game. Makes you wonder. No. Makes you* think. *Like a puzzle. A pattern. Patterns can be seen. What can you see? The ground. The leaves. The trees. The trees. Trees.*

Why haven't you looked up?

Herbert let his eyes climb. Some of the trunks stretched off the screen; others ended in a splay of limbs. At the top of the screen through the mishmash tangle, Herbert saw an outline, clear as day, formed by the intersection of branches at straight angles. A big, fat arrow pointing due east.

Haven't looked up because danger is on the ground, he thought.

He saw another leaf-covered pit at his feet—like the one he fell into on his first go-round.

*Not danger…*distractions.

Herbert smiled and started east.

He went slow, raising his torch to see the tops of trees every few steps or so. He found another arrow pointing north and began to move faster. Herbert stopped worrying about pits and humanoids and horse-goat hybrids altogether. No distractions here. Not on this hidden path through the endless black and white forest.

Now west.

North.

East again.

Never south.

He walked over the tunnel where he had been crushed to death —or maybe a different tunnel. The world seemed endless.

Now a rocky hill.

Now running *out* of the forest.

A narrow path rose before Herbert, climbing and cresting between two great stone monoliths. Perhaps guards, or prisoners, or gods—old and terrible ones, Gog and Magog. Lodestones of the universe from a time beyond space, now here, in this game, glowing dully like amber embers.

The path shortened. The stones glowed brighter, a burning orange. A fire in full roar.

The stones faded to orange on black.

Now fear. The face of the tiger. Clawing, ripping, roaring right through the screen and into his chest and throat.

Now. He can't turn back.

Now. He's stuck at the bars.

Now. In the mouth of the tiger, because—*da liegt was du suchst*—*there lies what you seek*, and whether it has come for him or he for it doesn't matter because NOW...apocalypse...NOW...lightning...NOW YOU SEE...everything...*JETZT. SIEHST. DU.*

The castle.

Herbert tore himself away from the screen with a gasp and flung the sweat from his brow. His heart triphammered. The second he walked past the monoliths, their glow extinguished, leaving him in darkness before the castle on the hill.

Herbert's fear reverberated within him, gong-drum echoes of the voice that spoke from the machine telling to *see*, loud and clear and dominating, an alien bellow in his own head.

Now, he was inside the tiger's cage.

But beneath his fear, Herbert felt an electric sensation, the one that comes to a boy somewhere he isn't supposed to be, doing something that he isn't supposed to.

HLP didn't *play* games. He *won* them. And Herbert knew he was close.

He walked forward. Slowly.

The gates of the castle rose, tall and impenetrable. They opened outward, creeping and soundless, to expose a widening crevasse. It filled with flashing shots of neon, changing colors rapidly before settling on orange. Orange alternating with black. Other colors, innumerable and vibrant, bounced and blasted out of every window and skyward space of the castle—a scene of silent, ominous gaiety. Herbert watched, mesmerized.

The colors went out. Herbert peered into the darkness. He readied his sword and shield.

A beam of neon orange projected outward from the screen and illuminated Herbert, so bright that we see him resplendent in all his mediocrity. The small teeth, the flat brow, the slight slouch, and the muddy eyes behind rimless glasses. His teeth are bared in a triumphant grin, or perhaps a dawning grimace. In his glasses we see the oncoming of what looks like a freight engine pounding through a dark tunnel. Something very bright and very big and very fast.

The orange light grows brighter still, changes from a prison searchlight to a lighthouse beacon to a flare pulled from the surface of the sun. As it intensifies, it flickers through the colors of the neon rainbow, shifting with increasing speed until they lose definition, become an unworldly shade: neon black. A color that shouldn't be possible. But here it is, and in its terrible glare, we see Herbert shining, and something unthinkable reflected in his lenses.

SIEHST DU?

DO YOU SEE?

The voice pounds into Herbert's head. The bright colors create heat, and the heat starts to cook him.

JETZT SIEHST DU.

We see. Although Herbert's glasses are melting, we see. In their runny surface, we see a reflection, an imperfect mirror of rippled water. Curving oscillations cover an image that eludes definition. An armored foot. A braced chest plate. A horned helmet. A flashing doom glaive. Each turns a uniform shade of pulsing neon black.

JETZT. SHIEHST. DU.

Eyes alight within the recesses of the helmet, growing larger in the running glass that drips down Herbert's waxen face. Eyes that replace Herbert's when his explode. Eyes that become tigers, striped black and orange.

The strange black light becomes too bright, but before we avert our own eyes, we see it move. It crawls out of the machine, as solid and weighty as a block of clay pushed through a tube, still maintaining the screen's dimensions as it approaches Herbert.

We hear a muffled shriek, the pop of a firecracker beneath a pillow. When we look again, the Arkade is now empty save Otto, who stirs at the sound but does not wake.

The next day, school lets out at ten after two.

By twenty past, the first of the afternoon crowd is already in the Kastle Arkade, Geoff and Tommy among them, glancing around with subdued apprehension.

"Do you think he'll show?" Tommy asks.

Geoff nods. He gets a birch beer from Otto, who miscounts his change and gives him an extra quarter. The boys sit at their table in the foyer, their backs to the door, looking over their shoulders every so often.

"What if he doesn't?"

"Where else would he go?"

Tommy shrugs.

"All he has is this place. At least you got your date, and someday soon, Brooke Shields will get my letters. She'll realize what she's missing." His smile fades as quickly as it appeared. "But, well, I feel bad about what I said to Herb."

Tommy frowns and nods.

A startled yelp makes them whip their heads up to see a crowd gathering around a chubby boy named Brendan Stewart at the back of the Arkade. Otto stands beside Brendan, mouth agape.

They exchange a confused glance and rise from the table, walking down the aisle of lights and sounds, pushing through the buzzing boys to see what has Brendan yammering.

"Alright, Stewie. What's got your goiter?" says Geoff.

Pug-nosed Brendan Stewart stands to one side, his face flushed and pink with disbelief as he points at the screen of DER NEONRIT-TER. The top of the screen says *Bestenliste*. Ranking first, at *Nummer Eins*: HLP.

Tommy grabs Geoff by the shoulders and shakes him as he jumps up and down, yelling, "He did it! He did it! He did it! Can you believe it?"

The crowd catches Tommy's enthusiasm, and he and Geoff find themselves tossed about by a sea of jubilant, raucous, roaring nobodies who now have something to shout about. Something largely absent from a world that walks them by. Hope.

Otto yells that everyone plays free for the day, and the first one to find Herbert gets free play for a year. He hurries to the phone to call Twin Galaxies and report the new national record while kids scatter like marbles off the crack of the shooter, hollering and proclaiming the name of their restored god all over the town of Valeville, Illinois.

Tommy looks slightly punch-drunk and Geoff feels the same. All the jostling must have knocked his head good, because the *Bestenliste* screen seems wavy to him. Like everything's been jinked out of place a half an inch or so. Geoff thinks he sees HLP changing, shimmering, distorting.

He leans in closer to the screen and rubs his eyes.

HLP

But for a second, he swears it looked like

HELP

There it is. Flickering. Waving. Geoff rubs his eyes again.

HLP

The underline cursor used to enter the player's initials appears.

H_LP

HELP_

HELP M_

HELP ME_

Now Tommy and Brendan were looking and seeing.

The ME cut out, and the E flittered over the blinking cursor like a dying moth, struggling to stay on the screen. Growing weak, weak, weaker until it disappeared entirely, leaving only

HLP

The machine came to life with a metallic churning. Its cavernous guts rumbled as cogwheels ground and turned. The boys took a collective step back with a sharp inhale of breath that caught the smell and taste of something like boiling copper. Despite the sudden wave of radiant heat, goosebumps raised on Geoff's arms.

There was a jingling clatter in the coin return, a flash of neon orange in the slot, and the machine switched off. The heat and smell dissipated. The coin return button smoldered, a dull cinder.

With his heavy breath sounding loud in his ears, Geoff stepped forward and, without taking his eyes off the screen of DER NEON-RITTER, slipped his index and middle fingers into the slot and scooped out the still-warm coin. With measured steps, he backed away, not wanting to turn his back to the machine. The other boys looked as he raised his palm and unfurled.

The quarter came up tails. The War Bird in profile, spread large and proud. Geoff turned it over. In the dull light of the machines, they saw Washington was gone. Pressed up and flash-frozen into the metal, as if trying to burst out from the other side, was a plain, forgettable face wearing a pair of sagging glasses. It appeared to be screaming.

Otto lowered the phone and asked if anyone had seen Herbert.

ABOUT ANDREW PUNZO

Andrew Punzo was born and raised in New Jersey. His short fiction has appeared on *The NoSleep Podcast*, and in *Shadowy Natures*, *Every Day Fiction*, and other venues.

LATCHKEY
AMANDA CECELIA LANG

"The last kid who lived in my house disappeared," Jonah tells his fifth-grade teacher after school one Monday afternoon, just spits the Bad Thing right out.

Mr. Fetner makes a funny noise in his throat. "Did you say *disappeared*?"

"Disappeared and was never seen again."

"Well then..." Mr. Fetner closes his gradebook and raises an eyebrow at Jonah's ratty Velcro sneakers and too-big eyeglasses. When Jonah asked if he could stay after school, the old man probably never dreamt of this, probably thought Jonah wanted to cry about his D in math or all his missing homework.

But Jonah doesn't know who else to confide in. It's either tell Mr. Fetner or the police officers who show up sometimes at the 7-11 at the end of his street—the one with the MISSING posters and all the graffiti—only Mom said never to stop there, *always* go straight home, no matter how bad he wants a cherry Slurpee or to play *Pac-Man*. Bad Things happen to kids who talk to strangers and don't go straight home after school.

Only, that's not always true . . .

"His name was Billy," Jonah tells Mr. Fetner. "The other kids say a man in a clown mask crawled in his window when he was home alone. Billy was just sitting there in his chair watching his afternoon cartoons and eating a bowl of Trix when he got snatched. They say the bad guy took him to a basement somewhere and chopped him up into soup and—"

"I wouldn't put much stock into anything your classmates tell you," Mr. Fetner cuts him off, stern but still sorta nice. It's this same teacher-y niceness that made Jonah hope he might help. "I assume you're talking about William Walker? Hadn't realized you were living in his old house."

Jonah nods. "His bedroom, too."

"I had William in my class last year. Good kid, quiet kid, kind of like you, Jonah. He even had trouble turning in his homework on occasion. I'm sure the stories your classmates tell about him are quite spooky. But can you keep a secret?"

Jonah shrugs. He's kinda breaking a promise right now just by talking to Mr. Fetner.

"William's parents were in the middle of a nasty divorce and fighting over custody," Mr. Fetner says. "That means which one of them he would live with."

"Oh, I know what it means."

"Well, the police think his father took matters into his own hands. Kidnapped him, moved him to Canada. Awful, yes, but even William's mother believes he's still alive."

Jonah shakes his head. His stomach knots, his heartbeat races and tingles. The fluorescent lights glint jagged stars off his glasses as if the Bad Thing is happening right now. "But you're wrong. Everyone's wrong. I know what really happened."

"Now, Jonah…"

"I know because Billy told me!"

Mr. Fetner sits forward, kind eyes suddenly sharp and alert. His mustache twitches. "You've spoken to William Walker?"

A staticky, white-cold warning buzzes inside Jonah's ears and crackles downs his spine, freezing him solid for a short eternity. Billy said nobody would believe him. Billy said not to tell.

But he has to try.

"I talk to him every day."

Praying his friend is wrong about adults, Jonah tells Mr. Fetner all that's been going on at home after dark. He spits out every secret Bad Thing.

———

"So that's all I wanted to tell you," Jonah says with a mouth that's gone dry, as if the truth sucked the Kool-Aid right out of him. "If I disappear now, too, my mom will know I wasn't kidnapped—not in the regular way. You'll tell her, right? My mom and ex-dad don't get along very nice either, but my dad won't disappear me. He doesn't even want me."

"You haven't told your mother any of this?" Mr. Fetner says.

Jonah shakes his head. He doesn't want to make her even more sad. Not with her two jobs and two mean bosses. He promised to act like a big boy now, like the man of the house. He just never figured on the Bad Things.

Mr. Fetner sighs, and a heavy goober of melting hope sinks through Jonah's guts.

"You know, Jonah, sometimes when something scary happens that we can't quite explain, we invent big fantastical stories to help us feel better about the mystery." Mr. Fetner raises an eyebrow at him. "Do you understand what I mean?"

Jonah understands. Billy was right.

"Living in a new house might feel strange—heck, even scary— but a house is just a..."

Jonah's ears start ringing, drowning out his teacher's voice. Through the classroom window, a glint of low sunshine hits his glasses. Oh jeez, when did it get so late? He scoops up his backpack and glances at the hands on the clock above the chalkboard.

"Sorry, Mr. Fetner, I gotta go." He scurries from the classroom, fast as he can. Hot tears sting his eyes, and already he knows this is the last time he'll mention Billy Walker and the Bad Things to an adult.

Mr. Fetner calls after him, maybe something about doing his homework—but Jonah's head is too busy spinning, working out a math problem all his own.

Little hand on the five. Big hand just past the three.

A twenty-minute walk home.

The *1986 Farmer's Almanac* in the school library said today's sunset is at 5:47 p.m., and so far, it hasn't been wrong.

All that equals only ten minutes to prepare!

If he runs, maybe he can add a few lucky minutes to his time.

Too bad he's never lucky.

Right away, the slippery November snow-slush sucks at his sneakers, filling his socks with soggy wet ice. His puffing breath fogs his glasses and the sidewalks ahead. The traitor sun sinks faster from the sky, and the brick track houses around him glow orange and cold and alien.

As he passes the 7-11, he biffs it, slipping on ice and skidding on his knees.

A police officer on a coffee break laughs gruffly. "Slow down, kid!" Probably laughing like how Billy will laugh when he finds out Jonah tried to ask for help.

Jonah runs faster. No help for him anywhere, not even from his neighbors. After dark, everyone seems to go blind and deaf.

The sun is a half-ball on the horizon by the time Jonah reaches the cracked cement stoop of his front porch. This house isn't nearly as big or nice as the one they lived in with his ex-dad. They don't *have* nice things since the big jerk married a younger lady. Usually, Jonah feels pretty sad about that for his mom's sake, but today there's no time.

He fishes inside his shirt for the key he wears on a shoelace around his neck. His fingers feel like grape popsicles, and only now does he realize he forgot his coat and mittens somewhere at school. His mom will be upset if he loses anything else to the lost-and-found, but there's no going back now.

He rattles his key in the deadbolt then dashes inside, pausing only long enough to peel a bright orange envelope from the door. *Final Notice.* A fresh knot of worry ties itself in his gut as he locks the door behind him.

In the dim twilight of the living room, lumpy shadows crouch all around him.

Jonah gets straight to work.

He scrambles for the wall switch. The overhead lamp pops on and the living room brightens, revealing saggy brown furniture and as-yet empty corners.

Jonah throws off his backpack. Then, giant deep breath, he races on squishy shoes through the remaining gloom, flipping switches in the kitchen, the hallway, his mom's bedroom, the bathroom, the bedroom that used to be Billy's but now is his. He doesn't exhale until the whole house is bright and shadowless.

Next, he yanks open all the window blinds. His mom doesn't like it when strangers can see inside, especially at night, but Jonah keeps hoping maybe someone *will* see.

He forgot to check the clock on the VCR when he got home. Now that he does, he yelps.

Seven minutes until sundown!

He drags a kitchen chair into the living room and sets it up two feet from the 19" Sony TV his mom got in the divorce. The piece of junk has tin foil wrapped around its bunny ears, but Jonah wouldn't still be here without it.

Six minutes until sundown.

He dives for the shoeboxes he keeps near the TV. Each is clearly marked:

Good Guys. Bad Guys.

Normally the two forces would never team up, but as Billy once told him: extraordinary circumstances call for extraordinary measures.

Jonah dumps his action figures onto the rug and arranges them around the chair. One by one, even though his stupid hands won't stop shaking.

He-Man next to Skeletor.

Optimus Prime wheel-to-wheel with Megatron.

Luke Skywalker, Han Solo, and Chewbacca in a line-up with Darth Vader.

The G.I. Joe attack team mixed up with the goons from Cobra.

And last but definitely not least, Johnny Galaxy with Vamptor and Wolf-Dude, leading the whole squad.

Each tiny protector brandishes a plastic weapon, bravely facing the surrounding room.

Three minutes until sundown.

"Stand by, soldiers!" Jonah hops over his perimeter and beelines for his and Billy's bedroom. He lands on his knees in the corner and pries the metal air vent from the floor. As always, his stomach gives a sick twist and he's certain his secret weapon will be missing.

But as always, it's right where he found it after his first few nights in this bedroom—after weird cartoony dreams about a boy named Billy prying up this very same vent and hiding something amazing. Jonah reaches his hand in and feels that same electric tingle of awe.

He pulls out the VHS tape.

A Maxell T-120 with two hours of tape and a label with Billy's crooked handwriting:

it keeps the BAD THINGS away

Jonah books it back to the living room and slams the videotape inside the VCR.

Two minutes to sunset.

He takes a seat in his action-figure-guarded chair and switches on the TV.

His pulse buzzes with the static on the screen. With a tingly prickle of dread, Jonah hits PLAY on the VCR. The tape rolls.

One minute to spare.

"Oh, blast it!" He bolts upright and runs for the kitchen, kicking Chewie and Han down the hallway as he goes. No time to rescue them! Jonah flings open the cupboard. Never much to choose from. A dusty box of Rice-O-Roni. The last can of Chef Boyardee.

He grabs at a tattered box of Pop-Tarts. It's light enough to be empty, but there's a lone cherry tart rattling inside. Have to eat it untoasted. He snags the pitcher of red Kool-Aid from the fridge then slams back into his chair. His glasses slip down his nose. He pushes them into place just as the digital numbers on the VCR flicker to 5:47.

Outside his gaping windows, the sun disappears into Elsewhere.

Just like Billy Walker.

And just like they did for Billy Walker, the Bad Things come.

———

It always starts the same way.

The wheels whir inside the VCR. The snowy TV static flickers to a commercial for New Coke starring Max Headroom, the blonde AI with the digital stutter.

Jonah leans closer to the screen and clutches the Pop-Tart and Kool-Aid in jittery hands.

Somewhere deep in the house, hangers rattle and a closet door whooshes slowly open. A floorboard moans with horrible footsteps. If Jonah glances sideways, he might catch a tall, wiry, white shadow slipping from his bedroom at the end of the hall.

But he doesn't look; he keeps his eyes glued straight ahead.

Max Headroom thanks him for being a Cokeologist, then the commercial break snap-cuts to black. A squealing guitar solo rips from the TV. Cartoon thunderbolts and music notes flash across the screen, spelling out a jagged heavy-metal logo:

Johnny Galaxy and the Slashers of the Night Beasts!

In the kitchen, condiment bottles rattle as the refrigerator door pops open on its own. Cupboard doors groan and whine, and fleshy bare footsteps trudge across the linoleum.

Jonah's lungs scream, but he doesn't dare breathe.

Doesn't dare blink.

On the screen, Johnny Galaxy's logo explodes and a cartoon teenager with orange leather jeans and an acid-green mohawk leaps from the blast, brandishing an electric guitar. "Greetings, head-bangers! I'm Johnny Galaxy, defender of Darktopolis and leader of

The Slashers, the wildest garage band ever to headline this monster-infested city!"

Jonah mouths along on auto-pilot, like reciting prayers with his mother before bedtime—only now, he's heard by all the wrong ears. Without moving a muscle, he tries to shrink smaller and smaller. If he doesn't move, if he becomes the size of Johnny Galaxy on the TV screen, nothing Bad can get him.

Except he knows that's a lie.

The toilet lid clatters open. Unearthly wet footsteps. Slow movement in the hallway.

A long white shadow gleams along the edges of Jonah's glasses. Neck and limbs as thin and rubbery as linguine. Large pale head. Turning his way.

On TV, Johnny Galaxy thrashes out a power chord on his guitar. Lightning zaps outward, and between the *zip-zam-zolts*, the rocker's ragtag bandmates appear.

"Meet my friends!" Johnny Galaxy cheers. "Veronica Van Hell-Sing—The Slashers' fabulous, fearless drummer! Midnight Jones—born to chew bubblegum and tear up the bass! And every screaming girl's favorite heartthrob—Davey Oscillator on synth!"

Streaks of fluorescent color dance across Jonah's glasses, all mixed-up with the reflection of that approaching shadow. Sickly pale limbs slow-glide down the hallway, getting closer. Nothing Chewie and Han can do to slow the Bad Thing down. Maybe nothing his other soldiers can do either, not with a broken perimeter. He wishes he would've saved his fallen *Star Wars* buddies. He wishes Mr. Fetner was here to see he wasn't lying.

Another Bad Thing creeps at the edge of the kitchen. It grips the doorframe with too-long spidery fingers. Jonah's glasses slip down his nose, but he doesn't dare push them back into place. On the screen, his cartoon heroes become brightly-colored blurs.

"By day," Johnny Galaxy says, "we're high school seniors rehearsing for our next big show. But by night..." The rocker's sunny, instrument-filled garage turns foggy and spooky with moon-clouds. *Zip-zam-zolt!* Thunderbolts strike Johnny Galaxy's guitar and Midnight Jones's bass, transforming them into spikey battleaxes. Veronica Van Hell-Sing's drumsticks sharpen into stakes. Davey Oscillator's keyboard guitar glows with wavery toxic-yellow music notes. "By night, we become The Slashers! Sworn to defend our unsuspecting classmates from Vamptor and the other horrid night beasts of Darktopolis!" A purple silhouette materializes behind the bandmates, fanged, clawed, caped, and reaching.

Behind Jonah, the springs inside the couch cushions let out a slow metallic screech as something huge rises and stands. On the tip of his nose, the lenses of Jonah's glasses reflect the nightmare and swim with white-washed shadows. Unlike Vamptor and the other horrid night beasts, the Bad Things don't reach out with their reedy arms. They don't need to. As they close in from all sides, Jonah's brain screams: *don't look!* But even with his eyes glued to Johnny Galaxy's world, Jonah can't help but see the stretchy-huge grins filling the Bad Things' empty white faces.

Billy said those grins are hungry.

Billy said those grins can swallow a kid deep down into Elsewhere, the very bad place where they're from.

"Join us on our latest slamming-jamming adventure!" Johnny Galaxy raises his battleax and lightning shoots from the blade— right toward the audience! Jagged slashes of cartoon thunderbolts stab the glass of the TV screen and explode outward.

Zip-zam-zolt!

They strike Jonah squarely in the chest, but they don't hurt because they never do.

The Bad Things reach his action figure perimeter.

In a neon flash, Jonah goes from sitting in his living room to standing in the side yard outside Johnny Galaxy's All-American garage. Just like every day after school since moving into his new house, Jonah hears The Slashers in there, tuning instruments, warming up for their latest episode.

And just like always, a grubby cartoon kid springs up from behind a nearby shrub and rushes over to greet him.

"Jeez, dude, what took you so long?" Billy Walker says.

————

"You stayed after school to ask for help?" Billy snickers, pacing the shadows behind Johnny Galaxy's garage. Fluorescent purple music notes pour from a nearby window. "Wowsa, dude, you really are a doofus!"

Jonah hunches over in the cartoon grass, real elbows on real knees, still dizzy-sick from his mega-close call back in the real world. He straightens his glasses, side-eying the reflections of the Bad Things as they glide along the edges of his lenses, testing the perimeter with their linguine limbs. He forces himself to concentrate on Billy in front of him.

The cartoon kid wears the same Bermuda shorts and *Karate Kid* t-shirt he had on the last time his mother ever saw him. In fact, he looks pretty much like the picture on the MISSING poster at the 7-11. Hooked nose, milk-chocolate eyes, dirty mop of hair—only now the missing kid is a genuine cartoon hero, same as Johnny Galaxy and The Slashers. Sharp black outlines, bright video-arcade colors.

Billy takes an enormous crumbly bite of the Pop-Tart Jonah brought him. "What'd you think? Old Man Fetner was gonna go all Mr. Miyagi and save the day? Adults aren't dialed in to the right frequency. The Bad Things will walk right through them and swallow you up anyway. Face it, there's only one escape, Jonah-san, and you've already found it."

In Jonah's glasses, the Bad Things start circling, searching for an opening into this world. He hopes Luke and Vader will summon the Force and hold the line where Chewie and Han fell.

"They keep getting closer," he whispers, all quivery even though he tries to act brave around Billy. "I think they're gonna get me soon."

"That's what Bad Things do, doofus." Billy taps his paper finger between Jonah's eyebrows. "Keep returning to the real world and they'll eat you whole. One gulp! Gone! But it's like I told you an infinity-zillion times, they can't step foot in Darktopolis."

"You're *sure*?"

"*I'm* still kicking, ain't I?" Billy swallows the last of his Pop-Tart then takes a long swig of Kool-Aid. "Take it from me, Jonah-san, you should stay awhile."

Jonah watches him eat, ignoring the low growl in his stomach. Billy's way nicer when Jonah brings him snacks, so Jonah always does. According to Billy, the food here in Darktopolis tastes like ink and cardboard. Secretly, Jonah keeps hoping real food might turn Billy into a real kid again. But so far, it's just the opposite. It's always kinda strange and uneasy watching his friend eat. The shimmery ruby Kool-Aid changes to flat cartoon droplets the instant it touches Billy's mouth. Even his cherry mustache turns animated.

According to Billy, to stay here forever, all Jonah has to do is call out Johnny Galaxy's Power Words. Then lightning will transform him into a cartoon, like Billy. Sounds easy enough, but boy does Jonah's stomach like to twist around at the thought.

"I can't stay here," he tells Billy for like the infinity-billionth time. "My mom needs me to be the man of the house."

Billy snorts. "That's just what moms tell their sons when they're sick of taking care of them."

"Not true. My mom wishes she could be home with me."

"Think about it," Billy says. "How many minutes a day does she actually spend with you? Bet you could set an egg timer by it. She'll never miss you. Heck, she'll be relieved not to have to feed you and dress you and bother with you. Without you, she could quit her jobs, find a *new* man of the house, someone to take care of *her* for a change."

"Don't say that."

"Why not? She'll be happier without you, just like your ex-dad is happier without you."

"You're wrong," Jonah says, but the words taste like cardboard. For a kid that got himself trapped inside a videotape, sometimes Billy is wise in the meanest ways.

He sucker-punches Jonah's arm. "C'mon, don't be such a downer, Jonah-san. Look! There's a bad moon rising!"

Right on cue, the sun drops like a tennis ball from the sky, and when it bounces back up, it's a full silver moon. The sunny sky deepens to a spooky purple nightscape streaked with long arms of wispy midnight clouds.

Somewhere at the end of Johnny Galaxy's street, a lone wolf howls. "*Ah-woooo!*"

The two boys hurry up and peek through the window. Inside the garage, the drums cut short, and the guitars screech to silence.

"Hear that?" Midnight Jones cries.

"I'm catching wolfy vibes," Davey Oscillator says.

"Sounds like a bad moon rising," Veronica Van Hell-Sing agrees, just like she has infinity-billion times before. Billy winks at Jonah.

Inside the garage, The Slashers form a circle and wail the Power Words with rock-n-roll voices: "For the heroes of Darktopolis, power chords to power us all!"

The moon over the garage crackles with purple veins of electricity.

Zip-zam-zolt!

A neon thunderbolt blasts from the sky and electrifies the bandmates. Their street clothes morph into spikey heavy metal body armor. Their instruments sharpen into mighty weapons. Lightning splinters outward, electrifying the whole garage like those static-filled plasma globes they sell at Spencer's Gifts. Billy and Jonah press their hands against the window glass and their hair bristles like mad scientists.

Usually in this part, Jonah likes to puff up his chest and feel a rush of courageous power! Heck, sometimes, he even feels like he might be ready to recite the Power Words himself and go all looney-toon.

But tonight, all he feels are vampire bats fluttering crazily inside his gut.

A second howl shakes the night.

The Slashers high-five with their weapons then pile into their rusted-busted tour van. The muffler coughs a cloud of orange smoke, the radio slam-jams to life, then the van squeals tires down the driveway.

Billy and Jonah rush out and leap onto the back bumper, just like infinity times before. Usually, by now, Jonah stops seeing the Bad Things in his glasses and enjoys the ride. After all, this is the special extra-long episode where Johnny Galaxy first meets Wolf-Dude. It's one of the all-time best.

But tonight, those shifty white-washed reflections don't go away.

Tonight, lumpy bulbous heads tilt closer, breaching the perimeter, widening their mouths. If Jonah squints sideways, he'll be peering down the barrel of a bottomless black grin. There's no telling what Elsewhere will be like, but he bets there won't be cartoons or action figures or anything that makes life not-so-scary. Billy once said Elsewhere is just mountains of chewed-up, unwanted dead kids. And the still-alive kids who get sent there run around dirty, barefoot, and starving—*so* starving they gobble the legs off the dead.

And now it's Jonah's turn.

The Bad Things lurk closer and closer until—

Jonah's sweaty fingers slip from the back of The Slashers' van.

"Hey," Billy cries over the rock-n-roll and the wind. "Get a grip, Jonah-san!"

Too late.

Jonah topples back and hits the street in a dizzy-making somersault. Up becomes down, and the cartoon pavement tumbles around him, scraping grit into his knees. His eyeglasses pinwheel off and he jolts to a stop on his butt. The speeding-off-without-him-van and the bad-moon-rising fuzz into unrecognizable paint smudges.

Anything could be coming at him now—Bad Things, Vamptor, Wolf-Dude…

Jonah paws the ground for his glasses.

Blurry hands reach out of the blurry darkness.

With a scream like a wet burp, Jonah skitters backward on his butt.

"Jeez, doofus, it's just me," Billy laughs. "I've never seen anyone backflip off a speeding van before! That was actually kinda awesome."

"I told you," Jonah gasps, trying to get his wind back. "Something's different; the Bad Things are hungrier tonight. They're watching me right now."

"Of course they are. You're *inside* your TV."

Jonah shakes his head. It's not that. "Why aren't you afraid of them anymore?"

"Because, doofus. I've got better things to be doing. Here." Billy pops Jonah's glasses back onto his nose. The right lens is cracked into a spiderweb. In each of the hundred slivers, a Bad Thing widens its mouth.

Jonah's insides lurch and he yanks the glasses off his face, squelching his eyes tight against a sting of embarrassing tears. He shoves his glasses up at Billy. "I think they're breaking my perimeter. If you're not afraid, then just look."

"No flipping way!" Billy skitters backward. It's the first time Jonah's heard his voice crack. "Get away from me with those things! Those are *your* Bad Things, got it? I've already escaped mine."

"But I can't face them alone. If I do, I'm toast. I don't know how to stop them."

"Jeez, doofus, how many zillion-billion times do I have to tell you? Just say the Power Words, stay with me in Darktopolis."

"I can't." Jonah buries his face in the tattered knees of his jeans.

"Then you really *are* toast. And one day, the Bad Things are gonna swallow you whole." Billy faces the direction the tour van zoomed off in. "Now look what you did. The Slashers are getting away. We're gonna miss the first wolf battle!"

Down the street, howls and fireworks and power chords explode against the Darktopolis cityscape. Neon sparks dance across Jonah's squished-up eyelids. He already knows how Johnny Galaxy's fight ends. Heroes like The Slashers make bravery seem ultra-easy. He's watched them blast the fur off Wolf-Dude a zillion times and won't ever get sick-to-death of it.

Only, tonight feels different—like an egg-timer ticking down inside the buzzing goo of his stupid kid brain. *I want my mommy!* But he doesn't dare say it out loud, not in front of Billy. Instead, he just slumps there in the street, arms blanketing his knees, trying to hold still as ice even as he can't stop shivering.

"Sometimes, you're a major bummer," Billy groans, nudging Jonah's leg with his paper sneaker. But Jonah can't help himself. If he moves so much as a pinky toe, something Bad will happen. He knows it.

Eventually, the fireworks in the distance flare out and Billy gives up on dragging Jonah to The Slashers' next battle. Instead, he helps him to his feet—"Come on, Jonah-san, it'll all be okay."—and guides him, squelched eyes and all, back to Johnny Galaxy's garage.

Jonah sits on Veronica Van Hell-Sing's drum stool and buries his face in his knees. "If I stay, do you think my mom might be able to visit me here?"

Billy snorts. "Wowsa, you've got a lot to learn, doofus."

Only, for the rest of the episode, the cartoon kid doesn't say much—just paces restlessly, tapping his fingers across the drums and tunelessly plucking the strings on Johnny Galaxy's backup guitars.

At last, far-away lightning crackles outward from the moon —*zip-zam-zolt!*—and defeated howls vibrate the paper-thin air.

A power chord later, Johnny Galaxy's electric garage door hums victoriously to life and starts to rise. Headlights streak across Jonah's eyelids as an old beater rumbles into the driveway and coughs to a stop.

His heart gives a little skip, and before he knows it, a pale icy hand reaches out from the real world and squeezes his trembling shoulder.

"Hey there, Little Man, I'm home."

———

Jonah lifts his head from his lap and blinks at his mom's blurry silhouette. He scrambles for his glasses, eager to see her, but by the time he fumbles them onto his face, she's already turning away.

"Sweet goodness, Little Man, haven't I told you not to sit so close to the TV? It's bad for your eyes." In his splintered right lens, a hundred kaleidoscope moms glide dreamily across the living room. She peels off her yellow second-hand puffy coat, revealing her brown cashier's uniform like a bruised banana.

"I love you," he says, but his voice chokes on a lump.

"And just look at this place!" she clucks. "All the lights in creation blazing, toys scattered everywhere. You promised to pick up after yourself."

Jonah blinks. His *sorry* sticks in his chest. His action figures lie battle-blasted all over the living room, sprawled on their backs with plastic limbs twisted at spooky jagged angles.

"I see you've had dinner; that's good." His mom plucks the empty Pop-Tart box off the rug then heads for the backpack he heaped by the front door. "Did you finish your homework?"

"Yes," he lies, barely hearing himself. It's worse than he feared. The Bad Things actually destroyed his perimeter! The torn-off heads of He-Man and Optimus Prime stare blankly back at him.

"Oh God," his mom says, holding up the bright orange envelope he pulled off the door earlier. *Final Notice.* She presses a hand to her mouth as she reads the letter, growing paler and paler, like maybe it's more unfair papers from Jonah's ex-dad. Since the divorce, shadow-clouds always hover around her eyes—but now they darken to storm clouds.

No lightning, though. This one's a rainstorm.

"What is it?" Jonah asks, suddenly afraid. A new kind of afraid.

"Nothing," she lies. Her gloomy blue gaze drifts up from the paper and meets Jonah squarely in the eye—straight through his broken glasses. He braces himself for trouble—he promised to take better care of his stuff—but she doesn't seem to notice the shattered lens. In fact, she doesn't seem to notice Jonah at all. For a long second, she goes very far away, transported to an Elsewhere reserved just for adults. Then:

"Clean this mess up and get ready for bed." Her voice sounds suddenly all shook up like a can of Coke about to burst. "And turn off all these damn lights when you go!"

"But you just got home—"

But she's stopped hearing him. She disappears into the kitchen and starts banging the cabinets closed and cursing Jonah under her breath for leaving the refrigerator wide open.

If only she knew what *really* happened in there.

Jonah crawls around, collecting his busted-up action figures. His stomach gurgles, upset and empty. His knees burn from tumbling off Johnny Galaxy's van. Worse, the carnage in the living room shows how mean the Bad Things can get. Heads twisted backward. Limbs hanging loose on boney plastic knobs. Skeletor, nothing left but a muscular torso. Luke Skywalker, snapped in half and missing his lightsaber. Darth Vader, helmet crushed flat as the Empire. Jonah fills his shoeboxes like coffins, and when he finishes the head count, his heart sinks.

Han Solo and Chewie are MIA.

Vanished from the hallway. Vanished from sight.

The Bad Things got them. Took them Elsewhere.

Only Johnny Galaxy seems to have survived unharmed.

On the TV, the cartoon's end credits cut to commercials. The Trix rabbit appears behind a tree, spying on a group of kids with rainbow bowls of cereal. Billy sits with them. He turns and winks at Jonah, then the scene fuzzes with static and the videotape runs out.

Jonah hits REWIND, resetting the video for tomorrow.

While the VCR whirs, he hovers silently near the kitchen doorway. His poor mom sniffles, then the phone rattles off the cradle. The dial tone buzzes through the lonely house, as if she's trying to figure out who to call.

With heavy feet, Jonah slinks back to the VCR and grabs his videotape. As he retreats for his and Billy's bedroom, his mom says, "Hey, Vick, it's me..."

Icicles stab Jonah's back at his ex-dad's name. Even though eavesdropping isn't polite, he leaves his door cracked while he re-hides the videotape and shrugs into his too-small PJs.

Like always when talking to his ex-dad, his mom starts shouting almost right away.

"Because he's your son, too, damn it! You want him sitting here all alone in the cold and the dark? Please, Vick! How am I supposed to come up with a spare two-hundred bucks by Thursday? I'm already working fifty hours a week! I don't give a shit that you just bought a second honeymoon to Mexico! They're gonna turn off our electricity, you asshole!"

Every word is awful, but as Jonah crawls into bed, the part about the electricity squeezes him to a jittery pulp. He buries his head under the pillow, trying not to cry while he does the math. His ex-dad being a jerk plus zero money by Thursday equals three days until the power goes away and Jonah is toast.

At last, his mom slams the phone down so hard the bell jingles.

Footsteps in the hallway.

His door creaks open and a sliver of golden light shines in.

"Little Man? You still awake?"

Without mentioning his ex-dad, she pulls Jonah up into a hug and nuzzles his hair with her chin. "Who needs electricity, right?"

"I need electricity to watch Johnny Galaxy," Jonah whispers. He can't help himself.

His mom lets out a surprised bark of laughter. "Oh, Little Man, c'mon now. Cartoons? You can survive without Mister Galaxy for a little while, right?"

She won't believe the truth, so Jonah nods and hugs her back, hiding his sad-scared tears like a big man—even as he shrinks inside her arms, so, so small.

"Chin up. It'll be an adventure, right?" But she sounds like she's hiding tears, too. "We'll pretend we're camping. Flashlights, our warm coats, and mittens."

And just like that, piled high atop a heap of worries as tall as a mountain of chewed-up dead kids, Jonah remembers the puffy coat he lost at school.

———

Tuesday after school, Jonah searches the lost-and-found for his coat. He digs down so deep his feet come off the ground. But it's bad luck as usual. His coat has disappeared into Elsewhere along with his mittens and Chewie and Han. He holds up an ugly orange ski jacket that isn't his and considers taking it.

So far, he's in the clear. His mom didn't notice his missing coat this morning before leaving for her shift at the café. She didn't even spot the hole in his glasses where he'd popped out the broken lens. Though Mr. Fetner noticed—just like he noticed Jonah's ripped-up knees and missing homework. "I think it's about time I speak to your mother, Jonah," he warned him after math class.

And now this. Jonah holds the orange ski-jacket against his chest like his mom does at the thrift store. He frowns. The color reminds him of *Final Notices*. Plus, he doesn't want his mom thinking he's a burden *and* a thief. Besides, who needs a coat anyway?

Truth is, he won't get chilly on Thursday when the power goes out because he doesn't plan to be around that long.

Come Wednesday night, he's gonna say the Power Words and stay in Darktopolis. It's his only chance of escaping the Bad Things before the electricity goes Elsewhere. His mom might miss him for a little bit, but after a while, she'll be happier—like how his ex-dad is happier.

Jonah tosses the ski jacket back into the lost-and-found.

A spot of green flutters from the pocket.

Jonah blinks. A ten-dollar bill?

Ten bucks isn't much. Still, he imagines handing it to his mom and the sun-beam smile she'll wear, like he saved the day. Of course, he's not so dumb he thinks ten bucks could save anything, but it'll be nice to see her smile at him. He peeks down the hallway to make sure there are no teachers, then shoves the cash in his pocket.

And now he spots something else in the heap of lost goodies.

A tiny hot pink mohawk. Jonah glances down the hallway again then reaches into the bin. Can this be real? A brand-new Midnight Jones action figure! He pulls her loose, followed by a shirtless Davey Oscillator and a winking Veronica Van Hell-Sing.

With his Johnny Galaxy back home, they complete the band. With their power weapons, they can take the places of his disappeared *Star Wars* heroes.

He shoves The Slashers into his backpack then races home through the shivery snow. He ducks his head low, hoping the grey clouds won't flatten him with a thunderbolt for being a thief.

At home, he turns on all the lights. Pulls up all the blinds. Builds a new perimeter around the TV and VCR. He poses The Slashers first. Standing together, friends-'til-the-end, their plastic battle-punk armor gleams.

Next, Jonah performs emergency surgery on the daring heroes who fell trying to protect him. He pops arms and legs into sockets, screws heads onto necks, and explains the importance of this next battle.

"Tomorrow, I vanish from this world forever," he tells them. His brain buzzes with a blurry-eye headache, and his chest cramps at the thought of his mom hanging MISSING posters at the 7-11. But if he wants to survive Thursday's blackout, Darktopolis is his only choice.

"Guard the perimeter one last time, so I can say goodbye to my mom tonight."

Johnny Galaxy and The Slashers stare back at him with painted eyes.

Outside his windows, the sun drops from the world.

Jonah drops into his chair and hits PLAY.

———

The Bad Things have him surrounded. More than ever, at least ten but maybe two hundred. Long-necked, hideous and towering, their reflections crowd the entire left lens of his glasses. Their deformed roly-poly heads dangle over Jonah's action hero perimeter, peering down at him, grinning.

But tonight, he doesn't fall off the back of The Slashers' van.

"Woo-Hoo!" Billy howls beside him, his cartoony mop of hair whipping wildly in the wind. "This is your life now, Jonah-san!"

Well, it's not his life *yet*—he's still gotta say goodbye to his mom. But ever since Jonah told Billy about his decision to move to Darktopolis, Billy's been celebrating like Jonah's already called out the Power Words.

Johnny Galaxy cranks up the power anthem on the radio and swerves into the parking lot of an abandoned fireworks factory.

Evil howls shake the moon.

"Looks like we found the dog pound," Veronica Van Hell-Sing snickers.

"Let's muzzle those hounds!" Midnight Jones cries.

Billy and Jonah trade high-fives and leap off the bumper just as The Slashers burst from the van with their instruments blazing. Even before the fur and fireworks fly, thunderbolts and star-filled music notes explode above their heads.

Sparks of DayGlo color paint everything, including Jonah. The skyscraper city of Darktopolis shines, more neon than ever. Sharp, clear lines, dazzling colors. Jonah rubs his right eye through the hole in his glasses frame—and it hits him!

Even with his missing lens, his vision feels 20/20. He pulls off his glasses and nothing changes. "Whoa."

"What are you doing now?" Billy whines, tugging him toward the action.

"My glasses," Jonah says. "I don't think I'll need them in Dark-topolis."

"No duh, doofus. The food might stink but everything else here is grade-A awesome."

Just to be sure, Jonah holds his glasses back up. Stupid. All he sees are Bad Things hovering in a frenzy around his perimeter, their starving grins the size of black holes—like they know their chance at a big meal is running short.

"Get away, you jerks!" Jonah shouts. "Just stay back!"

At the sound of his voice, the Bad Things recoil and skitter around the living room as if he lit fireworks in their faces. It surprises Jonah, too. He's never dared speak to them before.

Quick as they scatter, they swarm him again like flies to dead kids. *But still...*

"Billy, check this out," Jonah whispers, holding his glasses out. "I think I spooked them!"

Billy slaps his hand away and his eyebrows darken to angry cartoon slashes. "I told you to keep those things away from me!"

"Don't be a bummer," Jonah says. "Say something to them. They can't get you. They're stuck behind my new perimeter. I got some new toys." Jonah tells him about his discovery in the lost-and-found.

"You found ten bucks?" Billy's eyes glitter with tiny cartoon dollar signs.

"Well yeah, but that's not the point. The action figures practically appeared like magic!"

"Forget that." Paper drool trickles from the corner of Billy's mouth. "Here's what you do, Jonah-san. Tomorrow, during your last day in the real world, you're gonna hustle that ten bucks up to 7-11 and buy us a celebration feast. Nerds, Bonkers, Big League Chew—the works!"

Jonah's stomach grumbles, but he shakes his head. "It's for the electric bill."

"Don't be a doofus, doofus. Two-hundred minus ten still equals lights out. Anyway, don't you think good-old mom will ask where you got it? Want her to think you're a thief?"

Shoot. Jonah can't argue with that.

He sighs. "Fine. I'll buy snacks. *If* you try on my glasses."

Billy's eyes flatten to angry tough-kid slits. "Jeez, what's your weird obsession with me and your nerd-glasses anyway?"

Jonah's mouth goes dry of answers—at least, dry of answers that might impress Billy. With a shrug, he says, "I don't wanna be the only one who sees the Bad Things."

Billy rolls his eyes. "You know, doofus, we're missing the best action again for this bologna." In the background, lightning sizzles and—*zip-zam-zolt!*—ignites the fireworks factory. Wolf-Dude yowls as fur and cherry bombs explode from the windows.

"I'll throw in some Pop Rocks," Jonah says.

"Fine, hand them over." With a sideways smirk, Billy snatches Jonah's glasses and shoves the frames onto his face.

Almost instantly, the missing kid's mouth scoops open with an enormous gasping scream. Before Jonah can ask what he sees, Billy flings the glasses across the parking lot. The remaining lens shatters.

Only, before it does, the wildest thing happens.

For a flash-instant, Billy Walker's cartoon face flickers with the fleshy nose, mouth, and eyes of a real boy.

———

"Your teacher called today." Jonah's mom flips the TV off so zippy-fast he doesn't even get to tell Billy and The Slashers: *see you tomorrow.*

Jonah blinks up at her. His fingers fly to his glasses. Both lenses lost to Elsewhere. In this world, his vision is still all blurry.

Only that's not exactly true. His mom's disappointment is crystal clear. He's let her down. Electricity-gobbling lights blaze all through the house. And in the living room, the bloodbath is brutal. Every last member of The Slashers has been chewed apart.

Jonah grits his teeth, bracing for his mom to shout at him like she does his ex-dad.

Still wearing her coat, she slumps into a puffy yellow heap on the couch and hides her face in her hands. She weeps real tears and shrinks smaller and smaller.

"Mom?" He puts his hand on her shoulder, warm and soft, not paper-thin.

"I'm so tired, Jonah." She lifts her stringy head. "How did I miss all this? Mr. Fetner said you haven't done your homework in weeks, and your glasses... God, just look at you." She flutters her hands at him.

"You're doing your best, but I make it impossible." She shakes her head. "And you've been telling wild stories? Missing boys and a magic videotape?"

"And the Bad Things," he adds in a whisper.

"Oh, Jonah, just stop! You're too old for boogeymen and imaginary friends. Don't you see I have enough to worry about?"

"But Billy Walker *is* my friend. And I might know a way to turn him real again before the power goes out—"

"Enough, Jonah, enough!" she snaps. "Just go to bed."

But he lingers, wanting to hug her and tell her about what happened when Billy wore his glasses. "Shouldn't I pick up my toys?"

"Don't bother. It'll be a while before you get to play with them again."

"I'm sorry, Mom," he whispers. "I love you." But she's too far disappeared in her own Elsewhere to hear him. He slinks down the hallway and closes the door softly behind him.

This isn't how he wanted their last goodbye to go.

But as Billy would say: there are no happy endings in the real world.

———

"Hey, kid, it's freezing out!" a police officer shouts outside the 7-11 on Wednesday afternoon. "Does your momma know you're out here without a coat?"

But Jonah's already learned his lesson about confiding in adults. He ducks his head, hurrying past the window of MISSING posters, and runs home hauling $9.75 worth of Bonkers, Big League Chew, Nerds, Pop Rocks—the works. Tonight, he and Billy are gonna become friends-'til-the-end and share the best-ever celebration feast.

Because tonight, Jonah is gonna say the Power Words.

If only his stomach didn't feel so sour.

If only he could stop picturing that flash-second when Billy's face turned real.

If only his mom hadn't stayed awake most the night, digging through the junk drawers and closets, searching for his ancient pair of eyeglasses from third grade. They were waiting on his nightstand this morning along with a note:

Little Man, I hope this gets you through the day. I love you.

After reading it, Jonah tucked the note into his pocket. Except for Billy's candy, it's the only thing he plans to take with him to Dark-topolis.

Arriving home, shivering, Jonah performs his pre-sundown ritual one last time.

Lights, shades, chair, TV. No action figure perimeter, though. His mom hid his Good Guy, Bad Guy shoeboxes as punishment for not doing his homework and being a lousy son.

Today's sunset is at 5:46.

At 5:36, with ten minutes to spare, Jonah writes his mom a note.

I'll love you forever.

At 5:38, he pulls up the metal air grate in his and Billy's bedroom. It's empty.

Jonah's heart drops out and hits the floor. His secret weapon —gone!

He races back to the living room. Praying, hoping. His mom sent him to bed before he could re-hide the videotape.

But the VCR is empty, too.

5:40—six minutes until sunset.

His mom must've hidden the videotape with his action figures!

Heart racing his feet, he rushes from room to room.

5:41

He bangs open cabinets.

5:42

He yanks open junk drawers.

5:43

He even flings the cushions off the couch.

5:44

But his mom must've hid the VHS tape Elsewhere.

5:45

He slams open her bedroom closet.

And drops to his knees in dizzy relief.

His shoeboxes peek out from beneath the hems of his mom's summer dresses. The VHS tape sits on top.

it keeps the BAD THINGS away

The lamp flickers. Jonah's glasses slip down his nose as he reaches through the gloom.

A floorboard creaks. Hangers rattle.

Two twiggy white legs materialize in the back of the closet.

Jonah's hand freezes on the videotape.

Pale spidery fingers part the curtain of his mom's dresses, reach down, and curl around the videotape.

He's never looked directly at a Bad Thing before.

At first, Jonah can only wheeze with a silent scream. The Bad

Thing's neck is long and scrawny like a rope tied to a lumpy balloon. It stretches its hideous black mouth—only not black, not really. Its mouth cavity is lined with the rotting corpses of dead kids.

"Get away from me!" Jonah cries.

At his voice, the Bad Thing recoils on its spindly legs, topples backward.

The videotape clatters free. Jonah snatches it and bolts toward the living room. As he passes the kitchen, several spidery white bodies tumble like newborn nightmares from the open cabinets.

Jonah slams the video into the VCR and pushes PLAY. Again, again, like punching the call button for an elevator.

At last, the wheels in the VCR whir. The static on the TV snaps to video. The Trix rabbit appears behind a tree, spying on children.

The end of the video! He never rewound it!

All around, the Bad Things skulk from doorways, corners, all the hidden edges of reality.

Jonah hits REWIND then jerks a glance over his shoulder.

A hideous long-necked creature with slimy fish-belly skin spider-crawls up from the couch cushions. It reeks like the blood of action figures and when it opens its grin the dead kids lodged inside that hellish twisty-slide throat scream out for Jonah to run.

But there's only one place to go.

"Stay back!" Jonah screams. "Stay back! *Stay back!*"

All around him, linguine bodies flail, clamping hands to bulbous skulls and toppling backward.

The videotape hasn't finished rewinding all the way, but Jonah smirks at the fallen Bad Things and hits PLAY.

————

It's the final battle between Wolf-Dude and The Slashers.

The moon hangs high and bright over the abandoned Lucky Dog pet food factory—a.k.a. Wolf-Dude's secret lair. High above, on the rooftop, The Slashers hang in chains over a giant steamy can of molten puppy chow. A caped figure with furry ears, a tail, and a spiked leather dog collar stalks back and forth, howling with villainous laughter.

"No more battle of the bands for you tuneless punks!" Wolf-Dude grips the lever that will release The Slashers to their bubbly meaty-dog doom. But Johnny Galaxy and his bandmates smirk and exchange secret glances. They always have a lightning-packed trick up their sleeves.

Meanwhile, Jonah climbs the fire escape to the roof, up and up, fast as he can. His time is running out! His glasses fill with spindly white static as the Bad Things stand and swarm closer.

But he doesn't lose his grip.

"Get back!" he cries, and the Bad Things stagger again.

Hopping onto the roof, he whips off his glasses and scans the chaotic standoff of fur and rock-n-roll. Wolf-Dude's four-legged minions circle the Lucky Dog can with slimy dripping tongues, eager to feast. Crackles of electric blue lightning gather around the moon.

In the murky shadows behind Wolf-Dude, a lost boy stands with tearstained cheeks, watching his favorite cartoon heroes for the infinity-zillionth time.

"Billy!" Jonah cries.

Billy whip-flips his head around and lights up at the sight of Jonah.

"I thought you ditched me forever." He runs over, scraping embarrassed tears from his cheeks with the back of his hand. "Not that I would've missed you or anything, doofus. Did you bring my candy?"

"Forgot the candy! The videotape is gonna run out soon! You have to put these on!" He shakes his glasses at Billy. "You have to make yourself look at the Bad Things! You have to face them. If you do, you'll turn real again." Fingers crossed.

"Are you mental? I don't *want* to be real again!" Billy shoves Jonah backward toward the edge. "I don't *want* to face the Bad Things!"

"Even if it means you get to see your mom again? Go to school? Be a normal kid?"

"My mom was never home! School was hard! The other kids tell spooky stories about me! Why would I ever wanna go back there?"

"Because *I'll* be with you." Jonah glances at The Slashers. Together, dangling over certain doom, the bandmates link hands. Jonah says, "And I have a plan—at least, I *think* I have a plan."

"The plan was to celebrate with candy!" Billy cries. "The *plan* was for you to shout the Power Words and hide out with me forever!"

"Just listen! In the real world, we might be able to fight the Bad Things. *Together*, friends-'til-the-end. We'll shout at them until they go away!"

Billy snorts. "Haven't you been paying attention, doofus? The Bad Things will never go away! Even if one *does* die, there's always another one to take its place."

Across the roof, the furry villain growls a final warning. Maybe Billy's right. Heck, even here in Darktopolis, Wolf-Dude and his pack arrived as replacements for Vamptor after The Slashers slayed him in a previous episode.

But that doesn't mean The Slashers stop fighting.

Together, the bandmates raise their hands and wail their Power Words:

"For the heroes of Darktopolis, power chords to power us all!"

The entire sky crackles with a neon plasma ball of moon-lightning and power chords and courage. A heavy-metal thunderbolt strikes the puppy food can. *Zip-zam-zolt!* A starburst of Lucky Dog's finest explodes outward, splatting Wolf-Dude in goopy brown slop. At once, his growling, starving wolf pack pounces, knocking him on his tail and slurping the muck off his dazed, spiral-eyed face.

Meanwhile, The Slashers flex their super-charged muscles and explode from their chains in a burst of high-fives. Johnny Galaxy, Veronica Van Hell-Sing, Midnight Jones, Davey Oscillator! Each shines neon with blazing inner strength. Together, they tap drumsticks, strum guitars strings, jam on synth, until a pulsing spooky tune fills the air around them.

Jonah does the math. One last song plus a final fur-flying show-down equals:

"The show's almost over!" He rattles his glasses. "Please, Billy, take them. Don't make me leave you behind. If it's between you or my mom, I choose my mom."

The cartoon color in Billy's cheeks heats to a boiling caldron red and he shoves Jonah again, inches from the edge. "You swore you'd stay here! You swore you'd bring me candy!"

"There's candy in the real world," Jonah promises, refusing to lower his glasses. "Have a look. The Bad Things are there, sure. But so are the Good Things. Maybe even secret powers we didn't believe we had."

"There's no such thing as secret powers in the real world, Jonah-san! There is no magic, no Good Things! Only liars like you!" Cartoon flames flare inside Billy's eyes and curls of steam rise from his ears. "I'll never go back to the real world! You can't make me!" He yanks the glasses from Jonah and hurtles them over the edge.

Maybe there are no such things as secret powers.

But that doesn't mean there aren't treasures in the real world that make you strong.

Jonah pats the letter in his pocket. "I'll miss you, Billy Walker," he says. Then he stage-dives like a rockstar over the side of the Lucky Dog pet food factory. After all, he isn't about to let the glasses his mom stayed up late to find get broken.

The factory zooms by, windows blurring into painted action lines. Jonah snatches his glasses from the air and shoves them onto his face a billion-zillionth of a second before smash-landing onto the rug of his living room.

"*Oof!*" He rolls onto his back, gasping.

The Bad Things peer down at him.

Misshapen skulls atop necks as long as arms. Each stands taller than the sky yet lurks close enough to cast an endless shadow. They breathe in deep with those cavernous hellscape grins, taste-smelling the scent of Jonah's terror.

"Go away!" he shouts. "Go away, go away, go away!"

With a chorus of furious wheezing screeches, the Bad Things recoil back.

Then they slingshot forward again and swallow Jonah alive.

———

Spiraling down the Bad Thing's twisty-curvy throat, shrinking smaller and smaller, Jonah prays to be back in his living room, back in Darktopolis, anywhere but Elsewhere.

He squelches his eyelids shut. But he can't stop seeing the nightmare circus of trash and body parts twisting past. Empty food wrappers, broken eyeglasses, mangled action figures, forgotten homework, bright orange *Final Notices*, puffy winter coats, VHS cassettes with black tape spilling out like intestines, all tangled up with the soupy remains of unwanted dead kids. Chopped-off heads, torn-away limbs.

At first, they're only strangers, faces from MISSING posters at the 7-11. But as he slides deeper, they become people he knows.

Mr. Fetner and the snickering police officers at the 7-11.

The kids at school who tease him about the house he lives in.

His selfish ex-dad and his greedy new wife.

And at the bottom, crouching in a pale, hungry-empty pit of loneliness and sadness and desperation, Jonah sees his mom.

"I'm so tired, Jonah," she weeps with a voice that echoes around him and through him.

At the sound, deep in the stomach cavity of Elsewhere, more shadows stir, hangers rattle, a door groans, and more Bad Things drift like phantoms from the gloom—colorless and spidery and long-throated as ever. Only, inside their gaping grins, the soupy carnage is slightly different: mean bosses, ex-husbands, icy houses, empty wallets, a troubled son.

His mom's Bad Things. They surround her.

It's just like Billy said. They're everywhere. They never go away.

But that doesn't mean Jonah will stop fighting.

"Hey, jerks, over here!" He rises on wobbly knees and puffs out his chest.

Because, sometimes, even moms need heroes.

Giant deep breath, Jonah whispers *his* Power Words:

"I won't run away, Mom. I'll be strong for you. I'll make you proud!"

Thunderbolts don't strike.

Jonah doesn't transform into a heavy-metal cartoon warrior with electric superpowers.

But something hidden and Good begins to shine.

He stands ready for the fight. But he doesn't rush toward the crouching figure. That hunched and boney shadow isn't really his mom—just his deep-down scary idea of her.

He knows where his real mom is.

He starts to climb.

Up and up, through the nightmare throat of the Bad Thing. Past all the worries that twist his stomach. Past all the hardships that make him hide. He won't cower in cartoons any longer. And he won't let the Bad Things swallow his life. His ex-dad, *Final Notices*, MISSING kids. Awful, scary, yes—but hapless villains compared to the blazing power of the Good Things.

Like the note in his pocket.

Little Man, I hope this gets you through the day. I love you.

Jonah nudges his glasses up and cranes his neck. Far above the tangled dark mess, the Bad Thing's half-moon grin glows with the hopeful light of his living room.

Jonah climbs and climbs and grows bigger and bigger.

Until he spills un-eaten from the Bad Thing's mouth. Until he hits the rug, gasping. Until the golden light of his mom's headlights glints across his glasses.

———

Late Thursday morning, while Jonah sits in math class, the power in his house goes off. Murky shadows and a misty white chill creep from the corners, filling the silent rooms. Deep in the house, hangers rattle, a closet door opens, and a spidery hand grips the doorframe. More follow, as they always do. They wander, linger, gather in the growing twilight and wait for Jonah to come home.

Later that day, a key rattles inside the deadbolt. The front door moans, and a dark silhouette with large reflective eyes steps inside. He almost reaches for the light switch then remembers the flashlight and fluffy warm blanket his mom left for him by the door.

Click. A beam of light cuts across the living room, briefly illuminating a white-washed forest of legs, arms, and necks.

Jonah whispers his Power Words.

Then, with a wobbly but brave little smirk, he heads to the kitchen table and unzips his backpack. And with his mom's blanket warming his shoulders, he settles in with his flashlight and finishes his math homework.

Just like the Little Man he's become.

ABOUT AMANDA CECELIA LANG

Amanda Cecelia Lang is a horror author and aspiring recluse from Denver, Colorado. She lives with her life partner, two ancient cats, and an ongoing existential crisis. As a die-hard scary movie nerd raised by the VCR, her favorite things are slashers, 80s nostalgia, and the rise of a fierce final girl. Her stories currently haunt several podcasts, including *Tales to Terrify*, *The Other Stories*, *Thirteen*, *Creepy*, and *NoSleep*, and the bestselling anthologies *Night Terrors* and *The Year's Best Hardcore Horror*. You can stalk her at amandacecelialang.com—just don't be surprised if she leaps out at you from the shadows.

DOTS AND DASHES
SHENOA CARROLL-BRADD

Out of nowhere, your car stops. The hybrid engine dies, the headlights blink out. Instinctively, you stomp on the brakes. The car's interior is as dark as the night outside now.

Your satellite radio went silent when everything else did, and the phone you grab from its place in the cupholder doesn't react to your touch. The screen remains black. You've driven this stretch of forested road a million times on your way to see your parents, occasionally contemplating the lack of streetlights. Terrible place to break down, you'd thought more than once before, flying through it with your headlights blazing. Just a thought, a what if, a *thank-God-it's-not-happening-to-me-right-now* daydream.

Only, now it is. And it totally sucks.

You know it won't do any good, but you remove the key, reinsert it, and press the power button a few times, just to be sure. The ignition doesn't so much as click. Same thing happens when you hit the built-in roadside assistance button on your unlit dashboard. Safest model on the road today, your dad said. But nothing responds. Everything is dead. Without a current, all the safety features are just decorations.

How could this happen?

You clutch the phone and hold the home button down for a few seconds, repeating the same hopeless prayer as when you tried restarting the car.

From the corner of your eye, out the passenger side window, something catches your attention. A flashing light. You turn your head to look, but now it's gone. As you go to try the ignition again, the far-off light comes back.

Someone's there, in the woods, blinking a flashlight off and on. You're not sure, but it looks a lot like the codes your dad taught you as a kid—dots and dashes made of light. Short and long bursts that created Morse code messages used by nerds, soldiers, and spies. You haven't practiced the sequences since elementary school, and you barely remember what the patterns mean, but you recognize the intent.

Someone's trying to communicate.

You've stopped right in the belly of the woods outside of town. Too far to continue to your parents' house on foot, and just as long of a walk through the cold back to the outskirts of what people consider "civilization" in this area. You crane your neck to look at the sky. The moon's a sliver up there, a fingernail clipping shedding hardly any light.

The smartest thing would be to stay put in your car and conserve the remaining warmth from your heated seats. Someone has to come along eventually.

The light in the woods flashes again. Dots and dashes. It's so hard to look away.

There aren't any other cars visible along this stretch of road, moving or not. Maybe someone else got stranded, like you, and they need help—someone whose electronics still work. You grab the wind-up emergency flashlight from your glove compartment and tuck your useless phone in your back pocket as you leave the car. You should put your small car into neutral and try to push it off to the side, in case another driver comes too fast from behind. Your parents drilled roadside safety into your head when you got your learner's permit more than a decade ago. You don't, though. On the slim chance someone else comes this way tonight, you want your car to stay where it is impossible to ignore. If their parents raised them to be helpers, like yours did, you're sure they'll stop and offer a hand. To you, and to whoever is signaling through the dark.

The flashlight codes continue, blinking between the trees like lightning bugs.

You wind the emergency flashlight as you walk, though the light never comes on. The whirring sound is loud in this quiet night, but it gives you something to focus on, something to do with your hands. Keeps you from feeling totally helpless as you follow the light into the woods.

You call a greeting, just once, to be friendly—you don't want to spook them.

Your call goes unanswered.

The Morse code continues. Maybe they didn't hear you. Your voice did quiver a little, like your greeting was more of a question.

You carry on.

The path you take seems straight as you duck under branches and feel your way around low growth, but by the time you reach the clearing where the lights are coming from, you're all turned around. You aren't sure which direction leads back to the road and your stalled-out car, as much good as that will do you. The flashlight code was your North Star, and now that you've arrived in the little clearing, the light, like everything else you relied upon, has blinked out.

Tall grass and scraggly weeds grow all around, some as high as your knees. No one's been here for quite some time. Your heart drops as you turn to look the way you think you came. That barely-there moon is no help, but maybe, if you're very lucky, you can find the way back by following the brush you trampled on your way here...

Your shoe clatters against something lying hidden in the grass and you bend to pick it up—a long metal flashlight with a wide head, retro style. You tuck the useless one in your front pocket and try this one. The button clicks sadly underneath your thumb, and faint moonlight draws a silver line where the glass is cracked. The bulb inside long since burned out. Figures.

A curled pile of something lays off to your right, little sticks and logs tangled in cloth, but you don't want to perform a closer examination.

That's it. There's no one here. No sign of whatever was making those flashes. Nothing at all, except a sudden sense of vertigo that makes your head swim and sends you down into a crouch with your head between your knees.

When the motion sickness fades and you're strong enough to stand, the clearing is different. The moon is brighter now, half-waxed and tipping into full, the grass still long but the trees significantly shorter. The comforting weight of your phone is gone from your back pocket, as is the emergency flashlight from the front. Your clothes feel different, and when you move, the fabric gives off an unfamiliar synthetic whisper. You're cold, like you've been waiting out here a while.

Up ahead, through the trees, a flashlight flickers. Short and long bursts, signaling to you as it draws closer.

You smell a sweetness around you, an artificial sugar-and-flowers perfume, and a fake strawberry stickiness smears your lips.

When you raise your arm to wipe your mouth clean, the flashlight turns on again with a quiet crackle. The sudden yellow glow illuminates a new, alarming fact.

The hand holding the flashlight is not yours. The bones are more delicate, the nails long and Day-Glo orange. It's at the end of *your* arm, though, and it moves when you do. The flashlight glass isn't cracked anymore. The rusty stain along its edge is gone.

And the sad, collapsed pile nearly covered with weeds that you didn't want to investigate before—the thing almost but not quite in the shape of a sleeping girl—that thing is gone now, too.

The approaching flashlight draws closer, moving faster. Who could be out here? Who would know to flicker the light that way, and why? You hear the footsteps, solid against the leafy ground, and the swish of brush and branches being pushed out of the way.

You don't call a greeting this time.

Something in the air feels different, locking you in place. You stare in the direction the footsteps are coming from, the flashlight bobbing and strobing as it approaches.

You grip the big flashlight with both hands, shining it straight at the approaching figure. Baby finger atop first finger, you arrange your hands on the ridged barrel like your dad showed you when you were tiny and learning T-ball, back when he could rest his elbow on your ballcap while he drank a celebratory beer.

Something feels wrong here, but it's hard to tell whether that sense comes from you or from whoever painted these fingernails neon. Either way, you're ready to pull back and swing as hard as you can.

The tall grass parts at last, and the owner of the other flashlight steps into the circle of your beam. He's young, probably not even thirty yet, with shaggy brown hair and an embarrassing mustache you recognize instantly. You've seen it in faded pictures and teased him for it. He looks you up and down. A chill runs over your skin. Those friendly eyes crinkle the same as they will ten, fifteen, thirty years later.

This is your father, as you never knew him. This is him in 1986, a few months before he meets your mother. Two years before she gives you life.

In this world you're standing in, you don't exist yet.

But he's smiling at you all the same.

"Hey, beautiful."

It's strange to hear your father call you that, in that tone. It makes your muscles go rigid.

He has the mustache from the Polaroids, but the beard he's worn all your life isn't there yet, and the little scar on the left side of his chin's missing. You always thought it was funny, the way it almost hid under his facial hair, but how, like a pencil's graphite sheen under marker, you could find the scar if you knew which angle to look from. You'd heard the story of the car accident many times, how he swerved to avoid a deer and how his face split open on the steering wheel.

Only, now that you're thinking about it, picturing the pale line running along his skin, you can't remember exactly which way the scar curves. Did it chart the curve of the steering wheel, as he said?

Or did it curve the other way, like the metal rim of the as-yet-unbroken flashlight in your hands?

"Sorry I'm late, baby." He raises a hand to shield his face from the flashlight's glare.

Strong and sturdy hands, even back now.

This is ridiculous. Whoever this is can't be your father. This dude just looks exactly like your father did several decades ago, right down to the so-out-of-fashion-it-might-just-come-back facial hair and the way he holds his shoulders as he walks. And, now that he's closer, the little mole on his neck, below the right ear.

All coincidences. They have to be.

Because to accept the other theory as true would be too much. Too much to admit you'd slipped back along your own timeline so far you wrote yourself right out of the story. Now here you stand, watching what? The prologue? The cold open?

He'd told you stories of his wild younger days, but he never talked about the girls who came before your mom. There must have been some. You never asked.

If you accept this world you're seeing, accept that you've been pulled through decades and into the body of another...what happens next?

If you do nothing and let this night unfold like it must have, at the end, your father walks away and eventually owns a ranch house with a TV in every room and two gassy pit bull rescues, Della and Donna. He'll lose most of his hair and gain half-again his body weight in gut.

And her? She'll stay here, sinking into the soft forest ground until the sun bleaches all the color out of her polyester windbreaker and her skeleton just looks like sticks and moss.

And what about you?

If she dies tonight, will you wake up back in your car on that unlit road? Or will you die here with her, two years before you're born?

What happens if you alter the outcome?

What changes if you help her, if you fight back against this man who gave you piggyback rides and took you to amusement parks and sat you down for way too many I'm-not-mad-I'm-just-disappointed talks?

You could help her get away, but what if there's a struggle and you accidentally hurt him? Kill him? That would doom you never to be born, wouldn't it?

Can you risk it?

"You're real quiet tonight. Not mad at me for making you wait, are you?"

He's lowered his own flashlight and it points to his denim fly as he tucks his thumb into a front pocket. He's slouching a little, to underplay the height difference between you two, but you aren't fooled. His loose, casual stance feels calculated. It feels like a rubber band pulled back so smoothly it seems like it might expand forever, but you know it has to break sometime.

It's going to snap, and you have to make up your mind quickly, before it does.

Who is this man you thought you knew?

You raise a trembling hand and push teased blonde hair behind your ear. "No, I'm not mad." *Just disappointed.* Your voice is soft and raspy. Sweet and shy. It's not a tone you've ever heard before. Remembering the pile of twigs, you remind yourself precisely why you've never heard her.

How did she become that detritus? Other than the flashlight, your father's hands are empty. It's possible he's got a pocketknife in those too-tight jeans, or maybe that's something he only started carrying after he became a dad. Your heart's beating super-fast— maybe she had a panic attack out here. An aneurysm. And he just left her? No, that doesn't seem right. None of this seems right.

Your father never hit you, never tried to strangle you or your mother. Still, those hands are strong. The one time you made him lose his temper bad enough to snap, he grabbed you by the arm and squeezed until you were in tears. You wore the bruises for a few days, but you never forgot.

Just like she hasn't. She was forgotten, but she didn't forget. And he doesn't seem to know she's not alone this time.

You're still not sure what to do. Buy yourself some time.

You clear your throat. "Do you arrange to meet girls out here often, just to keep them waiting?"

A flash of annoyance crosses his face. That grin reappears. So easy. So reassuring, until now.

Now it feels like a thin layer of ice over a pond, waiting for one wrong step to make it crack.

"No, baby. Of course not."

He comes closer.

You sidle back.

"You're my first, I swear."

Your skin crawls, but maybe it's true. You want it to be true.

But even if she really is his first, will she be his one and only? Was she just an accident? A mistake? A ghost you never knew your father carried with him?

Only, he didn't carry her with him. He left her here. Whatever happened, he never told anyone about it.

And the way he hasn't stopped smiling...it's eating away at your certainty. If she's the first, accident or not, will there be others?

Every passing second hits you like drops of sweat, each one ticking by in a heartbeat—a flashlight flicker—all counting down toward some predestined endpoint, a narrowing strip of possibility between crashing waves of doubt.

How much of your father's life is a fog? A lie?

Who even is this man standing before you?

Your father flashes his light into your face, drawing your attention back to him, back to this crucial moment in 1986 where two overlapping realities cannot coexist much longer.

"Hey," he says with a grin, tilting his head to better meet your gaze, like he did when you were too short to reach the kitchen countertops. "Not getting cold feet, are you, Delly?"

Delly. Della? Your stomach turns.

He named his black-and-white pit bull Della.

In remembrance of the friend who mysteriously disappeared one night? Was that his way of mourning, of keeping her memory alive?

The look on his face tells you no.

His other pit bull is named Donna.

Is the real Donna lying in a clearing of her own somewhere, waiting to be found?

Has he smiled every time you called his dogs by the dead girl's name, enjoying his own private joke?

Now you recognize the flashlight in his hand. Plastic-coated body, pebbled black with a stripe of red. That flashlight sat on a high shelf in the garage for as long as you can remember. No one ever brought it down or tried to use it. It sat up there so long it just blended into the décor for you. But for him? Was that dusty shelf a trophy case? A memorial to this night? This moment?

"No," you say to the man who will have raised you, but hasn't yet. "No cold feet here," you say to the man who's about to leave you rotting and forgotten for three decades.

Your thumb slides over the flashlight button, clicking it off for just a second, readying it for a new message. Then on again, lighting up his face with each flash. Peeling back the layers of memory yet to form.

Long. Short. Short.

Short. Short.

Short.

His smile fades. His eyes are hard and empty, unlike you've ever seen them.

You grip the flashlight tighter.

You've made your decision.

ABOUT SHENOA CARROLL-BRADD

Shenoa Carroll-Bradd writes fantasy and horror from her home in southern California. Her short fiction has appeared in more than three dozen anthologies and been produced for audio on several fiction podcasts. She makes some killer vegan bacon and has been learning German in order to sing along with her favorite bands.

THE DAY CAROLINE BLOOMED

KEILY BLAIR

The week Caroline swam in the toxic waters of Gulf Shores, Alabama, she gave her formal blessing to her husband's affair. She noted the slightest hint of flowery perfume when she leaned in to kiss Peter goodbye. The last time she'd worn perfume had been to a local charity ball weeks ago. He tasted like cigarettes despite supposedly having quit cancer sticks at her insistence.

She opened her mouth to comment, but a quick glance around revealed the prying eyes of the neighbors. Peter had agreed to ground rules just so this sort of thing wouldn't happen—so his indiscretions wouldn't be obvious to her—but now was not the time or place to make a scene. She could tell from the smirk on his face that Peter knew that. Instead, Caroline played her part, flashing a smile as dazzling and white as the sunlight reflecting off her Mercedes, the latest in a long line of gifts.

Peter reached up to tug at the string of white pearls around her neck, adjusting them to his content like an owner adjusting his dog's collar. His fingers lingered against her throat. Caroline's heart fluttered in her chest like a hummingbird's wings, blood roaring in her ears even when Peter turned from her and left her standing on their manicured lawn. No "I love you" or even a "Goodbye." She sucked in a deep breath, slipped into the driver's seat, and left.

At the end of the road, she took one look back. Another car joined her husband's in the driveway as though its driver had been waiting to see the Mercedes leave.

It wasn't until she was halfway to Gulf Shores that Caroline grabbed her wedding ring, slipped it off, and tucked it into a small black box she'd brought along just for the vacation.

———————

When she arrived, Caroline explored the beach house. There was plenty of white—the walls, the furniture, the appliances. Now and then, a splash of blue or yellow broke the monotony in the form of glass bowls and throw pillows. Caroline hovered by a painting of a woman relaxing in a chair at the beach, lips curved in a ruby smile. In her previous life as an interior designer, Caroline would've trashed that first.

She searched the dresser drawers but found them empty. Her fingers lingered on the vanity's beautiful cherrywood, feeling around until her nail dipped into a chip on the side. Where had it come from? Who else had used this room? A young couple, perhaps, on their honeymoon. A family journeying down to the beach to take a picture in white shirts and dresses. Perhaps a housewife waiting on her husband to finish with his mistress so she could return from a bleach-white beachside rental that reeked of antiseptic—more a hospital than a home.

A framed photograph of the beach house's owners and their kids sat on a table. As Caroline examined the children—especially the baby with its round, chubby face and brilliant blue eyes—an ache filled her chest. A hard swallow, a sigh with a little hitch in it, and she set the picture facedown.

There were only so many things Peter could provide: jewelry, cars, new dresses. Most of them wound up in the closets or storage rooms in the house, untouched. If not for her mother's illness, Caroline wouldn't have even considered dating a man like him, let alone becoming his trophy wife.

But now, he had her. Until death do us part.

By the time Caroline finished her tour of the house, the sun had sunk low on the horizon. She set about adjusting pillows and décor to give the place a sense of home. When she finished, the house could've easily been mistaken as one belonging to a couple and their rambunctious kids. The bedroom held pillows in complete disarray, the curtains flung wide to let in the dying sunlight, a large candle in a glass jar filling the air with the scent of sandalwood. If she couldn't have a home at her house, she would make a home here, just for the weekend.

A shrill ringing filled the air and Caroline froze. She spotted the source—a yellow princess phone sitting on an end table—and reached for it with shaking hands. She relaxed when her mother greeted her.

"I take it you arrived safely?" Caroline's mom asked.

"I made it just fine. Already settled in."

"Sheila told me there was another car in your driveway."

Caroline's lips pursed. Of course, nosy Sheila would call her mother, who had insisted on exchanging contact information with the first neighbor to say "Hello." She tapped her fingers against the counter in contemplation.

"Probably just Grant," Caroline said. "They were—"

"Don't lie to your mother. I told you before that you don't have to do this. The debt was my responsibility, not yours. A parent shouldn't depend on her child for money or have to watch her suffer in a miserable marriage."

Her mother's sigh, drifting through the phone, chilled Caroline. "You paid it off *months* ago, Caroline. Now get out of there and come home."

Caroline's hand rose to her throat, inches from the dreadful pearls. She unclasped the necklace with practiced fingers and dropped it onto the counter. A *divorce*? The thought alone embarrassed her. What would the neighbors think? Her friends?

They'd think she'd lost.

Caroline's grip on the phone tightened. "I'll leave soon, Mom. I promise."

"You always say that."

"I'm famished. I'll talk to you later. Love you."

Caroline ended the call before she heard the response. Before she went to bed, Caroline wiped at the makeup along her neck, revealing purple splotches she'd have to cover up again in the morning.

————

When she woke the next day, Caroline watched through the giant glass windows as red blossomed in the water like blood from an open wound. It spread over the next few hours until the shoreline turned dark with its growth. The moment she stepped on the back deck, the odor struck her. It was an acidic, low tide smell—vinegar, most people would say. Her manicured nails clicked against the railing of the deck as Caroline made her descent.

Caroline watched the red water from her beach chair long after the tourists had left, their whispers of "sickness" and "toxic" slathered across her skin like the beads of sweat falling onto her towel. Even under the shade of her umbrella, the sun latched onto her, draining every last drop of saltwater untouched by the red tide.

When Caroline walked across the white, hot sand, searching for clear water, the red followed her. Grains of sand nestled between her toes and sandals, rubbing at the exposed flesh. Algal blooms. Health officials always warned not to swim in waters coated with red algae, but Caroline couldn't help herself. This was *her* vacation—a way to fill the void Peter left in her with his every touch, every word.

After the last tourist left the beach, sometime around sunset, Caroline waded in, wondering if the toxins could seep through her flesh. If they did, would they find anything that Peter hadn't already poisoned?

————

Early the next morning, when the sun-drained tourists were still fast asleep in their nice, cozy condo beds, Caroline returned to the red waters. The sea was still warm from yesterday's sun.

She wondered how long it would be before someone took care of the red algae. Wasn't there always someone to take care of every-thing? Some government official pouring chemicals into the water to kill every living thing for miles? A cleaning crew who could scrape up the algae and purify the water, like one would a pool?

Caroline plunged into the surf. Every wave that crashed over her swept away another memory, another toxin. Catching Peter in their bed with some woman he'd met at a local bar. Dabbing a drop of blood off her lip after Peter had struck her. Her mother, wasting away as the disease ate her until she was paper-thin.

When the first rays of light touched the water and made it glis-ten, Caroline waded back to shore. Her flesh tingled, then burned, as her toes dug into the algae-slicked sand. Fire suddenly crept up her legs. Caroline raced to the house, leaving her beach bag on the shore, forgotten.

Blood ran from pinprick-sized holes in her legs, leaving tiny spat-ters on the tile in her wake as she hurried to the bathroom. She turned on the shower, stripping out of her bathing suit. A hiss slipped from between her lips as she touched the tender, weeping flesh.

Once the seawater was rinsed from her body, Caroline carefully stepped out of the shower and hunted for hydrogen peroxide to disinfect her skin. Instead, she found a half-empty bottle of rubbing alcohol. Caroline unscrewed the cap and tossed it aside, put her left leg into the sink, took a deep breath, and poured the clear liquid over her still-bleeding leg.

The violent sting caught her off guard and she slipped, gasping and clawing at the shower curtain, pulling the rod down as she fell. Sunlight poured into the room through the narrow window above the shower. The rays struck her skin, and the fire returned, racing through Caroline's entire body, filling every space within her with a searing burning sensation—an intense, blinding pain that eclipsed rational thought. Her scream bounced off the white walls.

———

The sharp sound of the phone ringing woke Caroline with a jerk. She pulled herself off the bathroom floor, wrapped herself in a blood-smeared towel, and trudged down the hall to the living room.

"Hello?"

"You sound awful," Peter said. He sounded agitated. "I thought you were getting some rest down there."

Caroline cleared her throat, but it made her voice even hoarser. "Is there something you need, dear?"

"I need you to cut your vacation time short and get home," he said. "The house is a mess."

Her fingers tightened around the yellow plastic until her knuckles whitened. Before she could respond, she heard Peter slam the handset down, ending the call. In a fit of unexpected and uncharacteristic rage, Caroline threw hers, ignoring how its cord uncoiled like a sea serpent and how it cracked against the wall. Shocked and surprised by her sudden outburst, too reminiscent of Peter's behavior for her liking, Caroline dropped to her knees, snatched the cord, and yanked, returning the handset to the cradle as gently as her shaking hands would allow.

The gentle sounds of the waves crashing against the shore drifted through the open kitchen window. Caroline stood and walked to the sink. Her trembling fingers reached into the cabinet for a glass. She started to fill it but couldn't stop herself from downing the water before the glass was even full.

After her third glass of water, she realized something was missing.

Caroline opened another cabinet and found the salt. She poured a heaping spoonful of it into her fourth glass of warm sink water and then drank. The glass slipped from her fingers as she went to fill it a fifth time, striking the floor and shattering. She knelt to pick the pieces up, only to slice her finger on a shard. Rusty red slime leaked from the wound for a heartbeat before the skin closed, sealing off the ooze, keeping it from leaving Caroline's body.

Caroline gasped and tripped backward against the sink, as if she could distance herself from her own finger by jumping away from it. A ray of sunlight stroked her shoulders, and the powerful impulse to feel the sun on her skin overwhelmed her, pushing the horror of the red slime from her mind entirely. A crawling, tingling sensation danced along Caroline's flesh.

The sun meant warmth. *Life.*

Caroline raced out onto the back deck, panting as the morning sun blazed down on her exposed skin. The towel slid off her body, pooling at her feet. She thrummed with energy, her heart racing. Pleasure crashed over her in waves. She felt full. Complete. *Sated.*

"Daddy, look!"

Caroline's eyes opened in time to see a little boy standing on the beach, pointing in her direction. The boy's father followed the gesture with his gaze, then cursed and covered the boy's eyes. As other tourists turned to see what the fuss was about, Caroline quickly snatched up her towel and covered her nudity.

She jumped back inside the house, slamming the door behind her as laughter and shouts erupted into the salty air. Once the curtain shielded her from public view, she clutched it for support and laughed, feeling lighter than she'd felt in years.

Her thirst flared up again.

Three glasses of warm saltwater later, Caroline stood naked in the kitchen, knife poised above one of her arms. She slashed in a quick, fluid motion, releasing more of the red slime from her body. Again, the wound healed completely within seconds.

Caroline stared down at the ooze still coating her skin where the cut had been and dipped her finger into it.

Algae.

Inside of her.

Caroline's stomach lurched. She ran to the toilet and vomited rusty red saltwater. The taste lingered in her mouth—vinegar, salt, dead fish. She heaved once more.

The phone rang, echoing down the hallway. Caroline wiped her face on her way out of the bathroom and answered with a voice hoarse from the saltwater and vomit.

"Yes?"

"It's been an hour. Why aren't you on your way home yet?"

"I'm sick."

"Quit making excuses. I told you to come home. You better get on the road."

The call ended. Caroline shook, a laugh bubbling out of her throat. That was it. He would not push her around anymore. She'd leave—

You always say that, Caroline.

No. She wouldn't leave him.

If her mother could endure cancer, Caroline could endure Peter. She couldn't survive the whispers and stares, the thought of her neighbors' laughter behind closed doors as she trudged out of her expensive, cozy house to move back in with her mother, a childless *divorcee* in her late-thirties. The women at her book club would bring her faux pity casseroles and baked goods, then one—or more—of them would jump right into bed with Peter. Surely, he'd replace her with a younger, more attractive woman before the ink had dried on the divorce papers.

Her humiliation would be unbearable.

Caroline cleaned herself up as best she could then pulled on the white cotton summer dress that Peter always complimented. She wrapped the pearls around her neck once more. After examining herself in the mirror, she realized the bruises ringing her throat had faded completely, negating the need for her complicated makeup routine. She coughed, spraying a bit of algae onto the sink, then dabbed at her mouth and brushed her teeth so hard that her gums bled (though they promptly healed). A swipe of pink lipstick, and she was ready.

————

After a few hours on the road, an ache formed in Caroline's body. Blackness crept into her vision, causing her to swerve the car all over the road. Each time she drank more of the saltwater she had prepared before leaving, the ache drifted away and her vision returned. Sunlight helped, too, though the car's tinted windows filtered out most of it. Early in the drive, she'd rolled down the driver's side window and left her arm out until it turned pink with sunburn.

Now, she stood before her front door, key in hand as the lock clicked.

The stench of acrid smoke in the foyer struck her first. Peter waited in his office, just off the entryway, seated in his favorite leather chair, cigarette in hand. He blew out a cloud as Caroline approached. Last time he smoked in the house, it had taken her weeks to get the scent out. Weeks of scrubbing, trying not to think about how she was breathing in the same toxins that riddled her mother's body with cancer, trying to forget her mother's medical debts piling high.

"The house looks fine," Caroline said.

Peter shrugged, bringing the cigarette to his lips, then blew the smoke toward her, a knowing smile on his lips. "The sheets need washing." He tossed the cigarette on the floor and crushed it underfoot, blackening a small spot on the carpet.

Caroline clenched her fists at her sides and lowered her voice to a growl. "I am not your maid."

The words slipped out before Caroline realized she was speaking.

Their eyes met.

The moment Caroline moved to run, Peter grabbed her and slapped her face, his chunky gold ring splitting the skin on her upper lip. Pain crashed over her like a tidal wave.

Peter blocked the doorway, so Caroline darted to the window. She shoved aside the curtains and threw up the sash, intent on calling out—crawling out, if needed. Sunlight poured into the room, striking them both. She sucked in a breath to scream but the light hit her, its warmth permeating every cell in her body, giving her *life*.

"What in the—" Peter shrieked.

Caroline turned.

A smear of algae lingered on Peter's hand, bubbling, burrowing. Now, he was screaming, shaking his hand hard as fresh blood dripped on the carpet.

Dazed, Caroline stared as the fluid soaked into the synthetic fibers, the sun at her back enveloping her like a blanket. She was going to have to scrub the spot for ages. The pain in her lip had already faded, the split closed up and fully healed.

"What did you do to me?" Peter demanded.

Caroline's brow furrowed. Before she could respond, Peter began to shiver, then violently shake until he toppled to the floor. He gasped for air, taking great, heaving breaths that turned into a vicious coughing fit. Caroline watched as he spasmed, twisting and jerking his head against the carpet. Peter reached a hand toward her. Caroline watched his fingers close on empty air, watched red fill the whites of his eyes and ooze out of his mouth, watched him grow still.

———

The police had many questions for Caroline.

Did he seem sick?

Yes, she lied.

How long?

A few weeks, she lied.

He never went to see a doctor?

I tried to tell him to, she lied.

The official autopsy report asserted Peter had died of organ failure, possibly from the kidney transplant he'd had years ago.

After the funeral, Caroline flung open all the curtains, filling the house's many rooms with light. She and her mother sat in silence in the sitting room.

"Two toxic organisms can't exist as one flesh in one household," her mother finally said. "It was bound to happen eventually. I'm just so thankful it wasn't you."

Caroline considered this, then smiled. "That's an interesting thought. I've never considered myself toxic."

She brought the glass of saline to her lips and drank.

ABOUT KEILY BLAIR

Keily Blair (they/them) is a neurodivergent, queer writer and editor. They hold a BA in English: Creative Writing from UT Chattanooga, where their nonfiction won the Creative Nonfiction Award. Their fiction has appeared in magazines and anthologies such as *The Dread Machine*, *Dream of Shadows*, *Cosmic Horror Monthly*, *Good Southern Witches*, and *The Vanishing* Point. They are currently at work on a botanical horror novel. You can find more details about their work at www.keilyblair.com. They live in Chattanooga, TN with their husband, dog, cat, and four guinea pigs.

DESIGNS ON REDEMPTION
CHRIS DESTEFANO

The racks of bright, erratic patterns swayed with the bobbing of the anchored craft, making Gary nauseous. He had no idea when his mysterious, potential benefactor would make an appearance, so he couldn't waste any time prepping the pitch. He pulled different combinations of clothes from his case, arranging them in the exact layout to make his creations pop; seasickness and nerves be damned. The ensembles needed to pull together seamlessly—every detail perfection. A stray thread or a crooked stitch could sabotage his redemption. You get blamed for burning a kid to death, and you'll have to jump through a few hoops to get back on top.

The years following the incident had been hell for Gary. Ever since that kid, he had been forced to retreat to the dark corners of society, scrounging and scavenging with the bottom-feeders. Sure, he'd managed to beat the lawsuit and slip the criminal charges thanks to some slick, unscrupulous lawyers and just a large enough loophole in the Flammable Fabrics Act to mount a plausible defense; but slick and unscrupulous cost big money, which left him with nothing. Worse, the bad press proved more difficult to shake than the criminal investigation, and the reputation stuck. His label had folded, and he couldn't find work with even the lowliest of the fashion houses. He'd skulked off into exile and waited.

Only recently did he emerge into the light to attempt to climb the ladder back to the top. A few writeups about his bold new clothing line, Tude Wear, reintroduced his name to the public. But printed alongside phrases like "ahead of his time" and "enigmatic visionary" were words like "disgraced" and "scandal-plagued." So, when a lawyer, Alan MacArthur, reached out with an invitation on behalf of an investor who wished to remain anonymous until they saw the designs, Gary agreed immediately.

He couldn't really blame the investor for wanting to remain behind their curtain—he wouldn't touch him with a ten-foot pole either—but of all places to pitch a new fashion line, why a fucking yacht? The light was absolute shit, and the constant, subtle motion of the huge boat caused the clothing to sway as if possessed by gentle spirits. Whoever the investor was, they obviously didn't know a damn thing about design aesthetics, which suited him just fine. He wanted this person's money, not their opinion. He'd make the pitch on a damn rollercoaster if they asked.

Gary popped another Dramamine tablet and refocused. He squinted, walking the displays one last time, taking in the purple tank tops and smoothing out the neon yellow and orange jackets. The pieces he'd brought represented the best of what he imagined as the future of streetwear over the next few years. If these didn't capture the investor's heart, he supposed repositioning denim jackets for the tenth time wouldn't help either.

Gary sighed and ran his hands through his thick, unkempt hair, his palms coming out damp. Time to get his shit together. He made a beeline for the sliding glass door that led out onto the deck, slid the door closed behind him, and settled against the railing. The breeze picked up, the salt-laden ocean air cooling the sweat on his neck and brow. He rolled up the sleeves of his white blazer and tugged at his T-shirt collar. The sounds of revelers on the decks above floated down to him, and he hung his head against the railing, pulling in long draughts of breath through gritted teeth.

This is what I get for dipping into the coke early.

Gary couldn't help himself, not really. He was fucking nervous, and drugs were everywhere on this floating party. Servers roamed the top decks carrying shining silver platters topped with champagne and cocktails. If any of the partygoers ducked below deck into the dimly lit quarters, they could find trays catering to more varied tastes. Quaaludes, cocaine, speedballs, uppers, downers, and everything in between—all laid out neatly for the revelers. A promising sign.

Earlier, Gary had downed a couple glasses of champagne to take the edge off and then did a bump or three of coke to level himself out. They hit him harder than he'd expected—probably the nerves. Normally, he would gladly indulge in the festivities until he staggered down the gangplank and vomited in a cab on the way home, but not tonight.

Tonight, he needed to be on his game. His A-fucking game.

The trick was to find the proper balance between sobriety and numbness. Too many drugs and he risked being muddled, hazy. Too few, and the memories crowded in. Flashes of court photographs. A charred t-shirt, stiff with dried, copper-toned blood. Wailing and gnashing teeth.

Gary retched over the side, emptying his stomach into the ocean with a series of splashes. He pulled his handkerchief from his jacket, wiped his mouth, and gave himself a spritz of Binaca.

Better. Time to get back to the party, maybe grab a rum and coke to refresh himself, and work through his pitch until summoned. He tried to pull the door open, but it wouldn't budge. He tugged again, leaning his weight against the handle.

Locked. Just perfect.

Gary cupped his fingers over his eyes and pressed his face against the glass, trying to see into the dim room. He settled back to light a cigarette and plot a new course topside when movement caught his eye.

There, in the center of the room, stood a figure. Gary could only make out the shadowy outline of a person standing, motionless, amidst his creations.

Gary knocked on the glass.

"Hello? I locked myself out. Can you be a hero and let me back in?"

The person didn't respond, didn't even turn to acknowledge him.

Gary pounded his fist against the glass with a bit more force and raised his voice. "Hey, can you hear me?"

The figure turned slowly in his direction. Gary could make out a slight movement of their hands, accompanied by a flicker, then the flame of a cigarette lighter sputtered to life. Whoever was in that room, amongst all his precious designs, was literally playing with fire.

Gary's nausea returned with magnified ferocity. He thumped his fist against the glass as hard as he dared.

"Get away from my work!" he screamed through the door.

Still, the pattern of pop, sputter, darkness continued, the flame jumping into existence then dying before it illuminated any of the intruder's features.

"Put down that lighter!" Gary pulled at the door, veins straining in his forearms.

Panicking, he looked around and spied one of the room's over-sized windows ajar. He rushed to it and pulled it up until he could throw himself through the opening, tumbling to the floor in a heap.

He scrambled to his feet, intent on confronting the interloper, only to find himself facing an empty room.

Gary scowled and briefly searched the small space but saw no sign of the lighter-toting phantom. With a last glance around, he returned to the hallways to find the lawyer and a vodka rocks, to get his presentation underway before he fully cracked.

The ship's halls were narrow and claustrophobic, with only dim floor lights to guide him out of the bowels of the craft. Gary ran into several dead ends and backtracked a few times before admitting he was lost. The corridors' dimensions felt off, as if they were too long for the hull housing them. The boat was big but not big enough that he shouldn't be able to find his way out.

Gary took a few deep breaths to slow his racing pulse. *Nothing's wrong,* he told himself. *Just calm down; you'll find a way out of here in a minute.*

After a few more random turns, he came to the juncture of four hallways, each leading off into hazy darkness. He couldn't remember passing this way, nor did he understand how these damnable hallways could stretch so far.

As Gary stood there, frozen, pushing down his anxiety, a noise reached him. At first, he barely registered the sound against the constant background thrum of the ship, but as the noise repeated itself—*dragclick, dragclick, dragclick*—the familiar cadence captured his full attention. The unmistakable sound of someone rolling the spark wheel of a Zippo, then flicking the lid closed.

Gary squinted down each hallway. Each staccato beat—*dragclick, dragclick*—drew closer. Finally, at the farthest reaches of the hallway opposite him, he spotted the brief flicker of a flame.

"Have you been following me?" Gary called into the dark, his voice but a tinny echo in the tight quarters.

No response.

Gary felt a flash of anger, but his fear quickly surpassed it as he watched the flame jumping a little closer to him with each *dragclick*. He did not fancy himself a courageous man. If this person meant to intimidate him, they were doing a fine job.

Gary fled, turning down random hallways, deeper into the bowels of the boat. Pursued by the sound of the lighter, he gained no distance from his dogged stalker.

He came to a set of stairs leading up to a closed door. Breathless and dripping sweat through his bright blue t-shirt, still pursued by that regular *dragclick*, he clambered up the steps and fell against the door, pushing down the handle.

It opened. Strobing multi-colored lights and the blaring synth and guitar of a wild party scene assaulted Gary's senses. He reeled against the contrast, tried to orient himself, then staggered into a sea of writhing bodies that knocked him about on the crowded dance floor. Though still half-blinded by the lights, Gary spied a bar on the far side of the room and moved in that direction. The press of revelers and the low ceilings made him claustrophobic. As he shoved dancers aside, they paid him no notice, instead flowing back like water in his wake.

Gary's momentary relief at having escaped the ship's dim lights and muted halls dissipated with each pulse of the music. At the center of the dance floor—halfway to the precious safety of the bar —he found breathing room. The crowd formed an unbroken circle around him, leaving him several feet of wooden floor to himself.

Exposed.

Like flipping a breaker, Gary's claustrophobia transformed to agoraphobia.

The flashing lights seemed to focus on him. He held his hand to his eyes, shielding them from the pop-flash of the strobes, and saw a pillar of stillness among the swaying, living wall's first row. A black-robed figure, hood drawn, faced Gary in its own bubble of quietude.

Gary stepped back and looked for a break in the crowd. He wanted nothing to do with any weirdo wearing a cloak to a yacht party.

As he whirled, Gary spotted a second cloaked stranger amid the throng, then a third, then a fourth. They all stood still, immune to music and movement. He could feel their stares beneath their dark cowls.

Had his coke earlier been laced with a little something extra?

Gary plunged back into the crowd, bowling over dancers in a mad dash toward the bar. He crashed into its edge, the impact knocking the air from his chest. Sucking down oxygen, Gary seized the bronze rail ringing the wooden counter to avoid collapsing.

The bartender raised an eyebrow at him. "You alright?"

Gary held his hand up, one finger raised, and nodded. After a few more breaths, he managed to stand upright again. As he did, he twisted to look back to the dancefloor—no signs of pursuing robes.

"Vodka, neat," he sputtered. "A double."

The bartender reached beneath the bar and pulled out a bottle, pouring the clear liquid into a crystal tumbler. Before he could finish, another man reached across the bar and laid a hand gently on the bartender's wrist. Gary watched as this interloper, an older man with silver hair and a well-manicured mustache, shook his head at the young server.

"Please, Daniel, won't you grab something a bit more sophisticated for Mr. Diaz? Only the best for one of our guests of honor this evening." The graying gentleman's voice cut through the din.

The bartender dumped the vodka. "Yes, Mr. MacArthur." He pulled a stylized bottle from the shelf behind him, a brand that Gary did not recognize.

Gary examined Mr. MacArthur, the lawyer he'd only spoken with over the phone. He'd expected a mouse of a man who existed only to do the bidding of his wealthy employer. Instead, Alan MacArthur was tall and powerfully built, poised and imposing despite the deep-set lines of his face. The lawyer's attire harkened to a statelier era, forgoing the brash power suits—which Gary himself refused to include in his collections—in favor of a dark three-piece suit.

"I've been looking for you, Mr. Diaz," MacArthur said, smiling. He extended his hand. Gary took it, and the lawyer's huge hand enveloped his own; it felt frigid, as if it had just been pulled from extended time in a freezer. "Are you alright, Mr. Diaz? You look a bit unwell. You're sweating."

Gary released the other man's hand. "Oh, yes, I'm fine. Just a bit hot from the crowd. I was looking for you, as well. It's nice to put a face to the voice." He grinned at the lawyer, hoping he still conveyed his usual, disarming charm.

The lawyer nodded. "Our patron's parties are always wonderful affairs. Guests tend to enjoy themselves quite vigorously." MacArthur extended an arm, indicating a doorway set off to the side of the bar. "Shall we? I'm sure you're eager to finally meet your host."

Here was his shot. *Pull it together, Gary, pull it together.*

"Absolutely. I've just got to fetch my designs from downstairs."

MacArthur shook his head. "That will be taken care of. Don't waste that drink, Mr. Diaz. It's a rare dram," he called over his shoulder as he headed toward the door.

Gary grabbed the glass and followed.

The party's cacophony fell away as they entered a room resplendent with deep red velvet curtains, plush carpeting, and dim wall sconces. Cognac and cigar smoke overlaid a more unsettling scent that Gary couldn't place. A gentle murmur of voices rose from well-dressed guests. The crowd was thickest at the far end of the room, where someone was holding court amidst a circle of eager listeners.

"Let me introduce you," offered MacArthur.

Gary wished he'd had a second to comb his hair and gather his thoughts, but he'd roll with it. Here came his only chance at a first impression, the difference between success or continued obscurity. He took a long sip from his glass to steel his nerves before tailing the towering lawyer across the room.

The crowd parted for MacArthur and background chatter quieted. The other guests watched Gary closely, dozens of sets of eyes tracking his movements. He swore he could detect something in their gazes. Jealousy? Eagerness?

Before Gary could divine an answer, he found himself in the center of a circle for the second time that night. Seated on a couch before him was a striking middle-aged woman whose green eyes blazed at her enraptured guests. This woman curated every detail of her image, every stitch of her clothing, to command a room, to radiate control. Gary's eye for design went into hyperdrive at the sight of her perfectly styled hair and bright red power dress, with its wide, black-peaked lapels and angled shoulder pads clearly intended to draw all eyes to her. She looked at him with a broad smile on her face.

"Gary Diaz," MacArthur said, "please meet Miss Andrea Bethel, our benefactor and hostess this evening."

"Miss Bethel, it is a pleasure to meet you." Gary offered his hand to the woman.

She stared through him for a long, terrible moment. The entire gathering paused, breath held as though awaiting a signal. Just as Gary thought he would have to drop his arm and wilt into the floor, she stood and wrapped him in a warm embrace. He suppressed a flinch at the intimacy of the gesture before she pulled away and studied his face.

"Gary Diaz, the pleasure is all mine. I've been waiting so very long to meet you. Longer, I suspect, than you know."

"That's very flattering, Miss Bethel. Thank you."

"Of course, of course. Please, won't you sit with me?"

As he took a seat next to her, the room sped back into motion, and the murmured conversations resumed as guests milled about. MacArthur lowered himself into a seat in an overstuffed armchair across from them.

Gary took another long sip of his drink. "Ever since I received your mysterious invitation, I've been eager to have a chance to speak with you, Miss Bethel," he said, readying his pitch.

"You'll excuse the cloak and dagger, I hope. With your reconstructed reputation still a delicate work-in-progress, I felt it prudent to use Mr. MacArthur as my intermediary."

"I understand. All of that is behind me now. I'm focused on introducing my designs back into the world, on giving my art a chance to thrive again." Gary had rehearsed this particular line well over the past few months.

"Is it?" she asked.

"Is it what?" He panicked for a second. Perhaps the drink was stronger than he expected. His face felt slightly numb.

"That awful situation with that young boy, the trial—is all of that behind you?"

Gary had prepared for these sorts of questions. Hell, he'd answered similar lines of interrogation dozens of times. Now, he was struggling to dredge up his canned, diplomatic responses. He felt the urge to tell this woman the truth—how he woke up every night to the ghostly evidence photos fading into his bedroom ceiling, how the dead boy's name sat forever on the tip of his tongue, repeated over and over again when Gary sat alone in his apartment, how he told himself every day, like a prayer, that it had been an accident, how—

yes—the dyes and chemicals he used to give life to his vivid colors and patterns *were* flammable under specific circumstances, but those mixtures were what separated his work from the rabble, elevating his garments from cloth to art, causing his rivals to lower their eyes in shame.

How could he have dreamed that the particular chemical compounds in a specific brand of roman candles would also act as an accelerant in his dyes?

Swallowing the truth, Gary attempted a somber look. He sighed. "It was a tragic accident, and my heart goes out to the boy's family. What happened was awful, but the trial and acquittal were a long time ago, and I'm moving forward with my life. It's time to come out of the shadows."

His potential patron clasped her hands together and leaned forward. "Out of the shadows? What an interesting choice of words."

When she said *shadows*, the lights dimmed, and the edges of the room withdrew from sight. That feeling of numbness spread from Gary's face into his neck and back. He rolled his shoulders to shrug off the sensation.

"So, now you wish to emerge, triumphant and redeemed, the prodigal son returned from self-imposed exile?"

"After a fashion," chuckled Gary, trying to brighten the conversation. "Yes. Despite my innocence, I still feel troubled about the young man's death. I may not have been responsible for it, but he was wearing my clothes, and I've experienced some mental trauma. I had to work through my pain on my own, away from the public eye, through my designs." He raised his glass and drained it.

"Yes, I saw that in your new work," Miss Bethel acknowledged. "But I sense in you less an exorcism of trauma and more of an obsession with guilt."

Gary frowned, confused again. How fucked up was he, exactly? How strong was that drink? "You've already seen my clothes? Wh-where?"

"Here." She stood.

Gary tried to follow suit, to pull himself to his feet, but his legs were shaky, tingling with pins and needles. He stumbled.

An iron grip closed on his left arm. MacArthur offered him a full-toothed smile, with a touch too much glee in it for Gary's liking, and hoisted him up. "I should have warned you—the drink is a bit strong. No matter, come along, come along."

Gary leaned against MacArthur's bulk as they followed Miss Bethel. The guests had lined up, forming a pathway that led to a black door that bore ornate, carved runes and symbols. He didn't like the look of that door.

The lights in the room dimmed again. Gary felt like a model on a catwalk, with only the route in front of him illuminated. As he walked past the guests, they each pulled the hoods of their black cloaks over their heads.

Miss Bethel reached the door and pushed it open, stepping into the inky darkness beyond the threshold.

Gary tried to pull away from MacArthur but couldn't; his limbs were too heavy.

"Come now, Gary, we've gotten this far. Time to give Miss Bethel your pitch," MacArthur chuckled, dragging Gary through the door and shutting it.

For a few moments, Gary was blind and the room was boneyard quiet as MacArthur propped him against the wall just to the right of the door. The strange scent from the outer room was stronger here—sulfur and ashes.

"Mr. MacArthur, would you get the lights, please?" Miss Bethel's voice, somewhere close.

A flare of light erupted in response. MacArthur held a large wooden club aloft, fire licking its tip. He moved to the corners of the room, lighting wall sconces as he went, revealing a small space devoid of anything but a large pile of rags at its center sitting inside a large, etched pentagram with unlit black candles at each of the star's points. Painted on the walls, in a dark red substance, were glyphs akin to those carved into the black door.

"What is going on?" whispered Gary, his tongue a heavy slug in his mouth.

"Don't you recognize your art?" the woman replied, no trace of a smile on her lips now.

Gary squinted at the material on the floor and recognized the rags. They sported colorful patterns. His color and designs. All of the clothing over which he had toiled for so long now lay in a wrinkled heap.

"My clothes. What...the fuck is this? Who are you?" he sputtered.

Andrea and MacArthur set to lighting each of the five candles around the pentagram.

"When those fools acquitted you, I was furious for a long, long time," Miss Bethel said. "All of my prayers to a deaf God went unanswered. No life for my nephew, no justice for his family." She looked up from her task. "I searched elsewhere for answers and realized that for all of America's Satanic Panic, the Devil is just as cold and distant as God. That's when I found Lord Mastema."

"Hail Mastema!" shouted MacArthur, standing up to inspect his work.

Miss Bethel drew close to the lawyer, nodding her approval at the chalk scrawls on the metal floor. "Thank you, Alan. Would you make Gary more comfortable and tell the others it's time to begin?"

MacArthur grasped Gary by the shoulders, lifting him from the wall and laying him atop the pile of clothes with surprising delicacy. Gary could only follow the man with his eyes as MacArthur gave a chivalrous bow and stepped away.

Miss Bethel knelt before Gary as quasi-Gregorian chanting began outside the door, a low, ominous hum that made Gary's bowels twist and his eyes water. "Before he fell, Mastema persecuted evil on God's behalf. He can smell your guilt, Mr. Diaz."

The chanting outside the door suddenly grew quiet.

"Guilt is not the question," she said.

A familiar sound replaced the twisted chorus outside.

Dragclick.

Dragclick.

The torch flames ebbed to low, shifting orbs of blue fire.

The door creaked open. Gary couldn't see anything beyond the blackness—a void. As he watched, a figure stepped through and approached Miss Bethel's kneeling silhouette.

She continued. "This is a matter of your redemption. Have you acted on your guilt? Have you changed? Have you *truly* been redeemed?"

Miss Bethel pinched a corner of the cloth below Gary's paralyzed arm and rubbed it between her index finger and thumb. "Are these garments any different from the ones in which my nephew burned alive?"

The cords in Gary's neck pushed against his flesh as he tried in vain to answer, to nod, to apologize.

The figure from the void held up its hand. The small ember of a Zippo lighter snapped on, emitting more light than it should have, fully illuminating its bearer.

Behind Miss Bethel stood a fifteen-year-old boy.

The flesh of his face, neck, and upper shoulders was pale, untouched, but the rest of his body was a charred ruin. Split and blackened flesh encased his bare arms, oozing blood. The boy wore the tattered remains of a neon purple tank top, which clung to his torso by a single thread. Where the boy's stomach should have been, a large scorched circle revealed a deep wound with raw and jagged edges. Within that hole glowed a still-burning star from a roman candle.

"Lord Mastema knows your heart, Gary, and his flames will judge your works."

The boy stepped forward, holding the Zippo lighter out toward the best art of Gary's life. Gary pried his eyes away from the flame, from the boy, from Miss Bethel, and settled his gaze to his left, on the brightest blue shirt he'd produced. A worthy centerpiece for his triumphant return collection, now even more beautiful under the fierce, colored spectrum filling Gary's sight as his clothing throne became his pyre.

ABOUT CHRIS DESTEFANO

Chris DeStefano was cursed by a warlock at a young age, after meddling with forces he did not fully understand. He is now fated to one day spontaneously combust and is plagued with a recurring nightmare in which he is a very mediocre exorcist. He currently lives, works and writes in New York, NY with his wife, daughter and two black cats. You can find his work on thedreadmachine.com and in *Cosmic Horror Monthly*.

WELCOME TO CAMP KLEHANI!
CALEB STEPHENS

I stare at the cheerfully carved letters tacked over the door and groan: Welcome To Camp Klehani!

Fat camp, Jesus...

I'd fought hard not to come, but I knew it was over the moment Mom got her hands on that glossy flier with the kid smiling down from an exercise bike like it was a rollercoaster. She'd been having whispered conversations about my weight with Dad for over a year now. I'd moved well beyond "big-boned" territory. Still, I thought the cost alone might save me from going. I mean, a thousand bucks is no joke, especially for a cheapo like Dad, but he agreed immediately.

Yay.

I slap at a mosquito with a stinger the size of a coffee straw and stroll into the lodge. A mounted deer head takes stock of me from the far wall, its dull, glass-bead eyes oozing disapproval.

"Name?" mutters a girl from a rickety folding table. She glances up as I lug my suitcase over, and my voice clogs. I've never seen someone so beautiful. A fountain of frizzy blonde curls spills over a purple scrunchie, her eyes an electric, lake-water green. She has a heart-shaped face and lips that sparkle beneath a thin layer of bubblegum pink lip gloss. "Name?" she repeats.

"Um...Bobby. Bobby Bacon."

I hate my name, by the way.

She arches an eyebrow. "Seriously?"

A snort rises behind me. "Pfft, Bacon? At fat camp? You can't make this shit up!"

I turn toward a kid stuffed into a black *Metallica: Ride the Lightning* tank top. Well, "kid" isn't exactly the right word for him. He looks more like a man-child with a pair of honey-baked hams for arms and a massive gut bulging out over a ripped pair of Jordache jeans. A river of acne pocks his face, and he has a weak chin that's hard to differentiate from his neck. In other words, he doesn't have a lot of room to be busting my balls.

"I'm just joshing you, man," he says, slapping my shoulder. "The name's Cody."

The counselor rolls her eyes. "Can we get a move on, guys? You're holding up the line."

It's true. I didn't hear them come in, but kids are piling up behind us, sweating and puffing up a storm. A girl in purple Coke-bottle glasses flaps a *Seventeen* magazine like it's a fan; a pony-tailed Jennifer Connelly makes eyes at me from the cover. Behind the girl, a kid with orange hair crosses his arms and blows exasperated bubbles with his Big League chew.

The counselor holds up a pink slip. "Bacon. You're in Eagle Den. It's across the bridge at the far end of the lake. Don't fall in."

I snatch the paper from her and hustle away.

———

"Hey, Bacon, wait up, man!"

I turn and face Mr. Metallica. Cody. He stops to catch his breath and holds up a finger. "I'm in—I'm in Eagle Den, too. Looks like we're bunkmates. Where you from?"

"St. Paul," I mutter. "You?"

"Minneapolis. Hey, we're neighbors. You new here? I don't remember you from last year."

"Yeah. First time."

"I lost forty pounds last summer," Cody says. "Mom was pretty impressed, but"—he makes a ribbon of fat with his stomach and shakes it—"I gained it right back. Fuckin' Big Macs, man. They get me every time." He eyes me. "So, what's your story?"

I'm fat. End of story. "My parents made me come."

"Don't be so glum, chum," Cody says. "It ain't half bad here. I mean, the food sucks and all, but the rest of it is okay. And did you see Cindi back there? *Dayum,* she's hot, right?" He elbows me and winks. "*Right?*"

I can't argue that.

"She's the best part of this place. Sometimes, she tans on the dock in this little yellow bikini. *Gawd.* I brought some binoculars this year."

It's all sorts of wrong, but I already know I'll join in.

"The worst part is the mornings," he continues. "Waking up at the ass crack of dawn for all the exercise. It *suuucks.* Especially the burpees. Ugh. But they mostly leave us alone in the afternoon. There's a group of us that play *Dungeons and Dragons* if you want in."

Now *that* gets me excited, but I try to play it cool. Girls like Cindi aren't exactly into the D&D type. "Oh, yeah?"

He nods. "Yup. C'mon. I'll show you our place."

––––––––––

"Our place" is a shithole. It's cramped and drafty with cracks in the log walls large enough to see through and floors covered in so much grime, they might as well be dirt. Four twin-sized beds with green vinyl mattresses run the length of the room. I pick one near the back and toss my suitcase on it. I'm surprised. I'd been expecting bunks, but it makes sense. Bunk beds at fat camp are probably a major liability. A few loose screws and you're toast.

The screen door thwacks open to a Black kid in a blue denim jacket and a white kid with curls so thick, I wonder if they're home to a bird or two. The white kid drops his bag and issues Cody a mock salute.

"Hey, hey, it's the Codester!"

"Yo, Erik! Looks like we're bunking up again!" Cody stomps over and gives the Black kid—Erik—a series of high fives with lots of finger snaps and fist bumps—clearly something they worked out last summer.

"Yup," Erik replies. He jerks a thumb my way. "Who's the new guy?"

"Yeah, right. Erik and Matt, meet Bobby."

I know it's coming before he says it.

"Bobby *Bacon*."

I feel my cheeks flare up again. I want to punch him.

"No way? Serious?" Erik asks, his eyes bugging out. "Your name's Bacon?"

I exhale and struggle not to roll my eyes. "Yep."

"Dude, righteous! Bacon. I love it. Best name ever. I'm Erik." He strides over and shakes my hand. My palm comes away dripping with his sweat. He slaps the white kid on the back. "And this is Matt."

Matt raises a hand and is about to say something when the door bangs open again. This time it's a guy who looks just like Johnny Lawrence from *The Karate Kid*, but prettier, with biceps the size of grapefruits and spiked hair so peroxide-bleached it glows. A lanyard sways from his neck: *Tanner Holden, Camp Director*.

Even his name rocks. I hate him instantly.

"Bag check, maggots! Unzip 'em and rip 'em," he says. "And I better not find a single goddamn candy bar anywhere. No care packages or sweet treats from your Mommy, or you're all doing laps tonight."

He destroys Cody's bag first. Cody shoots me a quick eye roll as his clothes spray out like fireworks, his toiletries clattering atop the pile. Tanner moves to Erik's suitcase next and cocks his head at something, a *Playboy*, which he grabs and holds up. It's the Victoria Sellers issue. She leers from the cover with a red-gloved finger resting playfully on her lower lip. I gag. For some reason, she reminds me of my older sister, Sally, playing dress-up.

"Well, well, well, at least not everyone in here is a fag," Tanner says, running a hand through his spiked hair. I expect it to come away bleeding. He glances at Erik, then throws a fake punch. Erik flinches and sits down hard on his bed. Tanner howls with laughter and shakes his head. "*Psych.* I'm just fuckin' with you, man. Dinner's in ten. Be there or be square." He glares at the rest of us. "All of you." With that, he's gone, barging back outside.

Erik shoots him the bird. "*That* asshole is the camp director? What happened to Mr. Wilson?"

"Dunno," Matt replies with a shake of his head. "But I've never seen that guy before."

"Yeah, me neither," Cody adds. "Now that you mention it, I think the only counselor I recognize from last year is Cindi."

"Cindi." Erik and Matt sigh in unison. "Think she's dating anyone?" Erik asks.

"Probably that muscle head jerk," Matt replies. "Chicks dig the assholes."

"Forget him," Cody says, lurching for the door. "Let's go get some grub." He glances at me. "Bacon, be prepared. The food here stinks."

———

The mess hall stinks. Literally. It smells like wet cabbage mixed with dog food.

I grab a tray with food compartments stamped in it and set it in front of a lady in a hairnet ladling out spoonfuls of some formless brown mass. Her name tag reads *Mrs. Yoshika.* She regards me with all the enthusiasm of a Wal-Mart door greeter as she plops a scoop on my tray. I stare at it with my stomach in a twist.

"Ey, you want a second scoop?" she asks with a wink.

"Huh?"

"Okay. I give you one more." Before I can escape, she slaps another formless serving down. It looks like liquified meatloaf.

"What *is* this stuff?" I ask. There's nothing else—no bread or salad. Nothing. I'm not about to eat this crap.

She waves a gloved hand at me. "Go. Go."

"You better do what she says, man," Cody whispers, nudging me along. "She'll cut you."

We find a table near the back already jammed with campers. I wedge myself in next to a girl with mousy red hair and a face bleeding freckles. She gives me a glittery smile, her braces flashing. "Hi. I'm Lexi. What cabin are you in?"

"Hey, Bobby. I'm—" The lights go out before I can finish the sentence.

A deep rumble fills the room: a bass guitar thumping out the notes to "Another One Bites the Dust." Freddie Mercury tears in, and the lights snap on again. Tanner stands at the front of the room wearing mirror-lens aviators, one hand clutching a gleaming microphone over his head, his fist pumping with the beat. Counselors fan away on either side of him, the girls clad in a rainbow of neon spandex leggings. Purple. Pink. Baby blue. I stare slack-jawed. They look like they belong in a Coppertone commercial.

"Holy shit," Cody whispers to my right. "So many babes."

The music cuts off. "Welcome campers!" Tanner blares into the microphone. "This year's gonna be a little different." He grabs a tray from a boy tucking in to his pile of slop with gusto and tosses it across the room like a frisbee. "Who actually wants to eat this crap?"

"Not me. This food sucks," a boy shouts from somewhere behind me. Heads nod in agreement.

"What are you waiting for, then? Trash this shit!"

Cody stands first, grabs his tray, and slumps over to the garbage can. He shrugs and tosses it in. *Thunk.*

More kids follow. *Thunk. Thunk.*

We move, trays scraping off the tables, kids cheering and shouting in a mad race to the garbage cans. Mrs. Yoshika scuttles from behind the serving line, waving her hands and shaking her head furiously. A beefy counselor loops an arm around her shoulder and escorts her to the kitchen.

Thunk. Thunk. Thunk.

"Now *that's* what I'm talking about!" Tanner cries.

The music clicks on, Freddie Mercury back at it. More counselors burst through the kitchen doors carrying trays layered in hamburgers and hotdogs and bright green bags of Lay's potato chips. My stomach growls.

"It's all yours," Tanner says. "As much as you can handle! Eat up!"

Kids cheer and whoop, looking at each other with stunned expressions that mirror the one twisting over my face. High fives are in no short supply. Erik bites into a hamburger across from me, his fist full of fries. "This is bitchin'," he sputters, spraying food my way. He eyes my hotdog. "You gonna eat that?"

I dig in before he can grab it. I gorge myself. The meat is a little tough, but it's ten times better than the garbage Mrs. Yoshika tried to serve us. I mop up the burger grease with the fries and have seconds. The counselors keep bringing more, the girls winking as they pile our plates high.

Dessert follows in the form of ice-cream sundaes and chocolate cake layered in cream cheese frosting. Trays of cookies are delivered to each table. Mouths grow muddy with crumbs all around me.

I stop mid-bite. It doesn't make sense. The Camp Klehani flier advertised portion control and a well-balanced diet. This is anything but well-balanced. This is madness. But I'm not about to complain.

Tanner saunters over and crouches down next to Erik with his aviators off. He has gray eyes, which is strange. For some reason, I'd expected blue. They chat for a bit in hushed tones, Tanner ragging Erik good-naturedly about his *Playboy* again, jerking his hand up and down before thumbing his nose.

"You party, man?"

Erik goes blank-faced, a fat-kid asked to dance by the curvy head cheerleader. "I, uh—yeah. Yeah, for sure, man. Totally."

Something ripples across Tanner's cheek, a movement like an earthworm burrowing through dirt. I blink and rub my eyes, look back in time to see him dancing his way to another table. Erik catches my gaze and pops an eyebrow. "Holy shit, did you see that, bro?"

"Yeah...what did he say?"

"I um...I'm not supposed to tell."

"C'mon, man," I prod. "Spill it."

"Well..." he leans across the table and cups a hand to his mouth in a barely concealed whisper. "Tanner wants me to stay. After all this, you know?" He glances side to side like someone is listening. No one is. "He said I might score with one of these counselor chicks if I play it cool. He told me the brunette over there thinks I'm cute. Can you believe that?"

I can't. I can barely speak, I'm so jealous.

Dinner sputters out slowly from there. Kids filter outside in packs. Cody, Matt, and I follow. Erik is already planted at Tanner's table with a few other lucky campers, Lexi included. She notices me looking and flutters a wave as we tumble into the cool evening air.

"Dude, was that not *insane*?" Cody says. "Tell me that's not the craziest shit you've ever seen. I was wrong about Tanner. The guy rocks!"

Matt gives a hard nod, his curls bouncing. "Totally. So much better than Mr. Wilson's crew."

"Yeah, that guy never stopped with his stupid slogans." Cody throws up some air quotes. "'Give your body the proper nutrients and it will do the rest.' 'Eat well to live well.' 'Progress, not perfection.' Blah, blah, blah. Suck my dick." He says it in a high-pitched tone I take as a poor imitation of Mr. Wilson. Apparently, it's hilarious because they both double over with laughter.

When Cody comes up for air, it's with an, "Oh, shit."

"What?" I ask.

"We forgot Erik."

Tanner's invitation rings hot in my head. *You like to party?* I wave Cody off. "Tanner invited him to hang out." *And do some coke.* I'm pretty sure I remember the nose-tap thing from an episode of *Miami*

Vice. I'm also pretty sure Mom wouldn't be too thrilled to know about the extracurriculars going on here at Camp Klehani.

Matt cocks a hip to the side and crosses his arms. "What? No frickin' way. Erik? What'd he do that was so special?"

"No clue. I heard Tanner invite him, though. I think the *Playboy* got him in."

"No fair," Matt whines. "My Dad has a stack of *Penthouse* in his closet. If I'd known, I woulda swiped a few."

Cody claps him on the back and burps, spouts off a terrible British accent: "Alas, my good man, let Sir Erik haveth his time in the sun, for ours soon shall be nigh!"

"Huh?" Matt says.

"I said, forget him. We got us some D&D to play."

The prospect cheers me up significantly. We go back to the cabin and play until two A.M.

I don't think about Erik once.

————

We lurch from the cabin the next morning around ten, our eyes grainy with sleep. A piss-yellow sun hangs overhead, pinned to a cloudless sky.

"I don't get it," Cody mutters. "No stupid bugle? They always have us up by seven at the latest for morning stretch. I'm starved."

Matt yawns. "Me, too."

"They have all kinds of food out in the mess hall." It's a girl's voice, a hefty brunette in a pink and purple bathing suit with a towel clutched in her hand. "Everyone's heading up to the lake if you guys wanna come after you eat."

"What about fitness?" Matt asks, digging something from his ear.

"Cancelled."

"Rad!" His face buckles. "Wait...why?"

"Dunno. But I like it. See ya." She waves and trots off, bouncing on the balls of her feet.

I glance back into the cabin at Erik's bed, his bag still tipped on its side, vomiting a pile of clothes over the bare mattress. A lot of denim. His Walkman.

"Did anyone see Erik come back last night?" I ask.

Cody shakes his head.

"He's probably eating already," Matt replies, slapping his stomach. "I say we go join him."

———

Breakfast is another ridiculous spread of doughnuts, breakfast burritos, eggs, bacon, toast, and pancakes, which we devour before heading back to the lake. We spend the day staring at Cindi and the other goddess counselors. They're sprawled out in a field of golden skin on the dock, some with their tops unfastened. They mist each other with water bottles. They lotion each other's backs. Madonna chimes "Like a Virgin" from a boombox.

I feel like I'm watching soft-core porn; I want to run into the woods and masturbate. It's ridiculous.

Sometime around mid-afternoon, I think of Erik again. Cody has his shirt off, his man boobs glistening pink with an early sunburn. Matt's perched on a rock with his jeans rolled up over a pair of chalk-white thighs.

"Guys," I say, "don't you think we should do something about Erik? Shouldn't he be back by now?"

Cody shrugs. "He's probably at the cabin sleeping it off. Sex takes a lot of work."

"Like you would know," Matt says.

"Dude, I've totally had sex."

"With who?" Matt asks. "Your hand?"

I laugh. Cody glares at me.

"You think he *actually* scored?" Matt asks.

Cody picks at something in his teeth. "Probably."

I snap my fingers at them. "Hey, guys, forget about all that shit for a minute. What's going on here? Isn't this all a little weird? All this food? Everyone just doing whatever they want all day?"

Cody blows a raspberry with his lips. "Dude, relax. It's frickin' *awesome* is what it is. Matt, tell Bacon to stop getting his panties in a bunch."

Matt slaps at a mosquito and holds it up, squishes it between his thumb and forefinger. "Chillax, Bacon. It's not every day you get to—"

"My dudes!"

I jerk back to Tanner and two other counselors hovering over us with their shirts off, their abs rippling like they've just stepped off a Gold's Gym billboard.

"Who here knows how to party?" Tanner says before I can ask about Erik.

Matt's hand shoots up. "Me! Me! I know how to party."

Tanner smirks. "Hmm, I don't know, man." He looks at the other guys. "You think this kid can party? He doesn't look like he knows how to party."

The counselor closest to him massages his lips. "Yeah, I dunno..." He glances at the other counselor, a guy with olive skin and a square jaw. "What do you think, Dave?"

"I say we give the kid a shot," Dave replies. "What can it hurt?" A tremor runs through his face as he says it. More rippling worms. It happens so fast, I wonder if I've imagined it.

Tanner shoots Matt a Polaroid grin and claps his hands together. "Okay, kid, you're in. I'll stop by your cabin after dinner. You better bring your A-game, though. You *do not* want to disappoint the babes. Especially not Cindi."

Matt nods so hard, I think his head will pop off.

Cody's voice squeaks to life as they turn to leave. "W-wait, guys. Guys. Me too. I know how to party."

Tanner glances back without stopping. "Sorry, bro. Not tonight. You'll get your chance, though...*if* you play your cards right." There's something about the way he says it I don't like. It sounds more like a threat than a promise.

Matt's eyebrows pop so high, I'm worried they'll leap off his face. "Oh, my God. Oh, my God. I need to shower. I need—oh shit, you guys have any condoms? I think I might need a condom. I totally forgot to bring one."

"You suck, man," Cody says with a groan.

I don't hear a word. I'm too busy watching Tanner and his bros muscle their way down the shoreline. One thought picks at me the rest of the day and through dinner:

This is all too easy.

———

Tanner swings by around eight o'clock, wearing a black leather bomber jacket and his mirrored aviators. Tonight, he looks more like Ice Man from *Top Gun* than Johnny Lawrence. He takes a swig from the red Solo cup in his hand and clicks a piece of ice against his teeth. He raises his glasses, and I wither beneath his gravel-colored gaze. "Hey, Pudge. Where's the kid? He ready?"

"Um, yeah, he's—"

Matt bursts from the bathroom in a cloud of cologne. Brut. "I'm right here! Just, ah, you know, getting my game face on." He's in full-on party mode in a pair of frayed, acid-wash jeans and a purple track-suit top stamped in yellow and pink triangles. A black sweatband strangles his forehead, his hair curling over it like it's been freshly permed. He spreads his arms wide and wiggles his fingers. "Whaddya think? This work?"

"Sure, kid, whatever," Tanner says, indifferent. "The babes will love it. Now, let's go."

Cody blows an annoyed breath from his bed and rolls onto his side.

Matt eases past me with a dopey smile and a fist bump, mouths a quick, *Oh, my god.* They are halfway out the door before I stop them.

"Hey, Tanner!"

He groans to a stop. "You're killing me, Pudge. What?"

"Have you seen Erik?"

"Who?"

"The kid you took to"—I flash a set of air quotes—"party last night? He never came back."

"Ohhh, that kid. Right. He partied too hard. His parents came by and took him home. Guess he couldn't handle it." He makes a gun with his hand and cocks his thumb, fires it at me. "Now be a good little camper and go to bed."

He flings an arm around Matt, and they march off, his voice echoing through my skull.

His parents came by? No way. Erik told me they live seven hours away in some bumfuck town in Iowa. The itch hits again, the feeling that this place is a bunch of—

"Bullshit!"

I jerk back. Cody stands a foot away, tugging on his jacket and reeking of hair gel. "I'm crashing the party, man. No way is Matt cooler than us, Bacon. No 'effing way, bro. He doesn't even work out." He surges by me and stops, glancing back. His acne scars glow beneath the dim cabin light. "You coming, or what?"

———

We catch up with them before they hit the forest. The moon hangs above us in full, spotlight-white. Not a cloud in the sky.

Tanner still has his arm wrapped around Matt, but not in a fun, *hey-let's-go-get-you-wasted* kind of way. No, this is more of a *you-try-to-run-and-I'll-snap-your-neck* grip, not that Matt seems to mind. He bops right along next to Tanner, oblivious, probably thinking about which girl he's about to bang.

Except there aren't any girls. Only a dark wall of pine trees.

We hustle after them up a rocky trail winding through the ponderosa. Trees hem us in on both sides like giant slivers of bone, the branches filtering out the stars. We move as quietly as two fat kids can, which is not at all, but we're silent enough that Tanner only stops once, glancing back over his shoulder when Cody kicks a stone loose. We duck behind a jagged clump of granite before he spots us, and I want to tell Cody we should go back, that what we are doing is crazy. I can tell he wants to say the same, but neither of us wants to pussy out first. Teenage boy code.

My legs burn as we wind deeper into the woods, my quads trembling. I feel like I'm on a StairMaster. We hear the crackle of the bonfire before we see it, the pine boughs flickering with a dusty orange light that makes me think of every B-horror movie I've ever seen. The dumb kids walking straight toward the monster. I jerk Cody back behind some underbrush when we hit the ridgeline.

"What the hell, man?" he hisses, nearly tripping.

I point. "Look."

A fire the size of a small shed crackles downslope in a low bowl of earth. Campers and counselors circle the blaze, the female counselors wearing lace-white dresses with flower crowns planted atop their heads. It's not exactly party gear, but I have to admit they look pretty damn hot. Everyone has beers in hand, and a couple of campers are passing a joint. One of them, a Chinese kid I recognize from the first day in the cafeteria, takes a hit and coughs so hard I think he'll spit out a lung.

"Pfft. What a rookie," Cody whispers.

Tanner escorts Matt toward a cooler and snags a couple of beers, handing Matt one. Tanner cracks his and takes the entire thing down in one long pull. His burp rings through the trees like a grizzly's roar.

"Screw this," Cody says. "I'm gonna join them." He starts out, and I jerk him back.

He grabs my hand. "Man, Bacon, if you don't let go of me right now..."

"Shut up," I hiss, thrusting a finger. "*Look*."

He follows my gaze and his nose creases. "What the hell?"

The female counselors have formed a circle around the campers.

Tanner eases behind one of them, a blonde with watermelon boobs, and unzips her dress. Normally it would be the stuff of wet dreams, but the way this girl is moving, her limbs snapping back and forth, her jaw clicking open and shut so hard her breasts are bouncing—it's disturbing. The other male counselors do the same, each of them sliding behind a girl to remove their dress, the campers too wasted to do anything but stare.

Tanner tips his chin toward the moon and howls.

The sound is unlike anything I've ever heard—a piercing, inhuman shriek. Then he does something that sends a slug of acid racing up my throat.

He unzips her *skin*.

He starts beneath her hairline, at the nape of her neck, and pulls.

And pulls and pulls...

Down to her ankle.

What slides out is straight from hell. A glistening black tangle of arms and legs with two-inch teeth shredded to the gums, planted beneath four pearl-white, luminescent eyes. Serrated shards of bone extend from its elbows and knees. And it isn't alone. All of the counselors are ripping off their clothes, their *skin*. An army of black sludge bodies wriggle free, creatures with slick flesh studded in sharp splinters of bone.

"Holy fuck," Cody whispers.

The cafeteria kid is the first to scream. I'm pretty sure he pisses his pants as they swarm him. It's like watching a bleating cow tossed into a boiling mass of piranha. They go after his face first, their teeth shredding, slicing.

The other campers scatter.

Matt makes it to the treeline before one of the things hooks his ankle and drags him back. He screams like a girl as it tears into his calf.

Cody gags. Something hot splashes off his shoes.

"What are you two doing up here?"

My heart explodes. I jerk around to a dark figure and nearly black out before I recognize the voice. Cindi. I half-expect her to rip off her skin like the others before Cody's words ring through my head: *"She's the only one I recognize from last year."*

"What's all this noi—"

Cody clamps a hand over her mouth. *"Shhhh."*

Her eyes bulge and she claws at his wrist.

"We-we gotta go. They're *eating* them," Cody hisses.

Cindi stiffens, and Cody slowly lifts his hand. She smiles. "I know."

Black talons explode from the tips of her fingers. She sinks them into Cody's forearm and goes for his neck with her teeth. She comes away with a bloody chunk of his throat in her mouth.

I run.

Branches rip at my face, my arms. Rocks carve into my knees. Piles of deadfall slash at my shins. Adrenaline spurts through my veins and turns my legs to rubber. I stumble and fight through tangles of bracken, blind, save the moonlight cutting over the forest floor. Cindi tears through the brush after me...

...and shrieks

The other counselors answer her call with their own screams. Quick frantic bursts like gunshots. Metal on metal.

I know what that means. They're hunting.

I angle from the path and leap over a rotten log, my landing awkward and heavy. A hot bolt of pain rips through my ankle. The ground steepens, and everything picks up speed. I'm not running really; I'm being jerked downhill by gravity, my feet somehow keeping up, but only barely. I don't turn. Don't look back.

I know what I'll see.

Her joints click behind me, her limbs spearing the earth like a set of steel pistons, drawing closer. I feel her hot, rancid breath on my neck, her teeth grazing my skin.

I fall.

Rolling, rolling. Bashing off rocks and scree, the forest popping in and out in a series of flashes. Black. White. Black. White. Black.

My head cracks against a boulder and my vision supernovas for a second before I lurch into dead air.

I hit water. *Smack!*

My breath explodes, hangs above me in a thousand silver bubbles. I flop against the current.

The river. I'm in the river. The thought floats up as if from a dream. *Swim, you dumbass!*

I do, flapping and stroking, my clothes so water-logged, they drag me under. I slam into a pile of rocks and choke for air, gulp water instead. My vision blackens and curls at the edges, winks out.

Then there's air in my throat, beautiful air, and the rapids are slowing, dragging me toward the riverbank.

When my fingers hit mud, I almost cry out. I pull myself onto the bank and cough a lungful of river from my lungs. Upstream, a shriek carves through the trees. Another. I see the branches swaying, black forms leaping through the woods.

Broken and bleeding, I scramble beneath a hollow shelf of earth and wedge myself behind a dense curtain of roots. My breath comes fast, my ankle throbbing in time with my racing heart.

I'm pretty sure I broke a few ribs, and my forehead burns like crazy, blood leeching dark and sticky into my eyes. I barely have time to register its heat before I hear them.

They're horrifyingly fast. Their voices, if you can call them that, gutter and pop around me. Think of a train scraping over the tracks with the heat brakes screeching, only worse. *So* much worse.

One of them stalks closer, its teeth chattering—*click, click, click*. It snorts in a lurching, wet breath before blowing it out in a hiss. Silence. Air slides slow into a wet pair of nostrils as talons curl over the bank and set loose a shivering cloud of dust.

No, no, no, no, no...

I slap a hand to my mouth and bite the web of flesh between my forefinger and thumb until I taste copper. An oil-black head appears and lowers. A glowing set of milk-pale eyes.

A shrill cry rises in the distance. The thing above me jerks skyward and answers, and then it's gone.

My bladder empties.

I lay there the entire night and listen to them shriek. Spiders flurry over my skin. Insects burrow into my hair. I let them. I don't move a fucking muscle. At some point, I don't know whether from injury, exhaustion, or both, I succumb to sleep. When I wake, I'm covered in dew, the sun sparkling through the trees in a pink blush.

Matt's scream rips through my head, and I'm back to listening for them, my entire body rigid-stiff, my heart in a full-on thunder. I think of Cody's face, relive the panic flooding his eyes a second before Cindi smiled and tore out his throat.

I shudder and listen. Listen and shudder.

For hours.

Somewhere around mid-morning, I pull myself from my hiding place and limp downriver until I hit the highway, where I collapse on the shoulder beneath an ancient white pine. Half an hour passes before anyone stops. I'm busy rubbing my freezing fingers back to life when I spot the semi—a blue Peterbilt with an extended cab rumbling around the corner. It screeches to a halt, and the door kicks open to a face that's all beard and sunglasses beneath a John Deere ball cap pulled low.

"Need a lift, kid?"

I stare at him and consider running. He looks normal enough, but then again, so did Tanner and Cindi. It doesn't matter. Even if I wanted to, I won't make it another step. I nod and climb aboard. My arms are so bruised, it hurts to buckle my seatbelt.

"Jesus, what happened to you, son?" he asks through a mouthful of chew.

"The police...get me to the police."

"Looks more like I should take you to a hospital."

I fight back tears. "No. The cops. I...I need the cops. There were these things in the forest... Please. The police."

"There's a station in Spring Junction. It's just up the road. I'll drop you there. Whatever you need, boss." He pops the air brakes and we're off. We ride in silence. A picture of a woman, tan as a leather bag, sways from the rearview mirror. An army of bobble-heads clutter the dash and nod me to sleep.

When I wake, it's to a pounding headache and the back of my neck stinging like someone drenched it in battery acid. I finger it with a hiss and remember Cindi's teeth snapping as I fell into the river.

Jesus, she fucking bit me.

"You okay, kid?" The man asks, side-eyeing me through his glasses.

"I think so. Where are we?"

"Getting close now. Station's right up the road."

The gravel road, I realize as a set of cheerfully stenciled letters come into view: *Welcome to Camp Klehani!*

I leap for the door. The handle doesn't budge.

The man laughs and raises his sunglasses. His eyes shine the same wet concrete color as Tanner's. "Don't worry, Pudge. We ain't gonna eat'cha the way we did the others. Isn't that right, Cindi?"

I sense her rise behind me, feel a splash of her hot, musty breath spill past my cheeks. A cold metal finger slides across the back of my neck where she bit me. "Noooo," she says. "Noooo."

The trucker slaps a hand on my knee and squeezes, his teeth dripping with tobacco juice. "You see, kid. You're safe. You wouldn't taste any good." His smile broadens, and he glances back to the road. "Not now that you're one of us."

ABOUT CALEB STEPHENS

Caleb Stephens is a dark fiction author writing from somewhere deep in the Colorado mountains. His short stories have appeared in multiple publications and podcasts. He is currently at work on his next novel, a psychological thriller about family. Learn more at www.calebstephensauthor.com and follow him on Twitter and Medium @cstephensauthor.

BRENT LARSON

Toby Jones coasted into the RV park a good ten minutes late. Per usual, Jake, his mom's boyfriend of two months—and the person in charge of microwaving dinner—screamed at Toby, then grabbed him by the throat, which was new.

Toby had been fishing all day and was strong for his twelve years but couldn't break Jake's meaty grip. His vision started going all wavy before Jake's fingers finally relaxed. The man smiled vacantly as Toby huddled, gasping, eyes streaming.

"You tell your mom about this, and I might have to give her some of the same," Jake said. "You're just a useless jellyfish, Toby. Stick with that."

Three hours later, his mom crawled into the tent next to the RV where Toby now lived in perpetual exile. She explained in low, intense tones that they needed Jake. His airboat rides brought in money. She was getting better tips at the Moonglow. They'd get an apartment soon. They just had to stay the course. Toby kept silent.

When the lights in the RV went out, he unzipped his battered Jansport backpack. He was lucky it was August. He just needed T-shirts and shorts—and his flashlight, of course.

He pedaled the quiet streets to Bandy Park, coasting to a stop at home plate. His friend Andy arrived at 11:30 sharp, like always. They had first met in front of the only 7/11 in Bastille, not long after Toby discovered night time was the only reliable escape from Jake. The boys sized each other up without making eye contact as they stared at the ground. When Andy had asked about the loose straps on Toby's handlebars, he'd replied that they were for his creel, where he kept fish when he caught them.

"How often is that?" Andy had asked.

"Never."

Andy laughed, but it wasn't mocking. And Toby knew then that Andy would be his absolute best friend. Saying goodbye to Andy would be hard, but staying was no longer an option.

"Where d'ya think you'll go?" Andy sounded sad.

"Up to Saint Augustine? I dunno."

"Jeez, Tobes. That sounds dangerous. That's...wow." Andy sighed, looking small in his billowy Yankees jersey.

Toby kept his eyes down. "What I really need is money. I only got about twenty bucks." He wanted to cry, but he couldn't. Not in front of Andy.

Andy gave him a tentative pat on the back then lurched forward, holding his stomach.

"Hey, man," Toby said. "You okay?" Andy, who always looked a little sickly, seemed paler than usual.

"I'm alright," Andy said, gasping. "Stomach stuff." This happened often. Andy's family was obviously poor too, but sometimes Toby wondered if Andy was getting enough to eat. At least Toby's mom always made sure they had enough food.

Andy sat up. "Hey, hey, wait a minute!"

"What?"

Andy stood. "I have a crazy idea."

They biked north, up the two-lane highway, leaving the town of Bastille behind. Eventually the streetlights gave way, and only the moon illuminated the empty road as it cut through never-ending forest. They rode beneath the knobby limbs of twisted oak trees dripping with Spanish moss.

Whenever Toby asked where they were going, Andy smiled and kept pedaling.

An hour elapsed before they rolled up to a small faded billboard showing a little girl eating an orange. COME TO JACKBERRY FARMS! VOTED BEST OF '73! 20 MILES AHEAD.

"We're almost there," Andy said. Several minutes later, he slowed at an overgrown, unmarked road disappearing into the woods. Anybody not looking for it would have missed it.

"What's down there?" Toby asked.

"If what I heard's true, it'll solve all your problems." Andy grinned and pedaled into the trees over crumbling asphalt. The pair swerved around potholes and clumps of sawgrass for what seemed like miles before Toby smelled something pleasantly familiar—the fishy tang of the Intercoastal Waterway.

The boys broke through the woods and halted at the top of a small hill. The road descended, becoming a driveway. At the foot of the driveway was the largest house Toby had ever seen. A porch ran half the length of the first floor, covered in leaves and stringy moss. Dormer windows on the second floor stared at them. Open lawn surrounded the house, the untrimmed grass digesting the outdoor furniture whole. Behind the house, moonlight reflected off water. Halfway down the hill was a sign that said 'W lco to eabor e H ven!' and, in smaller letters, 'B Inv atio Onl .'

Andy stared, mesmerized. "I heard about it from the kids at school. Seaborne Haven. It was a hotel for rich people, but now it's haunted."

Toby licked his lips. "You been here a lot?"

"Nah. Never had a reason." Andy pointed to a sign halfway down the grade. "It only opened for one day." His voice lowered a couple of octaves. "They were drinking champagne to, you know, c-comenerate the occasion. No one knew something swam in through the waterway and crawled up from the basement—"

"Florida houses don't have basements," Toby said automatically.

"Yeah, well, this house does." Andy regained his sepulchral tone. "It took 'em, one by one, and dragged them down the stairs." He shrugged. "Afterwards, it just swam back where it came from. They say this place is cursed. But you know what that means."

Toby looked at him.

Andy grinned. "All the gold and jewels the richies brought with 'em are still there!"

Toby was painfully aware of his predicament. He certainly didn't want to go closer to the foreboding house with its double front doors, but he needed the money he could get from selling a pocketful of expensive stuff at a pawn shop in St. Augustine.

"It sounds like a…" Toby settled on a word he recently read in a *Hardy Boys* book, "… a hoax! People don't just forget about jewels lying around."

"People forget all the time." Andy sounded bitter.

Toby glanced at the house's upstairs windows. It was hard to believe there wasn't something looking back. Going there—going inside—was nuts.

Jake's voice flared in his brain. *Useless jellyfish! Useless!*

Toby pushed off to get away from it, coasting towards the dark shape of the house. The telltale squeak of Andy's bike followed as he slid through the parking lot, which ended at a cobblestone walkway leading to wooden steps.

Toby put his weight on the bottom step. It creaked, but only a little. The next step made no noise at all. The front doors were painted with gold coils, streaked and scarred from the wind. He reached for the knob. It felt gritty under his fingers, but the door didn't budge when he tried it.

Toby turned and continued to the end of the porch, passing a jumble of overturned rocking chairs. The single door in the wall there was locked, too.

As Toby descended the stairs, he saw Andy watching him, but he couldn't tell whether Andy looked relieved or disappointed. Toby picked up his bike and turned the handlebars back the way they came.

Operation Haunted Hotel was a bust.

Toby was halfway across the parking lot when Andy called, "Wait!" He turned and saw Andy looking back at the house. Toby followed his gaze, and a shiver wormed its way up his spine. Something was moving in the last dormer window at the edge of the roof. Drapes, blowing in the breeze.

"It's open," Andy said.

Toby's eyes settled on a gnarled dead tree next to the house. Its sturdy branches stretched over the porch roof. He dropped his bike in the grass and pried his flashlight from the Jansport. It was one of those nifty self-powered ones, so he gave it a few satisfying cranks, then wrapped the Velcro palm strap around one of the belt loops on his jean shorts.

Andy trudged over. "I can do it if you can."

Toby smiled and walked to the tree. Being alone for this would have sucked. He stepped onto the lowest branch and pulled himself up. Within seconds, he was parallel with the second floor. Two branches led to the roof, providing not just a bridge but a railing as well. Toby inched along until he hovered over empty space. He stepped onto the roof, cringing at the skittering sound his beat-up sneakers made on the asphalt shingles, and waited as Andy crossed and stepped carefully towards him.

Scritch, scritch.

As they reached the first dormer window, Toby wondered whether they'd see a disembodied face staring out, but the curtains were closed. He continued to the next one, then the next, stopping just shy of the fifth window with its filthy curtains stirring in the breeze. Toby took a breath, then swung a leg over the windowsill and ducked his head, his flashlight rapping against the sill.

Inside, Toby flicked on the flashlight. He stood in an empty hallway, ending at the top of a staircase. The place stank of mildew.

Something touched his shoulder, and he flinched, but it was only Andy. "Geez, man, I'm coming through...oop!" Andy fell against him, landing on the floor before bouncing up again, looking embarrassed.

Toby giggled. He clapped his hands over his mouth, but he couldn't stop.

"What do we do now?" Andy asked, laughing.

Toby looked around. The brass plate on the door beside him said 203. Next to it, he saw a weird design resembling an ampersand with an *X* over it. "Let's go in here."

The knob twisted easily, though the hinges squeaked.

Their sneakers sank into white shag carpeting, and Toby's flash-light illuminated a massive canopy bed covered by a deep red bedspread with several green pillows scattered across it like lily pads. There was a vanity by the door, so Toby checked the drawers—empty. Above it hung a painting of a sleeping naked woman and her baby. A brass-plated plaque on the frame declared: THE PEACE OF THE DEEP ENVELOPES THE FAITHFUL.

They explored further, finding nothing of note in the adjacent bone-white bathroom, with its tarnished silver fixtures, or in the bedroom's massive wardrobe.

Toby gave the flashlight a couple of cranks, the clicks sounding louder here in the stillness. Room 204 was identical to Room 203 in every way, except for the painting. This one was of a giant sinking ship: FORTUNE FINDETH THE REVERENT.

The painting in Room 202 featured an old man in a pinstripe suit, sitting and staring at the viewer. His bulbous eyes and heavy jowls reminded Toby of an uncharacteristically humorless Rodney Dangerfield. *I do not abide the presence of useless jellyfish,* the face seemed to say. The plaque under this artwork said: WISDOM IS BEGOTTEN OF HOLY AMBITION.

Room 201 looked different from the others. The stench of wild decay—probably from the wide swath of black mold stretching across the bathroom floor and up its walls—was overpowering. It covered the painting in the room, too, and rendered the plaque undecipherable.

Toby pulled the door closed, coughing, eyes stinging. "There's nothing here."

"Sorry, man," Andy said, studying his feet.

Toby clapped Andy on the back, then turned and shined the flashlight down the stairs. "Let's go look." Andy hesitated, then nodded.

They descended to the landing and gasped.

"Wow," Andy whispered.

Toby thought the room below would have been right at home in a German castle. A crystal chandelier—probably heavier than the RV—hung over plush sofas adorned with exotic afghans. Fur rugs covered hardwood floors. It wasn't a huge room, but someone had tried very hard to prepare it for royalty.

Toby stepped off the bottom stair and swept the flashlight's beam around. The sofas sat by a massive fireplace, and on the far side of the room stood a grandfather clock, its hands frozen at 2:14.

Above the fireplace hung a painting twice as tall as Toby. It was grouchy Rodney Dangerfield again, staring off into the distance and, apparently, not happy with what he saw there. Carved into the wall beneath the painting, Toby saw another *X* and an ampersand. Under it were the words, FROM OUT OF THE DEPTHS WE SUMMON THEE. And, under that, chiseled inelegantly into the mantel, a single word: GABONLAK.

"What's a Gabonlak?" Andy asked.

Toby gave the flashlight a few cranks. There were a couple of books on an end table by one of the sofas. He brushed the dust off one—*The Heart is a Lonely Hunter*. Under it, he found a textbook with a fossilized fish picture on the cover—*The Promise of Our Primal Ascendancy*.

Andy was peering into the fireplace. "You find anything yet?"

"Nothing good." Toby wandered into the adjoining room and Andy followed. A square table sat in the middle of the room, a ledger lying open atop it. A coat rack beside the front door was laden with moldy coats and complicated-looking hats. Wedged against the double front door, on its side, lay a three-tiered marble fountain. Half of its bottom tier was crushed as if by a wrecking ball. The finial atop the fountain was an odd, man-shaped fish creature that smiled with a mouthful of needles instead of teeth.

Toby put his foot on the fountain and leaned against it. It didn't move. Nothing was coming through that door again. "Or going out," he said aloud. It was the only thing he and Andy had seen since arriving that seemed out of place.

Meanwhile, Andy was searching one of the drawers under the table. Toby walked over and blew dust off the ledger.

Drs. Jim & Esmerelda Hardwick 4.8.52 Boston

Francine Marcos 4.8.52 Los Angeles

Jefferson Keystone 4.8.52 Ottawa

Brock and Amy Heller and son 4.8.52 Jersey City

Able Hildebrandt 4.8.52 Manhattan

Gen. Jack and Tilly Radner 4.8.52 Syracuse

Marilyn Cape 4.8.52 Chicago

Toby felt uneasy. He aimed his light at a hallway running under the stairs. "Let's go down there."

"Maybe we should split up," Andy said. "We could search faster." He produced a candle and a book of matches.

Toby wanted to say splitting up was a terrible idea, but he didn't want to sound weak. *Like a jellyfish.* Andy was right—they could find the treasure quickly and get out of this place faster. "Let's meet back by the front door," he said. "If you get in trouble, yell, and I'll come running."

Andy seemed to falter for a moment, then gave Toby a weirdly sweet and sad smile, "Bye, Tobes."

Toby watched Andy push open the glass doors, turn, and wave. Then he was gone.

The door under the stairs led to a small storeroom. Spray bottles sat on a shelf between a huge ball of twine and a box of Manger's Sugar Soap, all covered in cobwebs. Toby tipped over a small toolbox on the floor with his foot. Inside was a small hammer, screwdrivers, pliers—nothing valuable.

Toby found the door across from the storeroom locked, but the door at the end of the hall had no knob, so he pushed it open. It took him a minute to register what he was seeing.

Another chandelier hung over a long dining table, stretching the room's length. Most of the high-backed chairs were pushed away from the table. Some were overturned. One lay askew on the table itself.

Toby took a hesitant step, jumping when his foot crunched on something that cracked like a gunshot—a porcelain plate. A sea of broken china and silverware covered the floor. The doors at the far end undoubtedly led to the kitchen, but he had no desire to walk across a ceramic minefield. He backed through the door into the hallway and returned to the locked door. Why would anything be locked here? It wasn't like there was anything good left to steal.

Toby kicked the door, but it didn't budge. He stepped back and tried to put every single one of his ninety pounds into his next kick. Something splintered. On the third kick, the door surrendered.

Inside, Toby found haphazard stacks of luggage—all leather and boxy—and steamer trunks. A shoebox-sized red leather case with a tag that read "Francine Marcos" sat on top of one precarious tower. Another featured a tag proclaiming, "It's Howdy Doody time!" When Toby turned over the picture of a freckled puppet in a checkered shirt, he saw writing in a childish script: *A.J. Heller.*

Intrigued, Toby turned back to the Marcos stack of luggage and retrieved the little red bag. It was locked, so he went to the storeroom for the hammer and screwdriver. Three strikes, and the lock fell away in a small, broken heap. He opened the bag and knew the small mound of diamond necklaces, gem-studded rings, and ornate gold bracelets was worth more than anything he'd ever seen before in real life.

Miss Marcos hadn't traveled light.

Toby rolled a heavy pearl earring in his palm, his head buzzing. Forget Saint Augustine. He could buy his mom a house. No, a *mansion!* No more rusted RV, and definitely no more of Jake's stupid airboat rides.

A deafening racket—shattering glass and splintering wood— echoed through the building.

Toby leaped to his feet and ran to the front door. He waited breathlessly for Andy to appear, for him to laugh and say he'd backed into a statue or a lamp, but Andy was missing his cue.

Toby pushed through the glass doors his friend had gone through earlier. "Andy?"

On the other side of the pool table was a bar with long-handled beer taps and tall stools. Dusty bottles of alcohol lined a shelf, glasses hanging stems-up. Behind the bar, Toby saw a door, slightly ajar. *Andy must have gone through there.*

Toby sagged in relief and stepped onto a rug that looked like a dartboard, realizing too late he was falling.

No, not falling. *Sinking.*

Toby splashed down through the dark into putrid, lukewarm water, as salty as the Gulf. *I'm drowning! I'm drowning in the ocean!*

Then, Toby's feet connected with solid ground. He straightened his legs to find himself waist-deep in standing water. The flashlight, mercifully still strapped to his hand, bobbed unsteadily. Toby was shivering, but with the wobbling light, he could see he stood in a large, empty cellar. Giant, lumpy splotches stained the walls.

Toby took a couple steps, slipping a little as he kicked loose debris under the water. High above him, the rug hung limply from the ceiling. *Why would anyone throw a rug over a hole, unless...*

Unless.

Toby's heart began beating triple-time, and suddenly he needed his mother. He needed her very, very badly. But she was back in Bastille, dreaming, certain he was safe in his tent outside her window. She was home, with Jake. Despite his terror, Toby could still hear him. *Useless jellyfish.*

Toby took a deep breath and waved the light around more slowly. Against the far wall, he saw the weird *X* symbol painted on the concrete above the words GABONLAK WE RECEIVE THEE.

Some kind of mold-encrusted basket hung on the far wall, a couple of feet above the waterline. Beyond it, where the two walls should have joined, Toby saw an opening with ascending stairs leading to a closed door. Eagerly, he splashed forward, not caring how much noise he made, only to abruptly stop when he saw the water at the foot of the stairs swirling as if it were boiling.

A dark shape rose out of the water, unfurling until it reached its full height and stood. It was taller than a human. Toby couldn't see its face.

The figure moved toward him.

Toby stepped back and nearly lost his balance, sending water rippling away from him in tiny waves. However, the approaching figure didn't disturb the surface of the water. Toby could only tell it must be moving because the gap between it and the stairs widened.

A small white light appeared above the creature but did nothing to illuminate the thing's face. The light just floated there, dancing like fireflies at the Fourth of July picnic in the RV park by the ocean that the Jones family had called home years ago. Toby loved that park.

As his mind wandered, Toby realized that he wasn't afraid anymore. In fact, he felt good. As the creature towered over him, he noticed its face was still a huge inkpot under the merrily dancing, marvelous light. Something heavy and clammy settled on both his shoulders, but Toby did not pull away. The water was warm, and he felt content.

A wet, tangy smell, more pungent than saltwater, filled his nostrils, evoking an awareness of something ancient and foreign—and deep.

Toby screamed as a sudden, sharp pain seared his gut. The grip on his shoulders tightened, and Toby finally saw the thing's face—more hideous than anything he could have conjured in his worst nightmares. Bulbous, milky white eyes protruded from a narrow, scaly face. There was a hole where the nose should have been. Puckered lips formed a flat line, cutting across its mouth. The lips parted, and Toby saw teeth—long, spiny teeth like shards of glass, meant for shredding.

The entire room blazed with impossibly pure white light like someone had turned on the sun. Toby screamed again as pain exploded in every corner of his being. He looked down and saw a ball of pure energy. Toby thought it was emanating from the creature, but now he saw it was collecting in his own chest, giving off the light of a million candles.

The creature growled, and Toby felt his body exert, watched the ball of energy drift further out of his chest. As Toby's eyes flitted around the room, he saw Andy watching him from the top of the stairs.

Toby summoned every ounce of strength he had left. Every ounce that wasn't pouring into that ball of light. "Andy! Help!"

"I can't, Toby."

The ball in Toby's chest rose another inch, and the creature made a soppy, smacking sound. Couldn't Andy see what was happening?

He tried again. "Andy!"

Andy hung his head. He started crying. "I can't. I can't."

Even in the midst of his pain, Toby realized the truth, and his mouth suddenly tasted like bitter ashes. The creature had not magically drawn him to the Seaborne Haven or laid the trap for him in the game room. *Andy*. The game room trap was the handiwork of Toby's only friend.

Andy must have seen realization dawn on Toby's face. "It's been my turn long enough, Toby."

I'm going to die in this cellar. The hotel was a lost place, and he would be lost within it. His mother would search and search but never find him. Toby knew his disappearance would torture her every day, because then she'd be alone. Alone with *Jake*.

Toby tried to step away from the being and slipped. As he submerged, he was shocked to feel himself slither right out of the creature's grip.

The pain disappeared. The ball of energy snapped back into his chest, and Toby felt good again. No. Actually, this time, he felt amazing. This was different from the bliss of the dancing light. His mind was a laser, and he felt strong, strong enough to destroy Jake in a fair fight.

Which was good, because Toby hadn't inhaled before going under.

The flashlight's still on! He clicked it off and swam to the left. Something stabbed the water, grazing his leg. It took every ounce of Toby's self-control not to thrash away, not to splash.

How much longer could he stay under?

The creature shrieked a high-pitched warble. Andy's voice answered, thin and fearful, audible even underwater.

Toby reached out, and his fingertips touched something hard and rough. One of the walls. Behind him, he heard water rushing as the creature stabbed randomly. Toby fought the urge to stick his head up for one quick lungful of air. His chest burned. He only needed to swim along the wall to the corner and then he'd be at the stairs. He inched forward, grazing the cement with outstretched fingertips. *Too slow*, his mind gibbered—but then he reached the corner. *Just a few feet from the stairs.*

Toby reached down to steady himself, and his hand closed around something round and hard. *A human skull.* There could be no doubt. He had been tripping over human remains earlier.

The swishing water faded as the creature moved away from Andy, growling.

"I'm trying!" Andy said, close enough to hear. He sounded exhausted, even though the water distorted his voice.

My best friend did this to me.

Toby's fingers brushed a flat horizontal surface in front of him. A wooden board, rough and warped, covered in slime. *The bottom step!* Toby couldn't hear anything, which could only mean his pursuers were waiting for him to emerge.

The fire in his lungs grew unbearable. He felt blackness encroaching, much like when Jake had given him a hands-on demonstration of Toby's usefulness last night. Toby drew his knees to his chest and planted his feet. He forced himself to rise slowly until his head broke the surface. He inhaled the mildewed, salt-heavy air through clenched teeth, trying not to gasp.

Toby heard another warble, low and inhuman, further away, and took another slow breath. He felt the heat leaving his lungs. Would he be able to get up the stairs in time? Maybe he could distract them. There was, after all, lots of stuff on the floor to toss around. Toby reached down, and the flashlight scraped loudly against the concrete.

The creature screeched, and Toby shot out of the water as if from a cannon, then pounded up the rotted wooden slats. He flicked on the flashlight just in time to keep from running face-first into the door. Toby fumbled with the knob and crashed through.

He heard the creature thrashing towards the stairs. Toby looked around wildly—he was in a short hallway—as Andy yelled, "Toby, wait!"

Toby didn't. He stumbled against a small table with a mirror hanging over it. His eyes stared back at him, white marbles in his pale face. The door down the hall stood ajar, so Toby hurled himself through it, into the room with the trap rug. Toby shined the flashlight over to the dartboard rug—now hanging half-in the hole—expecting the creature to emerge, and sprinted away into the foyer.

With a yelp, Toby slammed into the guest book table with his hip. He heard a monstrous shriek, angrier this time. *It can't leave the water*, he realized.

Another scream, thin and piercing, followed the shriek. *Andy. Serves him right.*

Toby rounded the top of the stairs and almost fainted when he saw something at the end of the hall billowing towards him. *Curtains. The window's still open.*

He made it halfway across the branches bridging away from the roof before he stopped.

Toby wasn't afraid of the gap anymore. There were, after all, scarier things than falling out of a tree. The boys' bikes lay in the grass by the trunk. Toby stared at Andy's.

I know why Andy always hurts.

Toby willed his legs to continue across the gap. They refused.

I can't just go back in there. I need something new.

Toby didn't realize it until later, but—in that moment—he hadn't heard Jake's voice at all.

———

Toby cranked the flashlight strapped to his palm. The clicks ran together into a steady roar. His tube socks were now sludgy black. He could see golden light coming from under the basement door. Toby knew the source of that light, and it made him shiver with fear. On the other side, Andy wailed.

Toby turned the knob and eased the door open, unspooling a few inches of twine he'd peeled from the storage closet's cobwebs. The water below reflected the creature's light, casting bending, glowing shapes on the walls. Toby had also brought the screwdriver. He could stab with it, but he didn't plan on being within stabbing distance.

Andy whimpered, out of sight around the corner. Toby heard a wet smacking sound, like someone biting into a particularly juicy apple. He stepped onto the first stair, waiting for a creak. Silence.

Toby took the next couple of steps, uncoiling the twine as he went.

The smacking stopped.

Toby still couldn't see around the corner. Was it listening?

Jeez, what if it can smell me?

This time Andy's scream sounded high and reedy.

I need you to do that one more time, Andy. Sorry.

A few more steps, and Toby would be back in that horrible water.

What's the soup of the day? Why, you are, sir.

The creature made a purring sound.

Toby slithered down the rest of the stairs and slipped into the water. He inched his way forward. The creature stood less than five feet away. Toby could almost reach out and touch it. He froze in panic, but the creature's attention was on the moldy basket on the wall.

Its milky, bulbous eyes stared, unblinking as it held up a ball of light. If the one in Toby's chest had burned like a million candles, this one was a hundred. Maybe fewer.

The ball flashed brighter, and Andy hissed like he'd been burned. Toby could see him, pinned to the wall, covered with the dark splotchy substance. Only his face and shoulders were still visible. Toby figured the number of splotches dotting the walls would probably coincide with how many guests and staff had been present in the hotel on its opening night.

He retreated behind the corner, imagining the twine running up the steps, through the hallway, into the game room, and under the afghan he'd set at the edge of the rug trap.

Contrary to the opinion of some, Toby was a decent angler. He caught redfish and mangrove snapper all the time. But this one would be a first.

He pulled on the twine.

It held for a second, went slack, then taut again. A muffled clatter came from upstairs. Toby let out more line and peered back around.

The creature still held the ball of energy, but its face was upturned.

Toby played out even more line. His flashlight descended into view, the beam zigzagging back and forth.

The creature opened the basket and placed the ball of light inside, plunging the room into shadow. The only light now came from the dangling flashlight. Toby played with the line, and the flashlight rose and fell.

The creature moved toward it.

Toby took a deep breath and stepped out from the corner's protection.

He heard a gasp. Andy stared at him, eyes clear and astonished. They both looked over at the creature, its back to them.

Toby tugged again, and the flashlight bobbed. He reached Andy and grabbed a handful of the sticky substance, which had the texture of freshly chewed gum. Toby awkwardly pulled another section away, realizing the flaw in his plan—using one hand to play the line was costing him. He needed both of them to free Andy.

The creature stood directly under the hole and stretched a claw upward. The flashlight hovered out of reach.

Toby gritted his teeth. *This is taking too long.*

Andy met his gaze and shook his head. *Go. You tried.*

The creature made a high-pitched mewling sound and stopped reaching for the flashlight.

It's bored, Toby thought. *Maybe if I jig it harder…*

He jerked the line. This time, it snapped.

Toby stared in horror as the flashlight dropped into the water with a definitive *kerplunk*. The creature darted after it.

Toby threw off any semblance of caution and began pulling chunks of the sticky stuff off Andy with both hands, the submerged flashlight providing a bubble of light as the creature splashed around for it.

It can't see too good either.

Andy fell into Toby's arms. Toby cradled him awkwardly as he maneuvered back to the stairway. Moving stealthily through water was hard enough without a body to carry.

The thrashing behind them abruptly ceased, and the light grew brighter. The creature had found the flashlight.

"Cruh," Andy whispered, eyes squeezed shut. "Creel. Grab th' creel." The basket hung on the wall in front of them.

Toby jogged Andy's head up to his shoulder. The basket had no handle, so he wedged his fingers between it and the wall, then tugged. Nothing.

With another kerplunk, the light dimmed again. It had dropped the flashlight. Toby looked down at Andy's pinched face and gave the basket a violent yank. It tore free with a sucking sound.

The creature screamed. It was the most human-like sound the thing had made yet.

As Toby scrambled up the stairs, the creature plowed through the water after them, shrieking the whole way.

Toby slammed into the doorway, struggling to fit through while carrying Andy and the basket. They fell sideways across the threshold in a heap, and Toby jumped to his feet. The creature's huge black shape stood at the bottom of the stairs, bristling with angry energy.

He really can't leave the water, Toby thought, and his knees almost buckled in relief. Then he heard the wood slats groan.

It's moving up the stairs.

The soothing, small white light reappeared above the creature.

Toby slammed the door and twisted the lock, engulfing them in darkness. He fumbled around for the candle and matchbook he'd set by the wall earlier. It took him three tries to light one.

BOOM!

The door bulged outward. Toby's hands shook violently, but the candle's tiny flame remained steady. "Andy, can you stand?" he yelled, fumbling with the creel under one arm.

Andy was already on his feet, already running to the end of the hallway. "Come on, Tobes!" he yelled. Behind them, the door splintered.

They dashed into the foyer. Toby could see the hotel grounds outside the windows, bathed in moonlight, mere yards away. The creature crashed through the pool room door behind them as they ran up the stairs.

The boys made it to the open window. Toby scooped up his battered sneakers. "You go first," he gasped. Andy nodded and disappeared through the rotted silk.

Toby awkwardly juggled the basket as he threw a leg over the sill. He looked behind him and saw with a jolt the creature, at the end of the hall, staring back. All the spit in Toby's mouth dried up.

He heard a noise then, a repetitive *chup-chup-chup*.

It sounded like laughter.

Useless jellyfish.

"Screw you! I'm Toby the Destructor!" he yelled.

The creature screamed again. Toby heard thumping as it

approached. He sprinted across the slanted roof to the tree where Andy stood on the branch, his eyes bugging out. "Run, Toby! He's trying to…"

Toby waved his free arm. "Go!"

Andy squirreled across the gap. Toby stepped onto the tree limb, his heart beating a steady mantra—*move, don't look, move, don't look…*

When his feet touched the tall grass, he ran to his bike and shoved the basket between the handlebars, cinching the straps tight.

Andy had already mounted his bike. "C'mon!" he yelled, but Toby twisted around, scanning the roof.

Only the billowing curtains moved.

They both stood on their pedals, propelling their bikes uphill. They reached the top and looked back. "I never want to talk about this place again," Toby started to say, but a loud crash cut him off. The front doors—the ones Toby had thought eternally blocked by the overturned fountain—flew out of the frame and landed on the front steps. Toby glued his eyes to the dark, open rectangle of the doorway, expecting the dark shape to rocket out, but it didn't.

He turned to Andy, smiling, but Andy was staring at the house, eyes welling up, his face reflecting deep, deep weariness. Toby saw something old in his friend's eyes, too—old like the creature itself.

———

Another breeze gusted, warm and open. Toby never felt anything so wonderful in his life as he and Andy rested their elbows on their handlebars, studying home plate. The sky was graying with morning light.

"Toby," Andy said.

Toby dismounted, undid the straps holding the creel, and carried the basket over to the grass. Andy followed.

Toby expected the ball of light to burn as he lifted it out of its container and held it aloft, but it had all the warmth of a freshly baked cookie. The air hummed as it left his hands and hovered above their heads.

"Toby," Andy said again. "I'm so sorry."

"It's okay," Toby said.

"I was the last one. It said it'd let me go if I found another kid to take my place. Kids are stronger, I guess..." he trailed off. The ball of light dimmed.

"It's okay," Toby repeated.

"We didn't know those people. They wanted to...*give* us to that thing. But it turned on them. It took everyone. All of them." Andy looked at him steadily. "But now I can see my mom and dad again. Thanks, Toby."

"Sure, man." Toby's voice was gravel in his throat.

Andy took a deep breath. "So...bye, Tobes."

"Bye, Andy."

Then Andy laughed like a kid on Christmas morning. "Toby the Destructor."

Toby stayed there a long while, staring at the dirt. When he looked up, Andy and his ball of light were both gone. Tears cut tracks in the grime on Toby's cheeks.

No matter what had happened, Andy was still his absolute best friend.

Toby fished around in his pocket for a handkerchief, and his fingers closed around a hard bump. He pulled out the pearl earring and stared.

He'd been wrong, back on the hill. He *could* tell someone about Seaborne Haven. If a useless jellyfish like him had found one earring, what could someone stronger find?

After all, the door was wide open. And Jake liked money.

Toby would have to bait the hook carefully, but as he'd just proven, there wasn't anything he couldn't reel in.

ABOUT BRENT LARSON

Brent writes and produces short films, taking him to such far-flung locations as South Africa, Russia, Ukraine, Spain, and Shreveport, LA. His favorite project is still the zombie web series he shot in his garage in 2009. He is also the creator/writer of *Kayless* and the upcoming *CapeTown*, both for Silverline Comics. Brent lives in Orlando, Florida with two dogs, a cat, and a wife who thinks Alien is the best movie ever. In short, Brent has no complaints.

JAWS

CHRISTOPHER O'HALLORAN

Luisa should be at home recovering instead of at Tommy Rictor's party, but it's her birthday, and a little jaw surgery won't keep her from having a good time. Her whole face is rigid. Steel grates against her gums, her lips, forcing her teeth together, leaving only enough space to slip a straw in through the corner of her mouth.

Luckily, that's all she needs.

New Kids On The Block tell her to "stop it, girl," and she should listen, but instead sips more of her Fuzzy Navel. It doesn't burn her throat the way stolen nips from her parents' big bottle of vodka used to. It goes down smooth like Tang.

"Did it hurt?" asks Giselle, her own cup bobbing in her hands as she dips and sways.

Luisa shakes her head. It hurt like a bitch after, but not during the surgery.

"I was knocked out," she says, but with her jaw wired shut and music shaking the house, being heard is hard. Being understood is impossible. She teases her dark hair up, straightens the gold, sequined blouse so the large butterfly on the front stretches clear over her chest, and shifts in her leather skirt.

The house Tommy Rictor rents with his three best friends is jam-packed with people. It smells toxic, the various eau de toilettes, perfumes, and hairsprays making every flick of a lighter a potential explosion.

"Can you eat anything?" asks Giselle, hand full of ketchup chips. She looks beautiful in her dress coated in silver sequins, and happy. She stands a full head higher, despite modest platforms and Luisa's own four-inch heels.

Luisa can't ask for a better companion for her first post-surgery night out.

Can she eat anything? She shakes her head. Anything Luisa eats needs to be shot via syringe through the space at the corner of her lips. Her mom had to blend her birthday dinner. Nobody deserved Ensure on their birthday.

"That's for the best," says Giselle, grabbing her stomach and shaking it. "Maybe I need some jaw surgery." The sequins on her dress rattle faintly, reflecting light like a breaching salmon.

As if, thinks Luisa. She would change nothing about her best friend.

Giselle's chin is perfect, cute enough to pinch. When she smiles, it juts out just the slightest bit. Enough space for a hummingbird to land on. When the doctors explained how they'd be pulling her jaw forward to fix her migraines, Luisa silently hoped it would give her a chin like Giselle's.

"Bobby Dupree is looking for you," says Giselle. She takes her time with her words, clearly enjoying the monopoly she holds over their conversation. When she and Luisa chat, it's like two auctioneers competing at a championship level. Now, she can slow down. Luisa can't butt in.

Luisa sips her drink, and before she knows it, her cup is empty.

"He just got back from Expo," continues Giselle. "His uncle got him a job at Science World. It's like a giant friggin' golf ball right on the ocean. Hundred feet tall!" She puts the handful of chips in her mouth and chews, bouncing her eyebrows at Luisa.

Luisa rubs her jaw. It's not as swollen as it was, but it's still sore. The booze helps.

"Built a train in the sky. The rails go above the traffic." Giselle speaks with chips in her cheeks, making her look like an adorable rodent. The fourth member of The Chipettes. "What do you think they call it?"

Luisa knew what they called it.

"The SkyTrain," she says through gritted teeth, but she might as well be a mime.

"The SkyTrain," exclaims Giselle, the punchline delivered flawlessly.

Luisa's head swims. She's had one drink, but it was strong, and her stomach has practically nothing in it.

Then her cup is floating out of her hand, and Bobby Dupree is replacing it with a full one.

"Heya, Bobby," says Giselle with a knowing smile.

The world swims, time skips, and Luisa is sitting on a staircase next to Bobby Dupree. He's cute, but his nose is a little too big, his hair a little too thin. When he talks, his breath wafts across to her. It smells faintly of dirt.

"I'll be heading out to Vancouver for good as soon as I get the cash together," he says. Bobby has a jet-black Grand National that makes Luisa's heart skip a beat whenever she sees it. Would he be as cute if he didn't have it?

Would he be interested in her if he knew she had a kid at home?

"It's nothing like Winnipeg," he says, eyes distant as if recalling an oasis. "Right on the ocean. Everything's so much bigger. That city is going to be the New York of Canada. And I'm going to make it mine." He goes so far as to wink at Luisa. "Expo made The Red River Ex look like a playground."

She smiles, nods, and sips her Fuzzy Navel. It's sour and sweet and she starts to feel fuzzy herself.

Bobby looks at her shirt. Is he looking at the butterfly stretched out along the blazing sequins? Is he looking at the gold cross her mom gave her when she was sixteen—a last-ditch effort to bring her back to the church?

No, she knows what he's looking at.

"Look at this fuckin' thing," says Bobby, reaching behind him and pulling a stuffed bear out of thin air. "I nicked it from Woolco."

At first glance, it looks like a Teddy Ruxpin, but this one lacks the healthy plumpness. It exudes malevolence in a way Luisa can't pin down. Its fur is stringy and damp. Its eyes aren't the perfect sphere of a friendly teddy bear. They pull down in a sadly knowing way. As if it's been under the bed of an abused child and now can't see anything but the devastation in the world.

"I can't make it talk," he says. "Squeeze its belly, its foot. Nothin'."

As Luisa looks into its eyes, the room slips beneath a veil of darkness. Within her, there is pain—waking up from surgery in agony as her mother sobs for her girl. There is fear—giving birth at the age of twenty, her baby's father wanting nothing to do with them. There is frustration—being tied down with immigrant parents who can't afford to send her to school.

There are all these things at once, compounded and electrified by a despair that blocks out the upbeat music.

"What is it?" she asks.

"What?"

Luisa leans close and breathes in his Obsession. It's light. He hasn't bathed in it like some of the other guys in this place. Still, Obsession smells better on women. With this toy, ripped jeans, and airy fragrance, Bobby seems like a kid. Nevermind the car.

"What is it?" she repeats, mouth to his ear. It's stupid, her wasting so much energy on such a dumb question, but she's getting tired of listening.

Bobby looks at her. His big nose twitches as his mouth pulls up in a sneer.

"Dead," he says, and rips the things head off.

The skin stretches, stringy fur trembling before the fabric tears. Instead of fluff, a load of marbles comes out of its neck. They bounce on the stairs, rolling down the hallway where others dance to Boy George.

One falls into Luisa's lap. She cocks her head, lifting the marble to her eye. It's not as hard as she expected. She gives it a little squeeze, and it pops, grey jelly exploding over her fingers.

"It's warm," she says. Fat ropes dangle from the head, grey like the marbles. They might be the wires that make these bears talk, but they look thicker than any she's seen.

"It's been in my pocket," Bobby says, holding the toy away from him. "Kind of stinks, too. They expect kids to like this thing?" He tosses the head and body into the kitchen, aiming for the trash can, but missing the mark by about a foot. The smell of rotten eggs and garbage drifts away with the toy's corpse. "Want to make out?"

Luisa shrugs. He does have a cool car. Maybe he'll take her for a spin in it.

When he comes in, his lips are dry. He bumps them against hers. She tries to open her mouth, to get closer, but the wires keep her teeth firmly clenched. There is no way to get her tongue through.

Bobby tries anyway. His tongue darts against her teeth, an aggressive worm.

"Can you—" he says, dirty breath choking Luisa.

"My jaw," she says, but he's not listening. His tongue frantically probes at her teeth, looking for an opening.

Bobby winces and pulls back. His must have run over where the wires connect to her mouth. It's sharp in there. If you're not careful, that metal will bite.

Bobby touches his tongue with a finger. It's bleeding.

"I—I'm going to get something to eat." He stands. "I'll see you around."

As he departs, Luisa sips her Fuzzy Navel. Her second? Third?

Who knows. It's her birthday. She deserves to let loose.

Time slips. She's stumbling home, into her room. Giselle is with her. She hands Luisa a ceramic salad bowl.

"Don't wake Anthony," Luisa says, her words hissing through her teeth as she pulls her shirt over her head and tosses it onto the back of a chair she sometimes sits in to feed him.

Anthony sleeps peacefully in his crib. The five-month-old can sleep through anything, just like his mama.

Her stomach lurches, and Luisa learns how hard it is to ralph with your jaw wired shut.

———

Nothing moves in the night. The bungalow on Barker Drive is silent aside from the snores of Luisa's mother. Her father has once again made his bed in the basement.

Within the folds of Luisa's discarded shirt, there's a clicking unlike that of colliding sequins. The fabric moves, shuffling slightly and falling off the chair over which it was draped.

A grey marble tumbles out.

Luisa groans in her sleep and turns over. Anthony, feeling his mother's agitation, stirs as well but falls silent, saving Luisa—or more likely her mother—from soothing him back to sleep.

Something within the marble begins to vibrate. The movement carries it from Luisa's bedroom, and all three of them—Anthony, Luisa, and Giselle—breathe more easily.

———

In the morning, Luisa wakes cuddling Giselle. Her arms wrap around her friend's larger body. At just shy of five feet, Luisa's a backpack. Giselle's hair crunches as Luisa plants a quick kiss on it, breathing in the hairspray.

"Laundry?" she asks.

Giselle groans and slips under the blanket.

"My head," she says, muffled. Out comes her dress, sequins clicking together.

Luisa tosses her an oversized KISS t-shirt she uses as a nightie. "What," asks Giselle, "No Zeppelin?"

"I get Zeppelin," Luisa replies as she tugs on a black t-shirt with the band standing before a crashing blimp.

She checks for Anthony, but her mom must have taken him out. It's a service Luisa greatly appreciates; she sleeps through his cries.

Wicker basket on her hip, she leaves the room. The ceramic salad bowl is next to the kitchen sink, washed out.

"Finalmente," says her mom, Anthony bouncing on her lap, "sei alzata." Reagan's on TV, looking serious. Did another rocket blow up? No, he's saying something about Iran, and she doesn't think they have spaceships in the Middle East.

"Giselle is here, ma." Luisa gives her boy a kiss on the head. His hair smells a million times better than Giselle's. Something like freshly baked bread. If they could bottle that smell, make a cologne out of it, they'd make a fortune.

Drakkar Noir, Calvin Klein, none of them hold a candle to the smell of your baby's head.

"While she's sleeping," says her mom in Italian, "I'll speak whatever language I want."

"Sì, mamma. Tornerò presto." Luisa makes her way into the basement. Her dad is on the couch watching Kinsmen Jackpot Bingo. His cards are laid out on the coffee table, dabbers to the side. He pushes tobacco into the red, plastic cigarette loader, then slides it home into the paper tube pressed to its mouth.

"Are you winning, dad?" asks Luisa.

He says nothing. He's still mad at her for getting pregnant.

Luisa tosses her shirt and Giselle's dress in the big, metal sink—sequins have to be washed by hand, that was a lesson she only needed to learn once—and dumps the rest of her laundry into the washer. In goes a capful of Tide. Soap dust puffs into her face and makes her sneeze. It's agony on her jaw, and she has to take a moment to let the pain pass.

Washer running, she turns to the basin and begins to fill it with water. She'll let the sequined clothes soak and take care of them when she comes down to switch the laundry.

A grey marble floats in the water, bobbing up and down in the force from the stream. One of the beads that filled Bobby Dupree's weird toy. It must have been caught in her shirt.

Luisa scoops it out and tosses it in the trash under the sink. It leaves her fingers oily, but a quick rinse in the water fixes that.

On her way back, Luisa's dad tosses her a stuffed animal.

"Tell Joe if he doesn't clean his shit up, he's going to get a smack."

Luisa smiles. She looks at the thing.

It's another one of the toys Bobby had, the demented Teddy Ruxpin knock-off. This one doesn't look exactly the same. Like a cousin of Bobby's toy. It's a little shorter. Younger looking, though just as creepy.

These things are supposed to talk, aren't they? Its mouth looks like it's about to move. Like it *should* move. Luisa expects it to blink, but if it blinks, she might scream.

A shiver runs up her back.

"I'll tell him," she says, climbing the wooden steps into the kitchen.

Joe—clad in nothing but a long sleeve shirt and He-Man underwear—sits at the kitchen table, Giselle across from him. They both eat from overflowing bowls of Frankenberry.

"Dad says to clean up your shit when you're done with it, or you're getting a smack," Luisa says, dropping the weird bear on the table. "He says put some freakin' pants on, too."

"Yeah, right," says Joe, mouth full. "I don't have to wear pants in my own house."

"You do when we have company."

"I don't mind," says Giselle. "Underwear with cartoons on 'em are super cute."

Joe blushes. He's at the age where "cute" is no longer a compliment. His dark hair hangs over his eyes and he chews furiously.

"Chew with your mouth closed," says Luisa, grabbing a bottle of strawberry Ensure from the fridge.

"I am."

"Then why can I hear you?"

"It's crunchy!" Joe looks up and finally sees his stuffed animal. "What the hell is that?"

"Watch your mouth," says their mom from the living room in her accented English. "I'll wash it with soap!" Anthony coos his approval from her lap. Reagan still addresses America. Why they're watching it in Canada, Luisa doesn't know, but her mother likes the president.

"If the toy's not yours, whose is it?" Luisa asks. Her jaw is getting tight from all the talking. She ran out of Tramadol three days ago.

"Hey guys," says Giselle.

"I'm too old for stuffed animals," says Joe. "That's baby stuff."

"You have a million toys," says Luisa.

"GI Joes and Transformers, not baby stuff!"

"Guys," says Giselle, dropping her spoon into the neon-colored cereal. "It's moving—"

There's a blur of fur—a streak moving through the air—and Giselle's mouth is full with the stuffed bear. Her eyes shoot wide. She stumbles to her feet. Her chair tips and bangs on the cheap linoleum.

Joe screams, cereal spewing onto the table. Luisa would join him, but in her current state, all she can do is whine through her wired jaw.

The legs of the teddy bear squirm, kicking at Giselle's face. It slips further into her mouth, wiggling and pulling its way in until all that's left are its padded feet. They bang against her teeth.

Then it's gone.

Giselle falls to her knees, gagging. Her pretty, round face turns purple. She grabs at her throat as it swells up like an anaconda swallowing a boar. The bear creates ripples in her flesh as it maneuvers itself further in.

"Che cazzo?" Downstairs, Dad yells in Italian.

Luisa can't move. She learned the Heimlich in her babysitting course, but a living fucking teddy bear is not the same as a hunk of steak.

Luckily, Giselle seems to catch her breath. She's hyperventilating, but at least she's getting air. She rolls onto her back, tears streaming down her face. Her hands are on her stomach.

"Guys," she says.

Her stomach stretches, bigger than Luisa's when Anthony grew in there. The KISS nightie slides up and Giselle pulls it the rest of the way up to look. Her skin becomes smooth, shiny with sweat.

Then it bursts. The creature rips her open, pulling itself into the air. World's quickest C-section.

Giselle screams, birthing the creature with its nattering mouth of sharp, bloody teeth. It grunts and squirms, Giselle's flesh pulling up before sliding away from its body. The healthy glow fades from her face. Her mouth falls open, tongue lolling out and hanging against lips growing bluer before Luisa's eyes.

Giselle passes out. Her head falls back to the ground with a crack.

Bloody face snarling, the creature looks around. Its eyes land on Luisa's brother.

Joe looks like he's about to faint, too.

The thing lunges at him, springing off Giselle's torn torso.

Luisa doesn't think. She swats it out of the air before it can reach Joe. It slams into the salad bowl, sliding along the counter. The bowl falls and shatters.

"Che cosa?" Her mom comes around the couch, baby Anthony on her hip.

"Ma, no!" yells Luisa. The thing is looking at Anthony, those weird eyes locked onto the most vulnerable target.

Her son.

Luisa gets between them as it launches off the counter. It slams into her face. Her lips mash against her braces, against the wires clamping her mouth shut. She falls to the ground.

The creature mutters in a raspy voice. It pries at her lips but can't get into her mouth. The wires keep it tightly shut. Its paws are mittens, too thick to get anywhere. Her clenched teeth keep them out.

The bear looks Luisa in the eye, confused. Dark marbles within those downturned sockets expand and reach out to her. They connect with something deep in her body, leaving her frozen in every sense of the word.

Luisa sees space in those eyes. Stars and planets, gasses undiscovered on earth. Cosmic radiation that makes Chernobyl look like an Easy-Bake Oven. This creature is not a god, but it knows gods. Not the god represented by the gold cross around her neck, not the god that her mom prays to before bed and meals, but something full of anger and desire. Something of galaxies beyond heaven. Something that cares so little for humanity that it would leave them to lesser creatures such as the one trying to crawl down Luisa's throat.

She feels her head begin to lose weight. Her brain is carbonated, the bubbles slipping from her ears toward a heaven unlike anything in the holy book.

The creature is torn away. Her dad stands in the kitchen, holding the animal by its throat. He screams in Italian, but Luisa doesn't understand. At this point, she wouldn't understand English.

Anthony squalls. Her mother roughly puts him in her arms. Luisa holds her son, pushing herself back with her bare feet, and comes up against something soft.

Giselle.

Luisa lets her head fall back onto Giselle's unmoving chest. Her friend is still. Doesn't moan in agony, though the hole splitting her belly button leaks blood and something dark and pungent.

"Shhh," says Luisa, holding Anthony against her. He calms, pulling at her oversized shirt, trying to receive comfort at her breast.

Luisa reaches up and pulls Giselle's arm over her. Its weight across her shoulder is her own comfort. She turns her head to the side.

A mound of grey marbles grows from the hole in her friend's torso. They twitch with reptilian life. They vibrate while the alien toy wriggles in her father's grasp.

Ma grabs the thing by the waist. In a rare moment of cooperation, Luisa's parents yank in opposing directions. The thing squeals in their hands before it tears in half.

Grey marbles bounce onto the kitchen floor with wet plops. They land among spilled cereal, looking like Frankenberry pebbles that missed the dye process. The smell of sulfur and rotting offal fills the air, worse than a trip to the dump.

A handful of the marbles land on Luisa's chest, bouncing off her son's dark head. One rolls into the hollow of her throat. She picks it up and examines it.

"—and it will take cooperation with all who seek to rid the world of this scourge," says Reagan from the living room.

The marble looks back.

"Thank you, and God bless you."

ABOUT CHRISTOPHER O'HALLORAN

CHRISTOPHER O'HALLORAN—HWA and HOWLS member—is a milk-slinging, Canadian actor-turned-author previously published by *Hellbound Books*, *Tales to Terrify Podcast*, *The Dread Machine*, and others. Despite making the transition to writing, Chris still puts his acting diploma to use; he acts like a fool for chuckles from his wife and son at home in British Columbia. He's co-editor and contributor for the anthology *Howls From Hell* featuring a foreword by Grady Hendrix. Fans of stories about vein-removal and Phoenix-women against the patriarchy can visit COauthor.ca for stories, reviews, and updates on his upcoming novel, *Pushing Daisy*. Contact him there or on Twitter or Instagram @Burgleinfernal.

Chairs scraped as footsteps echoed down the corridor, and the class hushed as Mrs. Dunworth entered the room to introduce the new boy as Ryan.

"My name is Brian," he said shyly to Mrs. Dunworth, but she ignored his correction and sternly pointed at the seat next to mine. Infectious sniggers made their way around the room as the poor kid began to waddle towards me, pants half-mast, long black hair matted to his pasty white forehead. His breathing was more of a raspy wheeze. He reminded me of one of those ugly pug dogs, or "Puglies," as my best friend, Eddie, called them.

"Your new boyfriend's a bit of a porker, Tom, isn't he?" Richard Clark whispered across the classroom to me, screwing half his face up in a wink.

Richard was the class knucklehead—sleeves rolled up, always ferociously chewing gum, and sporting a military-style crewcut that you just knew had been in the family for generations. He labeled boys with hair longer than half-an-inch "fairies." I smirked at his comment, though, because that's what you do when the school bully cracks a joke. You just smirk.

"Can we have some decorum, please?" Mrs. Dunworth asked without conviction.

"Jeez, what's that smell? Did someone just shit out a dead skunk?" Richard's sidekick, Shane, commented. There was a ripple of forced laughter.

"It's Moby Dick over there," Richard said. "Smells just like your momma's pussy, Eddie."

Richard harbored a general abomination for all, but it's safe to say that Brian topped his hate list from the day the new boy showed up. Something about him rubbed Richard the wrong way. Besides, Richard had needed a new project ever since his last one, a poor kid named Eric Chaplin, had moved to a different school.

The new kid flopped into the chair next to me, exhaling heavily as the chair creaked in protest. The putrid smell of his breath washed over me, and a stale cocktail of his deodorant and sweat closely followed. His large, puffy areolas were visible through the front of his white polyester shirt, which strained under the pressure of his belly.

"Nice rack, new kid!" someone called out from the back.

"He's got bigger tits than you, Sarah," Richard hissed.

I wanted to step in, be Sarah's knight in shining armor, but I didn't. Sarah could look after herself.

"Why are you looking at the new boy's tits, Rich? Something you want to tell us?" she countered.

Brian didn't say anything else for the rest of the day. We did, though; we said a lot, and things would only become tougher for him. We all knew it. I felt sorry for the kid, but I've been on the receiving end of the class's ire, and I refused to return to the land of persecution.

"Am I a pussy?" I later asked my Magic 8 Ball.

As I see it, yes.

I frowned, but it wasn't wrong.

———

Brian was much smarter than me. Whenever the teachers forced a response from him, he nailed it. He always had his head in books, even on lunch breaks, which only intensified Richard's hatred of him.

It started as verbal abuse—the usual stuff: "bitch tits," "lard-ass," "jelly belly", "lunch-bucket," and so on. But when Brian didn't give anything back—not a single scowl, not one tear—things started to get very dark very quickly.

The first incident happened in the school cafeteria.

Brian sat alone, surrounded by his banquet, alternating his

attention from the crinkled packet of food in his hands to the books spread across the table. Slowly making their way towards him, deliberately scraping their chairs behind them, Richard and Shane sat down on either side of him until their faces were only inches from Brian's. He didn't acknowledge them or look up from his book, just casually shoved his fingers into his mouth for degreasing.

"What is *with* that kid?" I muttered.

From where we sat, a few tables away, Eddie and I could see Richard's face turning red. Even as they scooted their chairs further inwards—until their noses almost pecked at his cheeks—Brian offered them nothing.

"Shit," Sarah whispered. "Should we do something?"

"Like what?" Veronica replied, toying with her mountain of hair. "Boys will be boys, especially those two."

"I'll give Fat Boy credit; he's lasted longer than most," Eddie said. "But they all crack in the end."

"Anyhow, what were we talking about?" Veronica muttered. "Oh, duh! Bobby's taking me to the old drive-in this weekend, but I doubt we'll see much of the movie, if you know what I mean. *Big Trouble in—*"

"Shh," Sarah hissed, elbowing Veronica.

We watched as Richard slowly peeled the lid off Brian's yogurt carton, lifted it above Brian's head, and poured it onto his greasy hair.

"Richie's having yogurt-coated blubber for lunch," Eddie quipped, but nobody laughed. We gaped, mouths open, as the pale substance made its way down Brian's hairline and onto the bridge of his pudgy nose. He carried on eating his packet of salt and vinegar chips as though he hadn't a care in the world.

"You're a filthy fucking pig!" Richard shouted in frustration, loud enough to echo off the cafeteria walls.

"Oink. Oink. Oink," Shane added. They both walked away, kicking chairs in disgust and defeat.

"Pig's got balls, though," I muttered.

We carried on eating, listening to Veronica's detailed descriptions of Bobby Taylor's tattoos and how comfy his car's backseat was. I kept an eye on Brian, watching him finish his meal. Just when it looked as though he was done, he fingered the yogurt from his face into his mouth, and then literally licked the table clean.

We all knew the bullying wouldn't end there, and as predicted, the pranks and harassment became worse each time—tacks on the chair, steel rulers whipped against his behind, "dead" arms and legs. One time after class, Richard relieved himself in Brian's locker, drenching the slightly faded Michael J. Fox poster still there from when the locker was Eric Chaplin's. Brian looked at me with a somewhat bemused expression on his face when he found the damage, but I averted my gaze to my own locker, preferring Heather Locklear's blue eyes and comforting smile.

———

Richard was relentless, but there's no denying it; I played my part in events that unfolded that year. I should have done something, but to reiterate the verdict from the 8 Ball, I was a pussy.

The day before we all became infamous, we had double P.E. in the afternoon. The showers were a terrifying place—no separate cubicles, just a tiled room with shower heads on the walls and drains on the floor. We were all naked and vulnerable, and everyone was fair game.

Shane herded us all out. "Get out, or I'll fuck you up," he whispered.

I looked back in time to see him and Richard, each armed with a wet towel, begin lashing Brian. He remained silent even as his skin reddened. They whipped Brian until there wasn't a single white patch left on his body.

Still, Brian gave them nothing, silent to the end.

When Richard returned to the locker room, he looked pissed. "What the fuck are you hard-ons staring at?" he shouted.

I continued dressing, avoiding his gaze.

"I've had enough of the kid," he muttered under his breath. With that, he unzipped his changing bag, pulled out a switchblade, and dashed back into the shower area.

Nobody said anything. No heroes chased after him. Shane stood there with the rest of us, his lips parted and his face white as a sheet, as Richard rushed past him.

"He won't do it, Tom, will he?" Eddie whispered.

Shane snapped his head towards me for a response, but I was no longer sure what Richard was capable of.

The shriek took us all by surprise.

It wasn't like a movie scream. It was piercing, and the sheer volume made my ears ring. I felt it inside me, too, rattling so deep in my core that I had to grab the bench to steady myself. The shriek shook us all, I think. Every boy's face in that changing room was taut and pale.

Finally, Richard came back out, hands over both his ears. "Wow, that bitch can scream. I didn't even touch the grody sack of shit."

"Is it finished now, Richard? Are you *finished* now?" Eddie asked.

Eddie's newfound bravado sent a shudder rattling down my bones. Everyone froze—half or fully naked—aware that a line had been crossed. My heart skipped a beat as I watched Richard step towards Eddie, lips peeling back in a snarl.

"I'm sorry, fuckwit. Perhaps it was because I had my hands over my ears, but for a minute, I thought you were asking if I had finished." He let the blade rest against Eddie's right cheek. "Is that what you asked me?" His words sent spittle spraying across Eddie's face. "Is it?"

I thought about saying something, but there was a wild look in Richard's eyes.

"N—No," Eddie stammered, his flash of bravery now a distant memory.

"Thought so," Richard hissed. "It's finished when I say it's finished, dumb shit!"

"Sure, Richie. You're the boss."

Richard put the knife back in the bag. "If any of you say anything about this, I'll cut pieces off you. Do you understand?"

Everyone nodded.

Brian emerged from the showers, redder than a cherry Sno Cone, a contrastingly stark white towel wrapped around his ample belly. He ran straight for the door, not even bothering to collect his clothes.

"Run, Sloth, run!" Richard shouted after him. I knew he wouldn't let this go. He turned back to Eddie. "Tomorrow, you and your boyfriend—we meet straight after the bell, just inside the gates to the field. There's a hole in the fence bordering the old cemetery that Fat Boy uses to go home. Be there or be dead. I want to make sure the pig doesn't come back next year."

After zipping up our bags, Eddie and I collected our bikes and started the short journey to the arcade, our Spokey Dokeys silent as our legs pumped like well-oiled pistons. Explosions, groans, and cheers leaked out onto the street as we pulled up outside, but the sights and sounds from our favorite place, usually dopamine-inducing, still couldn't lift our mood.

We weren't prepared to give up, though. Dripping with sweat, we pooled our clammy coins together and claimed our machine: *Donkey Kong.*

"You first, Eds. Make it count."

I watched him feed his coin in, but he didn't seem right. The Def Leppard t-shirt he wore—the one I always teased him about because he didn't actually like them—looked far too big. The smattering of light hair above his lip suddenly looked silly and childish rather than cool. When Stacey Barlow, the best-looking and most popular girl in school, walked in wearing tight, fluorescent green Spandex leggings, Eddie only offered her a cursory glance.

"What are we going to do, Tom?" Eddie mumbled, moving the joystick around.

"I dunno. Richard's got me freaked out. Big time."

"Me, too. Why won't the school kick him out?"

"Not sure," I said, shrugging.

"I feel so pathetic when he's around, like a fucking dweeb! Kid's a real psycho. There's no telling what he'll do."

I watched as Eddie's pixelated Jumpman hopped over the barrels, but my mind was locked in on our Richard dilemma.

"Your turn," Eddie muttered, yanking the stick aggressively to the right.

We were both off our game. We couldn't get anywhere close to our high scores, but we kept pushing the coins in, anything to take our minds off Richard. Even after the money disappeared, we lingered. I preferred to be around the relentless bleeps and bloops and violent revving engines in this sanctuary of stale sweat and acrid farts than to be left alone with my thoughts.

When we parted ways, I gave Eddie a half-hearted high-five. Wheeling my bike next to me, I embarked on my slowest walk home ever. Home meant dinner, dinner meant TV, TV meant bed, and bed meant tomorrow. And tomorrow meant—

I didn't finish my food that night, even though Mom made my favorite: cheeseburgers and fries. I told her I felt sick and spent the rest of the night in my room staring at my *Karate Kid* poster, imagining taking Richard down with a vicious leg sweep. I could almost hear the rapturous applause erupting and Eddie proudly shouting, "That's my best buddy!" as the audience chanted my name and lifted me high into the air, carrying me to where Sarah waited with a gold medal and a kiss.

Usually, I'd read for a bit before bed, but this whole mess had my stomach in knots. I laid there, wondering how I could get out of it. There was no Mr. Miyagi on my street—nobody to teach me to wax on, wax off, and how to kick a bully's ass.

I couldn't win. If I chickened out and didn't turn up for school, I'd end up back on Richard's radar.

————

The last day of school should have been fun, should have been spent anxiously anticipating the long summer break, signing each other's yearbooks, and daydreaming about all the adventures we'd have. Instead, guilt and dread haunted my classmates' tired faces.

Even the teachers picked up on our morose mood. "Is everyone going to miss me that much?" Mr. Turnbull joked.

None of us laughed.

When the final school bell rang, I wanted to run home, but I met my clique—Eddie, Sarah, and Veronica—at the designated spot.

Richard and Shane were already there, sitting at the edge of the clearing, taking drags from their cigarettes, occasionally spitting balls of mucus into the tall grass.

"Fat Boy shouldn't be too long. I've watched him walk into the field a few times," Richard said before blowing an impressive smoke ring.

"What are we going to do?" I asked.

Richard looked at me with a manic sneer. "*We* aren't gonna do anything, Tommy Boy. You've just volunteered yourself," he said. He plucked his switchblade from his back pocket and thrust it into my palm. "Pig. That's what you're going to write across his chest, and if you don't, I'll write it across yours instead."

I smiled nervously, hoping he was joking. I felt the knot in my stomach tighten. "Richard, I—I—can't."

"Give me the knife back then," he said, "and I'll demonstrate how to do it."

"N—no."

"Give me the fuckin' knife back now, you pussy!" he shouted.

I wanted to stab him, to sink the blade into the side of his neck, and to watch him choke on his own blood. I looked at Sarah, who shook her head at me. I didn't have a choice.

"Okay, okay. I'll do it."

"That's my boy," Richard said, slapping me on the side of my arm.

"He's coming." Shane hissed. "Hide!"

The six of us nestled in the waist-high grass. I was certain Brian would be able to see or hear us. I prayed he would notice us and find a different way home, but he kept coming, in his own world, munching on a Snickers bar.

When he was only a few feet away, Richard stepped out of the grass to greet him. "Fat Boy! You left without saying goodbye. Didn't your momma teach you any manners before you ate her?"

No response. Richard's face reddened.

Brian stood there, forcing the remainder of the melting chocolate bar into his mouth.

When Brian began meticulously licking the inside of the wrapper, Richard's eyes bulged as if they were about to pop right out of his head.

"Tom, get over here!" Richard bellowed, but I couldn't move.

Shane crept out of the grass, a smirk on his face, and crouched down right behind Brian. Richard stepped forward and thrust his hands deep into Brian's chest with a grunt.

Somehow, Brian didn't move an inch. Not an inch.

Richard's face went lobster red. "Bring me the knife, Tom!" he commanded.

I looked at the blade in the palm of my trembling hand. I wanted to throw it into the long grass, to get it as far away as possible, but I walked over, unable to stop myself.

When Brian saw the knife, he opened his mouth wide and screamed so loud that I swear it made the trees shake and the ground tremble.

"Was that an *earthquake*?" Veronica shouted.

Brian started to back up and stumbled over Shane, landing hard on the grass.

"Come here, piggy," Richard said, grabbing the knife from me and approaching Brian. "I'm gonna make you squeal."

"Stop!" Sarah shouted.

"Yeah, Richard, you're going too far!" Eddie added.

"Shut the fuck up, losers!" Richard spat.

Brian opened his mouth and let out a series of sharp, piercing cries that quickly escalated to a deafening crescendo. The ground began to shake, and I thrust my arms out to keep my balance as a chasm opened in the grass before our very eyes.

The shrieking ceased.

To me, it was clear that this was a warning, not a plea, but Richard was oblivious, too far gone, lost in his campaign of loathing. He moved in again with the knife.

"No, Richard!" I screamed.

"You think you're so smart, don't you? But school's over now, Piggy. Time for a real education," he said.

The next tremor sent us all sprawling on the ground. Richard's knife sank into a yellow patch of earth only inches from Brian's head. Cursing under his breath, he pushed himself up, face twisted in hate. I saw a bead of blood run from his lips and down his chin.

"Was that you, fatty? Did you break wind?" He grabbed Brian's shirt and ripped it open. "Whoa, look at all that blubber! I think I'm going to need a bigger knife."

Sarah helped me to my feet, but another tremor shook the ground.

Undeterred, Richard put the blade to Brian's stomach.

Brian ralphed. A powerful spray of green bile hit Richard square on, covering his hair and eyes in thick, gloopy vomit. And then Brian spoke.

"My name is Brian."

Richard clawed at his face. "I can't see! I can't fucking see!" he screamed, rubbing relentlessly at his eyes, unable to displace any of the green substance. "Help—"

Another jet of liquid sprayed from Brian's mouth straight into Richard's, cutting his plea short. With his hands around his throat and his head covered with green spew, Richard began to let out a series of horrific, muffled choking sounds, maniacally hopping from one foot to the next. His moves became more exaggerated, and bits of his exposed skin started to turn deep red.

"Somebody do something!" Shane screamed, but no one did.

We watched as Richard's foot caught in the fresh crack in the earth, and he toppled headfirst onto the dead grass. He squirmed there, his hands still clasped around his throat. He looked so vulnerable.

"We—we need to get help," Sarah said, her voice trembling. She slowly backed away, and the others followed. I wanted to run, but my legs still wouldn't move. I was frozen, helpless, as Brian heaved himself to his feet.

"My name is Brian," he repeated, expression neutral.

Another disorienting tremor shook the ground as he turned toward my fleeing classmates. He launched a spray of green liquid that coated them from the waist down, bringing them to a sticky halt, setting like concrete. Some of it splashed across my feet and ankles.

"My name is Brian."

"Please, Brian. Don't hurt us," Sarah begged. We were trapped.

One by one, Brian looked each of us in the eye before pulling another Snickers bar from his right pocket and making his way back into the tall grass.

Richard's body lay in front of us—silent, unmoving, dead.

I glanced nervously at the others, seeking comfort but only finding mirrors of my anguish in their faces. Shane's bravado was gone. Tears flowed freely from his eyes. Without his commander, he was just one of us. Perhaps less.

Desperately, we started trying to free ourselves. No luck. The shit was rock solid.

"For fuck's sake," Eddie muttered, his voice shaky, as he tried to pull his leg from the solidified gunk. "Fuck!"

I started screaming for help, and the others joined in. We screamed until our voices went hoarse. We waited for minutes that stretched into hours until we were left exhausted and all cried out. There was nothing left to do but watch the sun drop from the sky.

It was torturous—the waiting.

My eyes kept falling on Richard. He looked just like a kid, one of us.

I'm not sure exactly how much time passed before the goo finally began to dissolve, but it felt like we were in that field for an eternity. It must have been early morning when enough of the stuff had dissolved for Eddie to finally drag himself free. I managed to free my feet too, and the others followed suit.

We hurried back to the fence, glancing nervously over our shoulders. My heart skipped each time the breeze rushed through the nearby grasses. What if Brian came back?

Our parents were beside themselves with anger. Mine had sent the police out looking for us. Even though our stories matched perfectly, neither the police nor our parents believed us. With plenty of people to corroborate our bullying, they accepted Brian's story that we'd ambushed him, but he'd managed to escape.

Richard's death stumped the adults. An autopsy determined he had died from respiratory failure and asphyxia, symptoms closely related to drowning, but there was no fluid in his lungs. The green stuff, of course, was gone. Richard's death was eventually written up as "unexplained," so there weren't any arrests, only ostracization from the community and years of prescribed therapy for all of us that involved nodding in the right places and agreeing our imaginations had gotten the best of us.

Sarah and Veronica were the first to move away, then Eddie. I remember fighting a tear as I waved at his receding face, which stared solemnly back through the rear window of the car. My parents refused to be run out of town, so we stayed. Shane stayed, too, but he was a shadow of his former self.

As for Brian, I kept my distance. He went on to graduate valedictorian.

Months of jumping through hoops and nodding in the right places, and they eventually considered me "cured." Since then, I've tried to live a normal life. Cancer has nearly won its battle, though, and it seems wrong to take the truth to my grave. Now that there's no threat of the funny farm lingering, I feel a duty to warn others.

My parents are dead, buried in the cemetery next to the clearing, and close to them lies my sister, who was taken from this world well before them—nothing sinister, just the wrong time and place. Some hick with a skinful, driving well over the speed limit.

I've nothing to lose.

The internet made it easier to track similar events—unexplained deaths and sightings, and related theories from hillbillies to doctors. Then a breakthrough. It was an arduous and painful task going through all the missing person pages for the last few decades, but finally, dating back to 1965, I found a picture of Brian—only this kid was called "George" and disappeared from his bed one night in October somewhere on the other side of the world.

There are thousands of missing people still unaccounted for, and it doesn't take a genius to know what's going on. I don't pretend to understand how it all works, but I know one thing for sure; *they* are among us—*with* us.

Life has been unkind to me. It's probably taken its fair share from you, too, but the events of that day have helped me cling to an unwavering state of childhood wonder. On the warm evenings, when I lean against the doorway, saying a prayer for my old friends, I can claim to understand some of the science behind the twinkling stars and the two-million-year-old light that makes it down to us; however, my mind still races with all the possible life forms out there, and the magic that hides behind the black veil.

ABOUT MARK TOWSE

Mark Towse is an Englishman living in Australia. He would sell his soul to the devil or anyone buying if it meant he could write full-time. Alas, he left it very late to begin this journey, penning his first story since primary school at the ripe old age of 45. Since then, he's been published in the likes of *Flash Fiction Magazine, The Dread Machine, Cosmic Horror, Suspense Magazine, ParABnormal, Raconteur,* and his work has also appeared (and set to appear) on many exceptional podcasts such as *The Grey Rooms, No Sleep, Creepy, Tales to Terrify,* etc. His most recent novella 'Crows' from D&T Publishing was published in December 2021, with lots to come in 2022, including his anticipated return to old folk horror with the imminent release of 'One Last Shindig' in April. Also, look out for Nature's Perfume in March from Journalstone Publishing!

AND THE UNIVERSE WENT ON

JASON P. BURNHAM

"Ran! Hey, Randy! I could use some directions here," says a voice from far away.

I'm adrift in a black ocean, a grey dawn on the horizon racing across the waves; its sinuous spirals pry open the darkness.

"Randy!"

I blink and wake in a different blackness: the dark night on a deserted two-lane highway, my long-time roommate, Clevon, in the driver's seat. I wipe spittle from the corner of my mouth.

"Oh good, you're awake," Clevon says with a sarcastic smile. "I hate it when you snore."

"Remind me why we're friends." I groan.

"*Best* friends," he says, correcting me. "We've been driving forever, and I wanted to make sure..."

"Clevon, look out!"

The back end of Clevon's yellow Gremlin spins out as he slams on the brakes, narrowly avoiding a deer.

Something resembling a grey, exuberantly pulsating lichen bulges from where the deer's antlers and neck should be, obscuring the reddish-orange coat and white spots underneath. It's so close I see its nostrils flare when it breathes, dyssynchronous from the throbbing of the grey mass on its head and neck.

"What's wrong with that deer?" I shout, and dissolve into a coughing fit.

Clevon looks from me to the dusk-darkened road, but the deer is gone. He adjusts his dark-rimmed glasses and rubs his neck with a pink, sunburned arm.

"I didn't see it very well—it was harder to spot than deer by the Golden Gate Bridge. What was wrong with it?"

"It had a weird-looking growth on it or something." I shiver, though I can't tell if it's from seeing the deer or my pneumonia. "Don't you think you should check the car for damage?"

"You want me out there in the dark with a mutated deer? I've seen that movie before."

"I haven't—how does it end?"

"Not well for one of us," he says and pulls the car parallel with the road. Grasses on the shoulder of the highway whip in the summer wind, lit only by our headlights.

"How far until your parents' place?" he asks, stretching his hands.

One of the last things my parents told me a few years ago, before I left for San Francisco, was to not get AIDS. Despite my caution, I failed them, and they haven't spoken to me since, which was at odds with the very last thing they said—how much they loved and supported me, no matter what I did.

This discrepancy is precisely why Clevon has agreed to chauffeur me home—it's harder to ignore a surprise knock than a phone call or letter. I want to talk to them again, one last time.

"Look for the treehouse, remember?" I say with another cough. Our friend Gaëtan had the same *Pneumocystis* pneumonia that myself and the other AIDS patients are getting, but his popped his lung, killing him almost immediately. It's usually slower to kill, like in my case, but the doctors say I can hallucinate if my oxygen gets too low —hence why I need Clevon to drive.

The Gremlin shudders as Clevon steers over the progressively rockier road.

"Slow down, Cleve, all the bumps make my body hurt," I say, raising my head off the passenger's side door.

"If we go any slower you might as well get out and push, save us a little gas."

I roll my eyes, and it makes me nauseated. He's been trying to keep the mood light—telling bad jokes, recounting funny stories. This isn't his first reconciliation road trip. He's driven several people from our dwindling friend group on their last voyages home to make amends—I think he does it because his parents don't talk to him anymore. He's never *said* that, but you get to know a guy.

I push myself up off the door. "I'll steer if it comes to that."

"Roger." Clevon salutes and grins. Cleve's got HIV too, but the doctors say his body is different and isn't progressing to AIDS—he has far more energy in reserve for things like salutes and grins.

The wind of the road blows through my illness-thinned hair as my mind and eyes wander among the shadows cast by the trees. I push back the film of exhaustion from my corneas and watch untrimmed grasses whip by in our wake. The *thud thud thud* of wind through partially open car windows bumps against my eardrums, enough pressure to revive my brain.

"Is this it?" Clevon asks.

I sit up. Too fast. My head spins, and the world darkens, my hands holding existence on the precipice of a black hole until I overcome its gravity and the road resumes its solid state.

"You okay?" Clevon asks.

"Yeah, yeah. Just a little dizzy."

Clevon shrugs. "Mailbox says 'The Tills,' so it must be your folks' place. Don't see much in the way of a treehouse, though."

I blink. "It's right there, Cleve," I say and point. After I was about fourteen, Dad used it more than I did because I thought high-schoolers were too cool for treehouses. Dad liked to write up there with the wind in his hair, birds chirping nearby.

Clevon slows the car and we turn right onto the long, graveled drive.

"Stop the car."

"What?"

Rotten wood dangles from the treehouse, planks amiss, the rope ladder at the center mildewed green with disuse.

"Cleve—look at the treehouse. Come around and help me out."

After staring up at the old maple for a moment, Clevon does as he's told. Wary now, his eyes survey the darkness creeping in like fog. A coyote howls in the distance.

The door opens, and I slide halfway to the ground. I push myself up, and Clevon puts one arm under my armpit to steady me.

"Thanks, I..."

My breath catches in my throat—not from pneumonia, but from seeing the treehouse's disrepair up close. A piece of wood falls from the tree and smashes into the ground near my feet. Clevon's fingers dig into my arm.

"Randy, you sure your folks still live here?" he sputters.

I grunt, half in acknowledgment, half in confusion, half in exhaustion. That's too many halves.

The coyote howls again, this time nearer, garbled somehow as it fades into the stillness around us. Clevon lowers me back into the car and sprints to the other side.

"Dad would never let that happen to the treehouse," I say, mostly to myself.

"How far to the house?" Clevon asks, voice shaking.

"Like two hundred yards."

"What if they're not home?" he asks.

"It's rural Missouri, Cleve. We don't lock doors. If they're not here, we'll just go inside."

Clevon stops short as the house appears from the penumbra.

"Their car is here," I say, trying to sound reassuring.

Clevon sighs; I think in relief.

"Help me out. Let's go knock."

As he extinguishes the headlights, a flash of grey appears on the nearest wall of the house. I blink and it's gone. Probably a floater. The doctors said AIDS patients sometimes have eye troubles near the end.

"Do you have a flashlight?" Clevon asks as he lifts me out.

I wheeze out a laugh. "Who brings a flashlight to a funeral?"

He squeezes my arm tighter than is strictly necessary. "You're not dead *yet*. Now tell me how we're going to see."

"We'll turn the lights on."

He scoffs, but his grip relaxes ever so slightly.

The house is as I remember it—a wooden porch, deck chairs and a table where we ate during the spring and fall when the weather was nice, a screen door to keep the bugs out.

"Can you stand?" Clevon asks, one hand on the doorframe.

I steady myself against the house. "Yeah." I lift my arm, the strange sensation of knocking at my own house reverberating through atrophied muscles.

"Mom, Dad?" I say, my voice trembling, more from anticipation than physical strain.

The longer the seconds drag on, the more anxious Clevon becomes.

"Mr. and Mrs. Tills?" Clevon shouts, voice cracking. He clears his throat in embarrassment and calls again in a deeper register.

The dark threatens to envelop us in the silence.

"Let's just go in—I need a nap."

Clevon smiles, but sweat lines his brow.

"Didn't know you were this afraid of the dark, Cleve," I say with a half-smile. I push the door open, and it creaks.

"What was that?" Clevon jumps back.

"Cleve—it's a rusty door hinge, calm down."

I call into the foyer and dining room adjacent, the cherry wood table draped with white linen, uncomfortable chairs tucked underneath. No answer.

The foyer has Grandpa Bill's grandfather clock. The one I hated when I was a kid because it was tick-tock-chiming every hour on the hour. It's silent now—why hasn't Dad wound it?

"Maybe some light?" Clevon asks.

"See," I say as the foyer light flickers on when I flip the switch. "Told you they'd work."

"Take your shoes off," I instruct Clevon while wriggling out of my own loafers, the white stone tiles cool under my feet.

There are winter boots out—Mom's doing. Dad would prefer all the shoes in the closet, but Mom gets cold easily and works in the garden in snow boots to prevent prickers from embedding in her feet. Their summer shoes are nowhere to be seen.

"Are we going farther than the foyer?" Clevon asks in my ear.

"Yeah, just... remembering," I say. "Help me to the couch."

"Don't you want to find your parents?"

I groan, my vision and thoughts hazy with memory, with malaise, with ill.

"Yeah, let's check their bedroom."

"Mom, Dad?" I call as we approach. Clevon props me up against the doorframe to their bedroom, and I turn on the lights.

A pointillist beach painting sits above their combined mirror-dresser. The bed is partially made, nightstands dressed per usual—Dad's side with books, Mom's with flowers (plastic because she got tired of replacing them every few days). The air isn't stale, but it isn't lived-in either.

"Do you smell anything?" I ask.

Clevon holds his nose up and inhales deeply.

"No, can't say that I do." His eyes narrow. "Should I? Does it smell like they're dead?"

I shake my head. "They're not dead. Nobody's here. They're just..."

Clevon waits, fingers drumming against the door.

"They're just, what?"

It clicks. "They're probably camping."

Clevon grabs my arm.

"Ow, Cleve, not so hard. You know I bruise easily."

But his grip doesn't relax.

"Their car is in *the driveway!*" He's got me by both shoulders now, face in my face, so close our glasses almost touch.

"Huh," I say. My brain swims as if I've just summited a mountain, the weight of low oxygen pressing my brain into a tiny ball in the center of my head.

"Huh? That's all you have to say? Randy, are you sure your parents even *want* to see you?"

Ouch. I feel Clevon dragging me down the hall, away from my parents' bedroom. I shoot out my arm and grab the doorframe as we pass my room. The abrupt change in momentum sends us both to the floor.

"What are you *doing,* Randy?"

"They *would* want to see me," I sob, tearless rasps muffled by the thick beige carpet.

"Ran, I'm sorry. My parents, you know..."

"I don't care about *your* parents; these are *my* parents and *my parents* love me." All the energy from shouting blurs my vision.

When the haziness clears, Clevon is sitting, arms wrapped around bent knees, rocking back and forth.

"I'm sorry," I croak. "I..."

Clevon has confirmed what he had never said in words—these reconciliation road trips are also about *him* finding peace.

"It's okay," he says. "I'm sorry, too. This trip is about you, not me."

"This trip is about *both of us,*" I say. Clevon nods and wipes a tear away.

I stare up from my position on the floor to the posters on my wall —Cheryl Tiegs, not because she's hot, but because she's glamorous, Freddie Mercury, and *Star Wars,* because even if Freddie doesn't like *Star Wars,* I do.

"I don't want to be the president."

"Randy?" Clevon bends close, puts a cool hand on my warm forehead. I hadn't realized I was so hot.

"Yeah?"

"Are you hallucinating?" he asks urgently.

"Freddie," I say and point at my wall.

"Who?"

"Mercury!"

Clevon finally looks at the wall. He slumps against the door.

"Queen! You were quoting Queen lyrics at me?" I can't exactly pinpoint his tone, but it's somewhere between relief and annoyance.

"Is this real life?"

Clevon hits me. "That's not even correct."

"Oooh-ooooooooo."

"Don't give up your day job, Freddie," Clevon says, then winces. I *did* give up my day job at the *San Francisco Chronicle*. Who needs a job when...

I push myself up and sit against the door. "Everything's fine," I say, motioning to my bedroom. "See, they didn't change anything. If they were mad at me," I pause, wishing hope into truth, "they would have turned this into a sewing room."

"Do your parents sew?" He asks.

"No, but they could."

Clevon sighs. "You really think we're safe?"

"I lived here my *whole life*. I'm fine. My parents are fine. Their friends sometimes pick them up in their RV and go hiking and camping." I stop to catch my breath. "They're usually only gone a few days. Worst case, they'll be back in a couple nights."

Clevon glances up and down the hall, still not totally relaxed.

"You can sleep in my room with me so you're not scared. Plus, if I have any bad dreams, you can wake me up," I smile. "Help me to the bathroom—we'll inquire as to my parents' whereabouts at church tomorrow."

"Church?"

"Only game in town on Sundays," I say.

I cry out when he flips on the bathroom light switch.

"What? What?" He nearly pushes me over.

"Sorry, I... I haven't seen myself in a mirror in a while. I look... *awful*."

In the mirror, Clevon's mouth opens and closes, knowing anything he says will be a lie.

I never thought I would look like this—my hair is wispy, almost grey where it should be dark brown. My glasses look far too big for my sunken face, anemic and pale white as though the bones were poking through. My beard somehow looks like it has gotten shorter, even though I haven't trimmed it. The bags under my eyes carry the weight of the world.

"Sorry, Randy."

"It's fine," says my reflection. "Help me to the toilet, then get out. I can at least pee on my own."

Clevon helps me to the cold porcelain, and I sit. It's easier than standing, and it means the sobs don't knock me over.

I wash my hands and trudge my way out of the bathroom, summoning strength in defiance of the living corpse I saw in the mirror. The hallway feels dimmer than it did, longer, greyer. The doctors were right about the fading vision.

Clevon takes his turn in the bathroom, but I'm asleep long before he returns.

———

Darkness, expansive. Floating forward, faster, faster.

Glinting grey walls—in out, in out. Corridors contracting, narrower, narrower still.

Floating no more, waves of wind washing over—still I go.

Shrinking, shriveling, smaller, an atom in a world ocean.

Black ocean, gone grey. Putrescent, bubbling, boiling barnacles prolif-erate, erase the ocean. Popping, planting, permeating

Just like...

"The deer!" I shout. I'm awake, soaked in sweat, shivering, somber.

"Hmmm?" Clevon says from the floor.

"The deer! I saw those grey things that were on that deer we almost hit—they were in my dream."

Clevon rolls over, mid-morning sun streaking through the window across his face, and he holds up a hand to block it. "What are you talking about?"

Then I remember that he didn't see anything unusual and feel embarrassed.

"Nothing, I... I thought that deer looked weird when we almost hit it, and I think I just dreamed about it."

"It was all a dream then, and it's all a dream now."

I nod, not convinced, not awake. "Why are you on the floor?" I ask.

"You were sweating something awful."

"Did you sleep?"

Clevon shrugs. "For a while, then you snored and didn't stop when I hit you, so I've just been laying here, waiting for you to wake up, wondering why your parents would leave the door unlocked when they went camping."

I sit up and regret it immediately. Sweat pours off me, and the world swims.

"What do you mean?" I ask, the words oozing torpidly out of me, fighting each other to be the first to return to silence.

"You said they leave the door unlocked, but would they really leave it unlocked while they were gone for a week?"

"Maybe... maybe they forgot—it's not like they lock it often." I feel suddenly less sure than I sound. It *is* weird that they wouldn't lock it if they were going to be gone for a few nights. "Maybe they're only out for the night. People at church will know where they are."

Clevon shrugs, perhaps as unconvinced as I. "Do we have time to eat before church?"

The thrush at the back of my throat and tongue has slowly eroded my desire to eat. Add to that the film of unbrushed teeth, and food sounds about as good as dirt.

"Yeah, but I'm not very hungry—I'm sure we can find you something, though."

"You should eat too," Clevon admonishes.

I nod. "I'll give it a shot."

Clevon stands and pulls me up without asking. "Bathroom first?"

"Yeah," I say. "But let's go to the one off the kitchen—no mirror in there."

We hobble down the quiet hallway, birds chirping distantly outside. The walls are the same—wood-paneled to waist height, the top half painted white and plastered with pictures of the three of us, of me as a kid, including a few glamorous ones with bad haircuts. Mom with her old horse, Dad and I building the treehouse. The treehouse... Why did he let it go to hell?

From the toilet, I have a view of the yellow, linoleum-flowered kitchen, white countertops, white cabinets above.

"That's weird," I say.

"What?" Clevon asks.

"Cobweb behind the toaster. Toast is part of Dad's breakfast every Sunday."

"Randy... *where* are your parents?"

I flush the toilet and push myself up. "Would you quit being a baby? We survived the night, didn't we?"

"Not much of a reassurance." Clevon rubs a chill from his arms and busies himself looking through the pantry.

Adjacent the pantry under bay windows sits our little, round breakfast table, placemats set for three, as if I never left. "Any powdered donuts in there?" I ask, remembering spilling the sugar onto those ribbed, light blue placemats. "I love licking the sugar off my fingers."

"Hmmm, don't see any."

Clevon walks to the seafoam-green fridge and opens the door wide. He slams it shut and backs away so quickly he almost falls. His arm is across his face and he is a little green himself.

"What, what is it?"

"*Yuck.* Holy lord! You don't smell that?"

I take a deep whiff. "Smell what?"

"*Whew.* I've never smelled a fridge so rotten, and my old roommate once let a cheese enchilada sit in the refrigerator until it turned black."

My heart sinks through the floor. They've been gone longer than a few days. Dad would never let his refrigerator spoil like that. Why didn't they take the car?

"Let me look."

"Go ahead, but you're on your own," Clevon says, stepping away from the smell.

I use countertops to support what little weight is left of me and pull the refrigerator's metal handle. I'm greeted by the smell of rot. As with the lights, the refrigerator still works—the air is cold. For the food to get this bad, they must have been gone for months, around the last time I talked to them...

"Oh God, Cleve," I say.

"I know, it's disgusting, right?"

"No, no. I think they left when they found out I had AIDS."

Clevon's face falls and he rushes over, supports me, though his face wrinkles at the smell.

"Can... Sorry, Ran, can we close the refrigerator?"

I'm too exhausted for tears, too heartbroken to cry.

"Yeah, sorry," I say, and start to close the door when something catches my eye.

A grey blob.

"Oh my God—it's the grey stuff that was on the deer!" I point anxiously at something that looks like it might formerly have been a meatloaf.

Clevon's arm is across his nose. "What?"

I point to the aluminum foil tin, the grey growth bubbling over the side of the spoiled meat container. "See?"

My hands are clumsy and careless and as I lurch forward, my finger hits something wet. I gasp, my expelled breath popping some of the grey bubbles as it wafts over the rancid meat. I look back at Randy.

"See? This was on that deer's face."

Clevon grimaces. "Randy, I, I think you're seeing things—that's just a gnarly meatloaf."

I look where I'm pointing and all the grey bubbles are gone. I pull back my hand and examine it as Clevon closes the refrigerator. For an instant, reflective grey goop strains toward Clevon at the tip of my finger, then vanishes when I breathe out, like it was never there.

Clevon watches me watch my finger.

"See, nothing."

I nod, shaken.

"Now that we agree, can we figure out where the hell your parents are?"

———

"They told me they would come to San Francisco when I needed them," I say, holding back a tear.

Clevon squeezes my knee from where he sits in the Gremlin's driver seat.

"We'll check the church, like you asked. If it's as popular a spot on as you say it is, surely someone there will know where they went."

I try to shrug, but am not sure if my muscles actually move.

"Do they let queers in church around here?" Clevon asks, only half serious, but I don't have the energy to respond.

The dry wind of summer rushes over me, threatening to wash away the few grains of life I have left. I pause for a moment in the sunshine, thinking the warmth of daylight might not be a bad 'last feeling.'

"Randy!" Clevon shouts, as if he's repeating himself.

"Hmmm?"

"Church is *this* way?"

The church is at the end of a wooded path. The founding preacher thought it was the perfect location, the church shrouded in darkness except for sunrise service, when the east-facing window reveals the light of God. It made for some spooky Christmas Eve services, back when we used to go.

"Oh, hush and keep driving," I say. As we get closer to the grove, even *my* heart catches in my throat. And I know it's my heart, because it feels much different from the thrush residing there.

"Where are all the cars?" Clevon asks.

I survey the parking lot, empty except for gravel, which leads all the way to four stone steps under white double doors. The surrounding church is white too, except for the stained-glass windows and the short brown steeple with a cross at the top. Adjacent is the town's small cemetery, shaded by evergreens. Sunday church is *usually* the hottest event in town, the *only* Sunday event—I've never seen it so empty.

"This is too weird, Randy. Where is everyone? I think we should turn around," Clevon says, hands shaking as he makes an executive decision.

"Go ahead, there's nobody here anyway," I grumble.

As Clevon turns, one of the stained-glass windows flashes grey.

"Cleve, stop," I plead.

He looks in the rearview mirror but keeps his foot on the gas. "We're leaving this town and going back to California. *Right now.*"

I don't fight, I don't argue. I can't take my eyes off the thick, pulsating grey bubbles surging out of the casings of the stained-glass windows and through the crack in the double doors.

"Cleve, let's at least stop for gas."

———

Clevon hasn't spoken since we turned around at the church-turned-grey bubble bath. I can't tell if he's pissed or horrified or both.

"*Clevon*," I say as we near a deserted station.

"What?"

"Can we stop for gas, please? Nothing's close in rural Missouri."

Clevon hesitates, stares a hole through the gas gauge and pulls into the station, stopping next to one of the two red metal pumps. The small, white-washed attendant station adjacent is dark and empty, a weather-worn lawn chair sitting just outside.

"Fine, but I'm not going inside to pay. I'm filling up and we're getting the hell out of here."

Now all I have to do is stay awake long enough to come up with a plan to get us to my parents' house—if I had known we weren't going back, I would have left a letter before we attended the church horror show. I need to leave them a message for when they come back; I need them to know I was here before I'm gone forever.

The gas pump *click, click, clicks,* like the seconds on my grandpa's clock that no longer runs, ticking away my seconds.

Ding.

Clevon is back in the car.

"I'm not going to make it, Cleve." My lungs press all the way from their apices in my neck to the depths of my intestines, stretching as far and wide as the bones will allow, desperately trying to extract a few more molecules of oxygen.

The tension in his shoulders is replaced by softness and he grips my hand.

"You're going to be okay, Ran. Let's just get out of here."

I push his hand away. "No, Clevon. I'm not. I'm not going to make it back to San Francisco. I might not even make it back to..." I cough, because of the threat of tears, but also because I was talking too long. My head swims, the sunlight feels too warm.

"Back to what, Ran?"

"Back to my parents' house," I cough again.

Clevon's eyes go wide.

"It's almost over for me. Take me back there, put me in my bed, and let me go. Cleve, I know—this whole thing is weird. After you drop me off, you can leave; you don't even have to wait for... Well, you know..."

Clevon's eyes are wet, and mine would be, too, if I had any moisture left in my body. My tongue sticks to my teeth, to the roof of my mouth, to my lips when I try to lick them.

"Okay, Ran. I'll take you. And..." He takes a deep breath. "And I'll wait with you until the end."

I half smile. "No, Cleve. You're a good friend, but you have to get out of this weird ass town before that grey stuff kills you or makes you disappear or whatever."

He cocks his head at 'grey stuff,' but doesn't say anything further and we drive to my parents'.

———

We pull into the drive at my Dad's favorite time of day: right when it starts to cool off and the sun starts to go down, but it's not too dark yet. A cool breeze blows over my fevered skin.

The neglected green rope ladder sways in the breeze, trying to free itself from the maple and decrepit treehouse above.

"Stop," I wheeze.

"Why?" Clevon asks.

"I changed my mind."

Clevon grimaces. "What do you mean?"

"Take me up to the tree house."

He blinks up at the dilapidated planks nested in the old maple's branches.

"Seriously?"

"You owe me for saying my parents didn't want to see me."

He exhales deeply, resigned.

"How am I going to get your butt up there?"

I shrug. "You're strong, you work out. Carry me. I barely weigh anything."

Clevon sizes me up. "I suppose you're right," he says and comes around the car. "You sure you want to do this? That ladder doesn't look too steady, and neither does the treehouse."

I nod. "Dad and I used to love it up there. Take me. Please." I cough and have to catch my breath before I can see straight again.

When I collect myself, Clevon is at the base of the tree and I'm slung over his shoulder, facing the grass below.

I'm not sure how he does it, as rickety as the ladder is. The world below me sways sickeningly. The green grass—the lawn I used to play on long before San Francisco, before AIDS—waves goodbye. I don't regret going; I just wish the government cared enough to do something for us.

We lurch upward and the ensuing nausea makes me glad I haven't eaten anything.

Now I can see the tree's base, its knobby roots like tiny brown people huddled together for warmth before they're suddenly overcome by grey bubbles. The bubbles surge from the church's direction, rushing up from the grass, taking over the tree.

I try to shout at Clevon to watch out, but all that comes out is "Hnnnngh!"

The grey corpuscles creep further up the tree as we go—growing, respiring spherules that lick at the bark. I reach out a dangling hand toward them. If Clevon can't hear me, I have to try to stop them.

The bubbles ignore my finger, and we move up another rung on the decaying ladder. As we heave upwards, the wind is knocked out of me. I watch my breath carve a path through the encroaching grey, bubbles popping in its wake.

Just like it did with the rancid meat in the fridge.

"Hngggnh!" I gurgle again at Clevon.

The world spins, and I'm weightless, floating across a threshold—Clevon has tossed me like a pillow into the treehouse. From my back, I stare up through green leaves at blue sky shading to purple.

Clevon scrapes his way onto the scattered planks and I hear him gasp.

"R-Randy?" Clevon stammers.

"Hnnnhgh?"

"I—I'm going to sit you up," he says matter-of-factly.

The world spins again, and then I'm propped against one side of the treehouse, beside a grey-covered shape.

"Ran, are you sure you want to be here?" Clevon glances nervously between me and the Gremlin down below.

I smile at him. "I've got to go."

"What? You want to leave?"

"Goodbye, Clevon. I've got to go," I sing, and point at the grey blob.

"Queen, again? Really?"

I wink at him.

"Goodbye Cleve," I say. "Thank you."

Tears well up in his eyes and he opens his mouth but doesn't speak. He squeezes my hand and hurries down the tree, scraping as he goes.

I watch the familiar grey bubbles in front of me, shaped *just so.*

"Dad?" I rasp.

The mass of grey turns toward me, three-quarters barnacle, one-quarter percent my father, Ed Tills.

The mass sways toward me, three-quarters malevolent, one-quarter pure love and joy.

"Dad?" I cry, though no tears come. In the distance, I hear the Gremlin's engine start and then fade away.

Just as Dad used to like, the wind blows through the leaves, the maple sings. The grey mass oozes closer, one hand sinuous putrescence, one hand human fingers. "GNnnnnnnnng."

"Ha, you sound like me," I say, surprised at the clarity of my voice.

The thing oozes closer. I should feel more afraid. I should be terrified.

But.

Part of this is Dad. Part of this thing loves me.

The Dad-barnacle oozes closer.

"Dad, I—I missed you. I'm sorry I broke my promise. I didn't mean to. I just—I'm so sad we haven't gotten to talk these last six months. I was so heartbroken when you didn't respond to my letters, didn't answer my calls. I felt like what I imagine all the other guys whose families ignored them on their death beds felt."

"Hngggggggggn."

"I love you. I'm sorry I didn't come home sooner. I'm sorry I didn't tell you to come to San Francisco when you offered. I'm sorry."

The hand of the barnacled arm and the human one grab my shoulders together.

"Dad?"

I watch as the grey spheres explode where my breath meets them. I breathe harder, faster, trying to erase the blight from my father. The Dad-quarter watches in surprise.

Dad embraces me fully, barnacled and real arm wrapping around me tight. Everywhere my exhalations touch, the barnacles pop and more Dad emerges. Finally, my breathing sets off a chain reaction.

Explosions swell and roar around us, then ripple down the tree and away. I hear a distant rumble, spreading out in all directions from the tree, until there's a sudden flash, as if a darkness has been lifted.

When I open my eyes, Dad holds me away from him—one hundred percent Dad.

"Randy, I missed you," Dad says, a tear in his eye. "I'm sorry we missed out on all those years, too. But I'm glad you lived your life, son. I'm proud of you."

"I love you," I cough.

"I love you too," he says.

"Where's Mom?" I wheeze.

He looks at his no-longer barnacled arm and smiles. "I think I know where to look for her—let's go check the garden."

I nod. "Okay, Dad, let's hurry." I cough again.

"Of course, Ran," Dad says as we embrace.

I'm aware of closeness, descent, wind across my face, then fingers, the smell of fresh dirt, my mother's voice. I smile at my family's embrace, and the world goes dark, as still as a placid black ocean.

———

A few weeks after Clevon made it back to San Francisco, a package arrived on his doorstep, a Missouri address on it he didn't recognize, but could guess.

He opened it hesitantly. Inside was a handwritten note resting atop some fabric.

Dear Clevon,

Thank you for being there for our Randy. We're forever grateful that he had such a good friend to lead him through the hard times at the end.

Underneath the note was a quilt square.

Randy Tills, 1962-1986

Saved the world and the world didn't even know it.

Now traveling at the speed of light among the stars.

Rest in Peace, son.

Survived by his father and mother, Ed and Martha Tills.

ABOUT JASON P. BURNHAM

Jason P. Burnham (he/him) is an infectious diseases physician and clinical researcher. He loves many things, among them sci-fi, his wife and sons, metal music, Rancho Gordo beans, and equality (not necessarily in that order). He also co-edits "If There's Anyone Left" a zine for marginalized authors of the sci-fi/spec community, with his friend Cindy M. Fields.

EVERY DAY'S A PARTY (WITH YOU)
CHRISTI NOGLE

Morning goes like a dream, just a nice hunk of quiche and a coffee with my favorite person. Frost and Christmas lights wreath the diner's dark window. We lean in and whisper because the handsome mystery man is stealing glances at us again from his booth in the back of the room.

"Looking at you," she whispers, her breath all warm and coffee-bitter.

"No, you," I say.

It took a long time to find my best friend, but I've found her. Gloria. She's divorced like me. She has a teen daughter like me, though her Mira is away at school.

Her song plays—that Laura Branigan song—so low you can't make out the words. I always thought Gloria was a name for a blonde, but my Gloria's colors are Snow White's. Her perfect little nose is red from her walk here.

The handsome man stares again and we whisper, we giggle.

The song changes to that one that goes, *Every day's a party with you, with you.*

"So how's Char been?" Gloria asks.

I sigh. "Not so bad last night, really. The other day she called me a monster, though. 'Mom, you're a fucking monster.' That's what she said."

"Don't swear, dear Sara," Gloria says, leaning back with a smirk.

"You're unattractive when you swear, dear," I say. Gloria's mother said that to her one time when I was over. We laugh now, remembering that, and then the tabletop vibrates.

"Got to go," Gloria says, checking her big black pager and rising from the booth.

"Your dad?"

"Who else?"

I stay a while longer nursing my coffee, but it's still dark when I leave Jack's Diner.

————

Moss Park is shaped like a Venn diagram. The park itself is the shape of a cat's pupil, a long pointed ellipse carpeted in an odd verdant moss. The pointy ends of the park are treed, but the rest is a field of moss crossed by walking paths, with a tall, white gazebo in the center.

I pass through the gazebo. The Christmas lights inside it are cherry and teal and lemony-green, like everything else in Moss Park. So beautiful, the big bulbs and tiny ones, all throwing their colors onto the white ceiling and the beams.

The town wasn't always this way. When Char and I moved here, it was all brown and gray and... poor. I remember the first day, walking lost, looking for the post office. Rain and dullness. I stopped for directions in a cruddy little convenience store in what amounted to a garden barn. I don't even think that store is still around anymore.

I cut across the park to the bookstore where I work. The owner, Mrs. Sylvester, is my landlady too; Char and I stay in the guesthouse behind her big Victorian. The old lady's so absent from my days, I seem to have taken over her place. It's like I am the owner of the bookstore now. Everyone treats me that way, just as everyone treats Gloria like she—and not her father—is the owner of Glories Jewelry on the other side of the park.

And whenever I go into the big Victorian to make dinner or to take a long, candlelit soak in the big downstairs tub, I feel I am the sprawling house's mistress, not Mrs. Sylvester. The feeling is complicated—a little guilty and a little blessed. I suppose the young overtake the old at a certain point, and that's natural.

———

Mrs. Sylvester and Gloria's broad-shouldered old dad are having words across the street. I can't hear what they're saying. She has just parked, must be coming into the bookstore to do paperwork, and he's caught her. Their stances are stiff like cats. I imagine growling.

And then Char approaches from behind me. She was so silent.

"Get a room," she yowls, looking out at the old folks, and we laugh.

"Why aren't you in school?" I say, but she only scoffs and sprawls on the settee, taking out her sketch pad. The inside of this place is all warm wood and book smell, and the windows are wreathed with frost and colored lights like all the windows in Moss Park.

The handsome mystery man walks past the bookstore and hesitates. It seems he's deciding whether to open the door, but as Mrs. Sylvester pushes by him, muttering like a crazy thing, he flinches away from her and leaves. I catch a flash of his baffled, sweet face.

"That was close," says Char, but I don't have time to ask her what she means.

The doorbells are jingling. Mrs. Sylvester's sweeping in on a cold breeze, already complaining. She'll want tea.

———

The days go harder then. It's almost Christmas, but we can't seem to find fellow feeling.

It's because of Christmas—all this mess. The people on their side of the park want white lights; the people on our side want to keep the cherry and teal and lemony-green lights that we've always had, and that is the root of the strife.

Gloria and I shop our way around the park, catching glimpses of the mystery man here and there. Tourists have invaded Moss Park. There are no available seats at Jack's. We look in at the strangers all cozy in their sparkly red vinyl booths until Jack brings us travel cups of coffee.

Last night Char said, "You are a monster." She rolled her eyes when I told her I'd called my mother a bitch once or twice, too—

"Not a bitch, a monster," she said.

My point was that she hadn't invented being a horrible teen. It's natural, normal.

But is it, though? Maybe that's why I'm not telling Gloria. Her daughter rides horses at boarding school and goes on overseas vacations.

My daughter, I see her doing something normal for a change, I see her coming in from a run and say, "It's so nice you like running, dear."

She says, "I wouldn't say I like running. It's more that I want to keep this body functional for as long as I can. Don't you?"

Is there something really wrong with Char?

And why can't I bring myself to share any of this with Gloria? It feels like the Christmas light argument has spilled over to us somehow. I notice when we're on her side of the park, the shopkeepers aren't as nice to me as they used to be.

We're looking at sweaters for the girls when we bump into him —the handsome man. He's on the other side of the table, touching the sweaters. I look straight into his face, and I think there will be a spark, but there's nothing.

"Oh, hello," says Gloria, and he looks baffled again, or I am getting a feeling of bafflement from him; I don't actually see his face.

"We see you in Jack's all the time. We've never met," I say, holding out a hand to shake, but he's stumbling backward and disappears into the crowd, just like that.

"Shy," says Gloria. "It's cute. You should follow him."

"You should," I say, but I get a little chill. His reaction, like he'd seen a ghost.

We don't follow him. We get matching Fair Isle sweaters for Char and for Gloria's daughter, who will be flying here in a matter of days.

I imagine bright-eyed Mira clutching hers to her chest, saying, "It's perfect, I love it, I love you, Mom."

Char, I know, will throw hers in the closet and never take it out. She wears black, always, and this sweater is all marled in teal, cherry, and lemony-green like the lights they're taking down all over Moss Park.

And the white lights are going up, whiter than white, dazzling like sparklers in summer.

Gloria and I are headed toward the center of the park when she stops. "I'll catch up," she says, and when she does catch up to where I'm watching men change out the lights on the gazebo, she has two tall cups. Coffee, I think, but it's not. It's a strange syrup. I cock an eyebrow.

"Cinnamon cocoa," she says, and we sip while we watch more of the lights come down.

"Out with the old," she says.

Far past the gazebo, near a treed end of the park, I see an old man and a woman arguing, gesturing wildly. Is he beating his chest? Did she just slap him?

I am glad that Gloria doesn't see.

———

"Skip work this afternoon," Gloria says over breakfast. "We're having a wrapping party at my house."

We're in Sylvia's Café, all silver sparkly vinyl and white lights and frost wreathing the windows. More cinnamon cocoa with berry tarts. No handsome men stealing glances in here.

"I can't skip. Mrs. Sylvester barely comes in anymore," I say.

"Just ask," she says.

I call and ask for the afternoon.

"Take the whole day," Mrs. Sylvester says. The old lady's a little breathless, almost giggling.

"Is someone there?" I say, but she only says it's fine, go have fun.

She'll get the store opened later or she won't; it hardly matters either way.

———

Gloria's living room is staged with a tree and candles, and the fireplace is lit. Silvers and blues, violet and white lights, the stink of wine and cocoa spiked with butterscotch Schnapps. Gloria's pretty sisters and cousins, her mom, a couple of young dads as well, all wrapping presents on card tables.

I clutch my meager bag of gifts and find myself a place to wrap.

Gloria's youngest sister isn't here. She's getting married soon, and her mother's going on about the blend of pain in losing her last baby and the joy in seeing her settled.

Gloria stiffens a bit. She must see it as a commentary on her solitary life.

When Gloria's husband left her—just about a year and a half ago, I suppose—it was like in a movie. For months she was puffy around the eyes and wore pajamas when she wasn't at work. But she snapped back. She snapped right back.

"Michael is the best. We just grew apart. It happens," she says.

They're wrapping the presents together so everything's color-coordinated. The wrapping paper and ribbons are silver, blue, and violet—like the room.

When I've wrapped my presents, I stand out of the way.

The white-lit Christmas tree is like a wall, like a hedge inside the house. Being near it gives me a feeling of dread. And it smells so strong, like a dark green candle.

The music video plays low on the television: *Every day's a party with you, with you.* Claymation supermodels crawl out of a wedding cake. They dance and merge. I feel a little exhilarated like I always do when that song plays, but I feel sad, too, like I'm looking back on a happier memory.

Gloria's mom says, "You're really settling in now. What's it been, two years?"

Almost.

"Moss Park is so great," I say. "You know, in the town we lived in before, there was a lot of crime. A woman and her daughter… "

"I don't know this is the right story for company," Gloria says.

I nod. "You're right."

A woman and her daughter were butchered. They disappeared, and the investigation ran on the news every night. They found them in the neighbor's backyard, just a slurry of blood and guts in a shallow hole.

The neighbor had been away on vacation.

They found blood evidence in the dead woman's bathtub, even though it had been bleached.

"How's Mira?" says one of Gloria's sisters.

"Thriving. I miss her something terrible, though," says Gloria. "Just knocking around this big old house all alone."

All eyes go to me again, and I say, "I wish I could have done something like that with Char. Not boarding school—I could never have afforded that—but I wish I would have pushed her to do sports. All she wants to do is read and sketch and mope, mope, mope."

"She's artsy," says Gloria.

"She hasn't grown—not an inch or a pound—since we moved here," I say.

"She's a great kid," says Gloria's mom, who barely knows Char at all.

She says the most horrible things to me, I don't say.

"Char has such beautiful hair," says someone else who barely knows her.

No image comes to my mind. Is Char's hair black, like her clothes? Brown? Blonde like Mira's? I can't say. I can't call up her face.

I'm turning toward the fireplace, toward the mirror, but I can't see anything in it. I turn back toward the tree.

"This is really something," I say. They look away. I guess it's lower-class to point out how nice things are.

———

It's dark and all are tipsy when I leave. On the way home, I pass the bookstore. Lights are dim inside, but I see Mrs. Sylvester's shape on the end of the settee, legs crossed. I imagine a pensive look on her face. Someone broad-shouldered looms behind her, closer and closer. His hand comes down.

I'm stopped, now, lit by Christmas lights. If anyone were looking, they'd recognize me. No one's looking. His hand slides down, over her breastbone. Her neck is arched and her arm is raising. She's pulling him down into a messy, groping kiss.

The wind feels hot on my face as I turn away. The white Christmas lights are all like sparklers, forked spikes coming off of them.

Passionate anger breeds passionate love, I think. But not real love. Real love is smoother.

Every day's a party; it plays in the street. Gloria's perfect nose, her little cold-reddened ears, her beautiful eyes all come to me in flashes.

I have time to walk, time to think and have a little romantic-comedy-style epiphany.

———

"Where were you?" says Char at the door to our guest house.

"So sorry, I should have tried to find a payphone," I say. I'm beaming and flushed, but I can't see her face. I'm not sure if it's some strange shadow striking only her face, but I can't see her at all. Her hair could be any color.

"You're not well. I can see it—hell, I smell it," says Char.

I have my hands on her shoulders now and am turning us, trying to turn her into the light, but I still can't see her. All I get from her is the mood—amusement, or scorn maybe. I begin to move away, but she holds me there. Her hands are on my temples. Like strange waltzers, we hold each other out at arms' length.

She says, "Listen, I hinted to Mrs. Sylvester that we might be going on vacation. Just in case."

"I don't know what you mean." I don't. It doesn't matter.

"You think you're in love with her? You're so deluded," says Char.

Am I crying? Can Char see what I've been thinking? I say, "I walked and I thought tonight, Char, honey, and I think I know what I want."

And maybe this is why Char's been so evil lately, why we aren't getting along—because she's jealous. She doesn't want Mommy's attention going anywhere else. Kids are always this way when a parent falls in love.

"You want to be her," Char says, and maybe that's true, too.

I think of our neighbor, back in that other town. I think of her screaming in the bathtub.

"You're poisoning yourself from the inside," Char says. "You're wearing out your brain."

She's on drugs, is all I can think. I break away from her and all goes dark.

———

Some long time later—dawn glowing through the sheers—I wake at the table, my mouth packed with rotisserie chicken. My hands are deep in the jelly of the cold carcass. Char sits gazing like a judgmental cat from the other side of the table.

"What are you looking at?" I say.

"Just making sure you don't choke on a bone," she says gently.

"I'm going. I'm going to Gloria, just as soon as I take a bath," I say.

"I think you better do just that," says Char.

I'm too full. I manage a few queasy steps, but with all the lights blazing, inside and outside, I drop.

I dream a double wedding, then, out in a lemony-green field of teal and cherry flowers, white dresses hot like sparklers—each of us with a copy of the handsome man—but the men fade away and Gloria and I seem to merge. Shudder apart, merge again like clay figures.

I see a massive, many-winged bat, each eye the shape of a Venn diagram.

I start awake into darkness. Char has spread a rough blanket on me. I think she's washed my face.

I rush out the door with mouthwash in my bloated cheeks, spitting it into the snow on the way to the street. Christmas lights swirl and spark. It's all coming apart.

It's just... my eyes are wearing out. Or my brain is wearing out, like Char said.

My brain is wearing out. I'm wearing out my brain. That's what she said.

————

Gloria's wearing off-white satin pajamas, the top open with a lace-trimmed cami underneath. I've never seen her without her makeup before, and she's even more beautiful.

I wait for her to invite me in.

"It's just as well you came over. I can't sleep, I'm so anxious, you know, for the holidays to get going," she says, but her eyes are weary.

Music plays somewhere. "Gloria," it was, and now it's changed.

Every day's a party, with you, with you, with you.

I'm not sure if I'm going to kiss her. The desire to do that, if it was ever there, is gone. It seems like something big has to happen, though, to explain why I'm here.

The oven timer goes off, and we move that direction, passing the

Christmas tree, which is now just a regular-sized tree with dim white lights.

Why'd you change it? I'm about to say, but I know, I know. I think of Gloria's family's stares as I praised the tree and almost laugh.

I've been wearing out the brain, placing colors on everything, glamouring myself somehow.

She takes sugar cookies out of the oven. Perfect pale angels and trees. The glass bowls of icing (cherry, teal, lemon-lime) sit ready alongside jars of nonpareils and cinnamon dots.

Pouring a cocoa, Gloria says, "I made the marshmallows. They might not be quite right."

It's the velvetiest thing I've ever had in my mouth, toffee and chocolate and something else, creme brûlée? The walls seem to be melting.

I'm not feeling well.

I go to kiss her finally, and she turns away. I feel her pulse like a drum on the ground.

"It's fucking hot in here," she says.

I wish you wouldn't swear, dear.

"We should go to your bedroom. It'll be cooler," I say, all low and flat.

"I can crack the window here," she says.

"I need to lie down. I'm not feeling well."

We walk down the hall, slowly. She's looking back at me. I enter her bedroom and go straight for her bathroom door.

"Oh, it's a mess in there," she says, but I shut the door. "Oh, okay."

I look in the mirror. Too thin, too old, no face at all. My hair, dry and frayed, dyed black like a parody of Gloria's.

The bathroom is nice—no doubt, but it's all gray and dull. There's a pubic hair on the toilet seat and a ring of hard water stain inside the bowl.

Back in the bedroom, I lie down. Gloria is sitting on the hope chest at the foot of the bed, looking through photo albums.

"This is what I was doing when you knocked," she says.

She passes me a picture of Char and Mira.

"That could be yesterday," I say.

"Oh no, Mira's a foot taller now, I bet," she says.

But Char's still the same. She takes care of the body.

———

I'm not seeing things right, but here's what I see: in the mirrored closet doors, the room is small and gray, the carpet plush but worn, the damask on the bed dated, not a suitable bedspread for Moss Park at all. I see me standing, her cross-legged on the hope chest lid. I take her by the scruff of the neck, lift her. In my hands, she becomes a husk. An outfit. A costume. In the mirror, I'm turning her in the light. I find the zipper, a fine hidden zipper like on a wedding dress. I unzip her, step inside.

I am not seeing things right, but it doesn't matter. Char was correct. I wanted in; that's all.

I look in the mirror; my hand on her throat, Gloria leaned back for a passionate kiss. Back arched, the satin falls back against her, outlining her curves. I aim for her lips and take her neck instead.

It's all over, all memory. The air is hot as it was in the kitchen and a smell is coming from the bathroom. A gentle knock on the door.

"Mira?" I say.

"Char," she says. "Is it all over?"

The satin is cool on my skin. The room is gray and empty. I look to the mirror, but it isn't there anymore. The shards are scattered all over the carpet, where there are rusty stains. The soles of my feet are dark.

"Open the door please, dear. I'm...decent," I say.

Char's wearing her Fair Isle sweater like the one I bought Mira.

I say, "Your mom was just here, dear. I don't know where she—"

"Please," says Char. "Just don't."

She comes into the room, bolder now. She steps over broken glass and looks in the closet.

"Now, honey, I don't think you should—"

Char moves into the bathroom. The shower curtain makes its quick sweeping sound.

"What's this in the bathtub, Mom?" she says.

My heart races and a feeling of guilt sweeps over me.

"What's in the bathtub?" I say, going to the door, but she meets me there. The curtain is back in place already.

"I'll get it cleaned up later," she says. "Just rest now. Take it easy." She shakes her head. "I guess if you could take it easy, we wouldn't have this trouble in the first place."

"I don't know what you mean."

She takes my head in her hands. Her bony little fingers poke around.

"You do something to the brain. You wear it out too fast. You don't use the memory, I don't think, but you use something else, the visualization part or something. I don't know that much about brains. Just let it be. Just close your eyes and lie down here a while."

She sits down on the hope chest next to me.

"Do you smell the blood on your pajamas? Can you feel it?" She takes my hand and touches it to the cuff of my other sleeve, which is damp. I squeeze the fabric and the moisture pools around my fingertips.

Before she can stop me, I'm up and in the bathroom. I shut the door behind me.

"You don't have to look," she says.

But I've already swept aside the curtain, taking in the tangle of blood and guts, the tortured, dyed-black hair.

Char is beside me. "You always choose the same general type, don't you? Maybe your own body looked like that long ago. Do you think?"

"We should go," I say, thinking of the mystery man. He wasn't handsome, really. Maybe he thought he knew this Sara woman. Maybe he did know her.

"You need a shower," says Char.

"Yes, and then we need to go. Get out of Moss Park," I say, a lump in my throat because I can't imagine leaving this place, though I've already left it, haven't I? When I go outside, won't everything be soggy and poor?

In the mirror, my face is already not quite the face I coveted. The eyes are still big and blue, but the skin has lost its glow. I shudder to think about what I'm doing to the brain.

Char strokes my hair, says, "We need to go get Mira. We have to pick her up at the airport."

"And then?"

"And then we have company coming. We get through Christmas, and then we go."

"You and me?"

"Gloria and Mira, yes... God, Mom. Try to stay with it just a little while," she says.

I am trying.

She strips me, shoves my feet into slippers, walks me to Mira's bathroom for a quick shower. I dry myself, and she wraps me in a fluffy gray robe. She sits me on the living room floor near the fire, leaves, and comes back with a fancy tray of hors d'oeuvres from one of Moss Park's pretty little shops. I was with Gloria when she bought it.

"That's for the party," I say, but Char's already messed it all up.

"I know, I don't normally eat this stuff, but it doesn't matter now, does it?" she says.

It doesn't.

I breathe in the meat smell, watching her feed like an animal. I can't really be her mother, can I? She's a relative, anyway, and she may be my only one.

"Go get the photo albums. I saw them in the bedroom," she says.

"Why?"

"So you can tell me who the people are. We're going to have a lot to do, to get through Christmas. It will help if I can pass as Mira."

But the thought crosses my mind: *this girl isn't anything like my Mira.*

"When's her flight coming in?" I ask.

Char frowns, finds the pink datebook on the kitchen counter and starts scanning. "One o'clock. The Christmas Eve party starts at…seven. We're in a tight spot. We have to keep them out of the master suite. They'll want to pile their coats on the bed and use the bathroom. Jesus. It's going to be rough."

She's getting greasy prints all over my datebook. I reach for it, and she puts it in her back pocket. I whimper when she wipes her fingers on the Fair Isle.

"I know you'll want to sleep until it's time, but you can't," she says. "If you sleep, you're going to forget. You're going to delude yourself. It's something you do with the brain, Mom. It always happens."

Char sits again. She takes her sketchbook from her bag and starts drawing. I feel like I've never been close enough to see her drawing before. It's just endless abstract shapes and patterns, all finely detailed, going right to the edges of the page.

I scoot around so we're sitting side by side. There are figures in it now, bats and weasels and slimy things. Her pencil moves so fast.

"Why do you do that all the time?" I ask, but she just keeps going. I watch, and the watching brings back something vague, like déjà vu, a little half-memory of some moment somewhere else, when I was something else.

"We're monsters, Mom," she says, and I see her, clear and full. For an instant, I see who she really is. I rest my head on her shoulder and try hard to stay awake and aware. The hair she wears now is gorgeous, long auburn waves. I wonder if she'll miss this hair, and there's another pang of guilt. She took such care of this body and now she'll lose it because of me.

The song is playing somewhere: *Every day's a party, every day's a party with you.*

The page is finished. She turns it and starts anew.

Soon we'll go to the airport. The two girls will go into the master bath. There will be a mess, but Mira will take care of it.

"Mrs. Sylvester?" I say.

"I left her a note. I don't think she's thinking of us right now, anyway." What a funny expression this girl has. I find her quite dear.

We'll get through Christmas. We'll go someplace new. I won't remember any of this later, but it's nice right now to have my head on her shoulder. It's nice to drop into the drawing with her.

"Oh, we still need to go over the photo albums," I say.

"It's fine. I'll just call everyone 'dear.' They won't notice."

I touch the page. "You'll keep doing this when you're Mira, won't you?"

"I'll be just the same. I don't change. Neither do you," she says, and I smile.

ABOUT CHRISTI NOGLE

Christi Nogle's debut novel, *Beulah*, is coming in early 2022 from Cemetery Gates Media. You can find more of her work in publications including *PseudoPod, Escape Pod, Vastarien, Fusion Fragment, Boneyard Soup* and *Dark Matter Magazine* and in anthologies such as *What One Wouldn't Do* from Scott J. Moses, *Humans Are the Problem* from Weird Little Worlds, C.M Muller's *Nightscript and Synth*, and Flame Tree Publications' *American Gothic and Chilling Crime*. Christi is an active member of the HWA, SFWA, Codex Writers' Group. Follow her at christinogle.com or on Twitter @christinogle

WHEN THE STREETLIGHTS GO OFF

P.A. CORNELL

What the hell am I doing here?

Andy and Sherry stopped walking for the umpteenth time to shove their tongues down each other's throats again.

Hello! I'm still here, you guys.

I should've stayed home and watched *Family Ties*, but like an idiot, I'd let Sherry talk me into going out. Now here I was, enjoying the status of "third wheel" to my so-called friend and the guy she *knew* I'd had a crush on all year—though after tonight, that was over.

"Guys, can we get going? How far is this place you said we could spend the night in, anyway?"

Sherry laughed as she pulled away from Andy, nearly losing her balance. Lucky for her, Andy was ready with a steadying hand—one I noticed rested a little closer to her right breast than necessary.

"Whoa, babe. Careful."

"I think I drank a smidge too much peach schnapps," she giggled.

"Nah, I think you drank just the right amount." He looked at me and added, "Keep your panties on; we're almost there."

We continued down the street, Andy starting up with the same few lines of "Living on a Prayer" he'd been singing over and over. I'd had enough of his off-key voice and grabbed the headphones hanging around my neck and positioned them over my ears. I pressed play on the Walkman, and let my mixtape drown him out.

We hadn't walked much further when Andy and Sherry halted again. I stopped the tape and pulled my headphones off.

"This is it."

He pointed to a dilapidated old house with wooden siding coated in the peeling remains of once-white paint. The windows—what remained of them—were boarded over. In the garden, the grass grew wild, and here and there were signs that read: "NO TRESSPASSING." Someone had spray-painted one of them with the words "The White House."

"No. Not here," I said, shaking my head. "No way are we staying here."

"Come on, don't tell me you believe those old stories," Andy said with a smirk.

"What old stories?" asked Sherry.

"You don't know about Mr. White?"

"Sherry only moved here a few years ago," I said.

"It's just some bullshit they used to tell us as kids. 'Don't go into that old, abandoned house, Timmy. A mean old man used to live there. He hated people going on his property so much that he shot a kid just for stepping on his lawn.' The kid's dad went nuts, came down here one night and drove the old man's head through a window, cutting him so bad he bled to death. They say he still haunts the place." He lunged at Sherry's face and shouted, "Boo!"

They both burst into laughter.

"Most of us," he continued, glaring at me, "grew up and realized the adults were just trying to scare us so we wouldn't go in there and step on broken glass or scratch ourselves on a rusty nail or some shit. There never was no Mr. White."

He was probably right about the story, but the place still gave me the creeps, especially this late at night. They used to say Mr. White would get you if you were on his property after the streetlights came on. Probably another lie our parents told to ensure we went home by then, but some childhood fears stick with you.

"Why not bulldoze the place?" Sherry asked.

"They've talked about it," said Andy. "But there's always some group of do-gooders claiming the place is historical and fighting to get it restored instead."

"Well, by the looks of it, it'll fall down on its own soon enough."

"Only thing that looks like it's about to fall down around here's you," Andy said, grabbing her in a bear hug and swinging her off her feet. Sherry screamed with delight.

I rolled my eyes.

"Come on, chickenshit," Andy said to me, steadying Sherry. "My friends and I spent the night here a bunch of times and nothing bad ever happened. Worse thing you'll see in there's a few spiders."

"Oh, you shouldn't've told her that," said Sherry. "Jen's petrified of spiders."

"Well, maybe Jen needs to stop being such a baby." He kissed her again, gripping her ass for a moment before pulling away and leading her up the steps to the front door.

I glanced at the house, taking in the dead tree out front and its bare branches, which looked like gnarled claws whipping in the breeze against a small, circular window near the roof. It looked like the only intact window on the house, and it was cracked open along a hinge near its top. Between the gap and the branches, the window offered a perfect access for rodents.

Great. As if this place needs more of those.

I turned away from Sherry and Andy, glancing across the street to where a payphone stood, illuminated like a glowing beacon of hope. I stuck a hand in my pocket and felt the coins Mom insisted I always have with me "just in case."

It'd be so easy to end this. I could call home and have her come get us. I'd be asleep on my comfy waterbed within the hour. But Sherry would never forgive me, and we'd both be grounded forever. I turned back toward the house and followed Andy and Sherry up the steps.

It's just an old house. The worst that can happen is mold triggering my asthma.

Andy held the door open for us. As I walked through, I noticed the doorjamb was busted near the handle. At least there was no way to get locked in—which gave me some relief.

"Watch your step, ladies. There's a few floorboards missing, so wait until I get the lights before you go exploring."

"Lights?"

Andy motioned to a room on the right. With some of the boards from the windows missing, just enough street light penetrated the gloom to make out a bunch of fat candles on the floor. Andy took something from his pocket and held it up. There was a flick and then a flame as he held a lighter out, swinging it back and forth like people did at concerts.

He winked at Sherry and bent over to light the nearest candle before pocketing the lighter. "See, babe?" he said as he used the lit candle to light the rest. "It's downright romantic in here."

"Romantic" wasn't the word I would've chosen. I remained by the front door, as Andy led Sherry further into the room—it had probably been called the "parlor" once. A set of broken French doors leaned against the wall, useless, waiting their turn to crumble into dust like everything else around here.

Directly in front of me, a staircase missing several steps stretched upward, and to its right, a hallway led to the back door. I sniffed, taking in the scent of musty wood and dirt. Dust covered every surface and cobwebs spanned all the corners I could see, hinting at countless unseen spiders.

I tried not to think about them as I entered the parlor. Near the candles, someone had laid an old and very stained mattress on the floor. The only other piece of furniture was a wooden cabinet in the corner of the room, its glass doors too dirt-covered to see through. The lone recent addition to the décor was a centerfold torn from a *Playboy* and pinned to the wall above the candles. It showed a woman standing against a pillar in a seductive pose, her fake boobs on full display. Someone had drawn a penis next to her mouth.

Puke.

Something was written in marker next to the centerfold, so I moved closer for a better look. It was a list of girls' names in three columns. Over each column was the name of a boy: Andy, Trent, and Nate. Next to each girl's name was a rating out of ten.

"I see you noticed our trophy wall," said Andy, laughing. "Let's just say you girls aren't the first ones to spend the night here."

"Gross."

"Don't be such a prude, Jen. Trust me—those girls enjoyed themselves. You can go ahead and write both your names there under mine. I'll fill in the rest later."

"Gag me."

"Suit yourself. I was just being charitable."

He reached for Sherry, pulling her onto the mattress with him and kissing her, but she looked like she was falling asleep. When he started to unbuckle his belt, I decided this had gone far enough.

"You don't actually think I'll let you do her right here in front of me when she's this out of it, do you?"

"You had your chance," he said, pulling Sherry's shirt up while she giggled and struggled to pull it back down. "Doesn't have to be in front of you either. Door's right over there."

I walked over and pulled him away from her.

"Hey!"

"Get off her!"

"Fuck you!" he yelled.

"If you think I'm leaving her alone with you, you're dumber than I thought."

"Fine." He stood. "I have better places to be than here, wasting my time with some drunken slut and her frigid bitch friend!"

He shoved past me and left, slamming the door behind him. The noise echoed for a moment, but then the room fell utterly silent. Even the street sounds had vanished.

Am I only just noticing now that it's been this quiet all along?

Sherry moaned and rolled onto her stomach, her face resting on a particularly large mattress stain. I walked over, pulled her up to a sitting position, then lightly smacked her face until she opened her eyes. She smiled a little too big.

"Hi Jen. Jenny, Jenny, Jen," she said, patting my face back. "Gawd, I have to pee. Where's the bathroom, Andy?"

"He's gone, and good riddance. Sher, we should go, too. There's a phone across the street. I'll call my mom and she can come get us."

"No. No, no, no, Jen," she slurred. "We'll get in *huge* trouble. My dad thinks I'm sleeping at your place. He'll *kill* me if he finds out we lied so we could stay out past curfew."

I wasn't eager for my mom to find out I'd given her the same story about staying at Sherry's either. It'd been such a stupid thing to do. We hadn't even considered that when the fun was over, we'd have nowhere to spend the night. Now, here we were, stuck with what passed for hospitality with Andy—Andy who was probably halfway home by now, and would soon be enjoying things like working electricity and clean sheets. *God, I need to get out of here.*

"Your dad won't kill you, Sher. I'll beg my mom not to tell him. You can stay at my place—so you won't even have lied. I'll be the only one that gets grounded."

"No way you'll get your mom to promise that. Besides, I'm too drunk. Gotta sober up first."

She had a point. If Mom saw her like this, she'd definitely call Sherry's parents.

Sherry stood—with some difficulty—and started walking around the room. "This place isn't so bad," she said. "Just need to find the bathroom."

She walked over to the cabinet and tried to open it, but the doors wouldn't budge. She wiped away some of the dust covering the glass with her sleeve, revealing that the back of the cabinet was mirrored. Never one to resist her own reflection, Sherry started posing and playing with her perfectly teased bangs.

She pulled her hair into a crimped side pony and puckered her lips. "God, I look hot like this."

The annoying thing was she did, too. Sherry, with her perfect blonde hair and Jordache jeans pinned at the ankles to accentuate her long legs. Of course, Andy had chosen her over me. *But she didn't have to kiss him back. She never even liked him before tonight.*

"Bloody Mary," she said, letting go of her hair. "Bloody

Mary…Bloody—you remember that, Jen? Remember when we used to scare the shit out of ourselves in the bathroom at school?" She laughed. "Bloody Mary."

I did remember. I remembered how much I'd hated that stupid game. Say "Bloody Mary" over and over and her face was supposed to appear in the mirror. We never saw anything, but it had still freaked me out. It was too much like something else that had spooked me as a kid, something I really didn't want to think about right now, in this of all places.

"That's enough, Sher. I thought you had to pee."

She ignored me and kept repeating the name, her eyes growing wide in the mirror.

And then they weren't Sherry's eyes. They were cruel and blood-shot, staring right into me.

The scream was out before I realized I'd opened my mouth, but I could already see those awful eyes were gone. It was just Sherry in the mirror, her mouth parted in surprise—until she burst out laughing.

"Oh my God, Jen! Take a chill pill!"

I felt the heat rise to my face. *What is wrong with me? A couple of drinks, a creepy old house, and I'm completely unraveling.*

"Andy was right. You really are chickenshit."

"Screw you!" I turned to leave, not caring if she followed. My anger made me pull on the doorknob harder than I needed to—and yet, the door didn't budge.

What the hell?

I pulled on it again, and when it still didn't move, I planted my left foot against the frame and pulled with all my strength.

The door remained closed.

"Are you kidding me?" Sherry said. "Did that asshole lock us in?"

"No. The door's broken. I noticed it on the way in. He couldn't lock it even if he wanted to. It's probably just stuck from the wood expanding or something. Help me pull it open."

We both gripped the doorknob and pulled, but nothing happened.

"The back door!" I remembered. I turned and was halfway down the hall before I noticed it ended at a wall. "But—I was sure I saw..."

I looked back at Sherry, then down the hall, which somehow seemed darker than it had earlier. Summoning my courage, I walked to the end and touched the wall. It felt as solid as a wall should.

There was no door. There had never been a door.

"I swear I saw an exit here when we came in."

Sherry let out a short laugh. "And I thought *I* was drunk."

"I'm not drunk! I saw it!"

"Well, there's no door now, and I still have to pee. Did you see a toilet anywhere, or did that vanish too?" She walked to a door to the left of the stairs and opened it.

Sure enough, there was a bathroom, though the plumbing probably hadn't worked in years. Sherry didn't let that stop her as she closed the door behind her, and I heard the distinct sound of someone peeing a minute later. I didn't even want to think about how gross that toilet was.

What is happening here? I walked back into the parlor and looked at the woman in the centerfold as if she could answer my unspoken question. She stared back.

Letting out a breath, I thought about what to do next.

That's when her lips began to stretch, slowly, not stopping where a smile naturally would. I watched, frozen, as she revealed teeth with jagged edges like broken glass, while her eyes grew wild and vicious.

Before I could cry out to Sherry, the woman suddenly looked normal again. Just a poster. I touched it to be sure. Only paper.

"What the hell is wrong with me?"

"Who are you talking to?" Sherry asked.

"No one," I said. "Maybe we can climb out one of these windows. Those boards are old. We might be able to push one of them off."

I walked to the window and found a gap in the broken glass and stuck my arm through to push on the board behind it, but it seemed secure. I withdrew my arm, careful not to touch the edges of the glass.

"Ow! What the hell?"

"You cut yourself," said Sherry.

"What?" I looked down to where she was pointing. Blood dripped off the fingers of my right hand. I pulled up my jacket sleeve, revealing a long cut. "That's impossible. I was so careful! And look, there's no tear in my sleeve." I showed her the jacket.

Sherry stared at my arm, then back up at me, her face screwed up in confusion.

The sound of rustling paper drew our attention to the poster. One of its corners flapped as if caught in a breeze, then it fell from the wall, right onto the candles, and caught fire.

"Shit! Oh, shit!" The breeze grew stronger and, as I stomped out the paper, the candles went out, too, leaving us in unnatural darkness. The lights outside still should've been able to penetrate the gloom as they had earlier.

"We have to light the candles again," said Sherry.

I silently agreed, but I remembered Andy pocketing the lighter. He'd taken it with him when he'd stormed out. *Damn it!*

"With all these candles, the guys must've left something to light them, right? Help me look." I got on my hands and knees and started feeling the floor around the candles, then moved along the wall. I could hear Sherry searching the space by the cabinet.

My hand hit something hard and smooth. I followed the shape up a curve, drawing my hand away for a moment when I touched what could only be laces. A boot. I pushed against it, and it didn't move, as if the weight of someone's leg were keeping it in place.

Sherry was wearing high tops. Not boots.

No, it's just the two of us in here. I let my hand slide up the surface again, feeling the leather...the laces...the knot...the top edge of the boot...and then—

"I found something," Sherry said. "I think it's a box of matches!"

I heard the unmistakable sound of matchsticks rattling inside cardboard, then the scratching hiss of a match being struck. Sherry smiled as she carried the match to a candle and then lit them all like Andy had.

I turned back to the boot but saw nothing. The light from the candles didn't reach that corner of the room. I turned and grabbed one of the candles, but as I neared the corner, it remained untouched by the light.

I began to feel cold. "Sher, are you seeing this?"

"It's probably just super moldy. Don't touch it."

I didn't intend to. The corner gave me the creeps. I could feel the cold like ice in my veins, so I stepped away. Some things are better left a mystery.

I checked the cut on my arm again. The blood had stained my jean jacket, but it seemed to have stopped. I wanted to clean the denim, but I had little hope of finding clean water here.

The light revealed other things the boys had left behind: more *Playboy* issues, a *Hustler*, a bottle of Jolt cola, and an empty beer can repurposed as an ashtray—but nothing to help us get out.

I handed Sherry the Jolt. "Drink this. It's warm but it might help you sober up. Then, maybe we can work on getting out of here. I'm gonna look for something we can use to break through the window boards or pry the door open."

I didn't wait for her response, just grabbed one of the candles and walked back into the foyer. She was still kind of out of it, anyway. I didn't want to go exploring too far on my own, but I checked the bathroom—holding my breath as I did—but there was nothing useful in there. I started pulling the spindles on the staircase. The third one I tried finally came loose. It wouldn't help us pry open the door, but it might do for the boards on the windows.

Back in the parlor, Sherry still held the empty pop bottle, its rim now marked with frosted pink lipstick. She was amusing herself by tearing off what remained of the label in tiny pieces and tossing them onto the candles to watch them burn.

I left her to it and went to work on the windows. First, I smashed out some of the broken glass, being extra careful to avoid cutting myself this time. Once the glass was removed, I pushed on one of the boards with the spindle, then tried angling it through the gaps to pry one of them off. They wouldn't budge.

I didn't understand. The boards on the windows had been there for as long as I could remember, exposed to all kinds of weather. I'd seen several on the ground outside that had fallen without effort from anyone, so why wouldn't these let go?

"Jen. J-Jen."

Sherry's voice was a barely audible whisper, and I almost ignored her, but something made me turn to see what she wanted. She stood in the middle of the room—looking more sober than she had all night, her face so pale that her blue eyeshadow stood out like bruises around wide, terrified eyes staring past me, just over my shoulder.

"Sher?"

She didn't speak. The bottle slipped from her fingers and smashed on the floor. The sound seemed to snap her out of it, and she ran from the room.

"Sherry!"

Her footsteps pounded up the stairs, faster than I'd ever seen her move. I wanted to go after her, but I was paralyzed with fear. For all I knew, whatever she'd seen behind me was still there.

I glanced at the cabinet to see if I could catch a reflection in the mirror, but the angle wasn't right, and Sherry had only cleared enough of the grime to look at herself. I turned my head as slowly as I could—just enough to maybe catch it with the corner of my eye—but as I kept turning, nothing appeared. Finally, I was facing the window again and there was nothing there.

I should've felt relief, but I didn't. Instead, I felt that chill again, and with it, the hair on the back of my neck standing on end. Even the little hairs on my arms stood at attention as goosebumps rose all over my skin. I couldn't see anything, but I knew I wasn't alone.

This time I ran, calling Sherry's name as I took the stairs as fast as she had, two at a time where there were gaps. In her state and with so little light, it was a miracle she hadn't fallen through the rotted wood. As I reached the second floor, I heard her voice.

"Jen! Where are you?"

"Sher?"

I turned down a hallway then heard my name again, back the way I'd come. I retraced my steps but now found myself looking down an identical hallway instead of stairs.

"Sherry?"

No answer.

I slowed, but kept walking. The hallway seemed longer than it should be, given the size of the house's exterior.

At the end of the hall, a little light streamed in through the cracks of a boarded-up window. I moved toward it, my right hand sliding along the wall to guide me. I'd read somewhere that even in a maze, if you kept one hand on the wall, you'd find your way out eventually. *God, I hope it's true.*

"Sherry!"

No response. Just impenetrable silence, as if the whole house were one of those sensory-deprivation tanks.

As I walked, I thought back to the stories about this house, trying to remember anything that might help me. When I was little, I'd been terrified of this place. Once, when my parents drove me by it, I swore I'd seen a face in one of the windows—which was why Sherry's Bloody Mary game freaked me out so much.

After that drive, I had recurring nightmares about Mr. White even though my parents said he couldn't touch me at home, and certainly not during the day. I remembered my father saying that as soon as the streetlights turned off in the early morning, the creepy old house's power would evaporate.

No matter what I'd seen tonight, I still didn't know for sure that the old stories were true, but I hoped Dad was right. *If we can just make it to daylight, we'll be okay. But I have to find Sherry first.*

The floorboards creaked with every step, and I slowed to make sure it was only the sound of my own movements I was hearing. The hallway grew darker, making it hard to see, so I held my free hand out to keep from walking into anything. I was making steady progress when my foot went through the floor and I started to fall, my ankle twisting painfully. As I did, I felt something hard and managed to catch myself on it before hitting the ground, which probably saved me from breaking my ankle altogether, but pain still shot up my leg and I screamed. I leaned on the object that had stopped my fall—a wobbly, wooden stool. When the pain had passed, I pulled my foot out of the floor and took a tentative step. My ankle burned every time I put weight on it, but I could still move—just not very quickly.

Great.

From behind me, I heard a light tapping sound.

I stopped, and the sound stopped too. I took a couple more steps and the sound resumed, then stopped when I did. I turned, straining to see into the darkness. The tapping sound resumed.

I turned and tried to run, but the pain shot up my leg again and this time I did fall. Behind me, the tapping gave way to a crash— someone had knocked over the stool!

I tried to get up, but my ankle was still throbbing. I dragged myself along the hall, trying to reach a spot where the light was a little brighter so I could see, but it was nearly upon me. I turned, resigned to face whatever was coming. The tapping gave way to another sound, so faint at first that I couldn't make it out, but then I recognized it: purring.

From the gloom emerged a cat. It trotted over and rubbed itself against my legs. Even in this dim light, I could see it was orange like that cat in the commercials. *Martin? No, Morris.*

"You scared the hell out of me," I told him. I scratched the cat behind his ears and picked him up, holding him close and feeling the comforting vibrations of his purr.

For the first time since entering the house, I felt calm. "Am I glad to see you."

He licked the end of my nose, and I rubbed my face against his soft fur.

"Where did you come from, huh, Morris? You don't mind if I call you that, do you?" I moved my ankle tentatively. Although it was still sore, I managed to get to my feet again, albeit awkwardly while holding Morris. "Come on, you can help me find Sherry."

"Jen!"

At the sound of Sherry's voice, Morris hissed and squirmed out of my arms, landing on the floor with a thud. He disappeared into the darkness. I thought about going after him, but Sherry was my priority. I followed the sound of her voice to a door at the end of the hall. When I tried it, I found it locked.

"Sherry! You'll have to let me in!"

She called my name again but didn't open the door.

Maybe she can't hear me? Maybe she's hurt!

I looked at the doorknob. It was the kind with a slot that you can use a flathead screwdriver to unlock. A screwdriver—or a coin. I dug in my pocket and pulled out one of the quarters. It fit in the slot a little loosely but when I turned it, the door unlocked.

I pushed it open and found a bedroom, complete with a fully-made bed, woven rug, and sheer curtains blowing in the breeze despite the boards covering the window. They looked like ghostly arms, reaching toward Sherry, who sat on the bed.

"Sherry, thank God."

As I took a few limping steps toward her, she raised her head and smiled too wide, exposing sharpened teeth just like the grin I'd seen earlier on the centerfold.

I stopped dead in my tracks. Squeezing my eyes tight, I tried to force the vision to fade, but when I opened them, the wicked grin was still there. Sherry stood. Her mouth opened, and from my friend came a man's voice, deep and vicious.

"YOU'RE...MINE!"

I was running with no memory of having turned to do so. My only thought was to get away *now*. Somehow, I reached the staircase and half-ran, half jumped down it until I reached the last step, where I lost my footing. I managed to reach out in time to keep from slamming my face into the floor, but only just.

I rose, expecting to be back at the front entrance with the parlor to my left, but a different room was where the parlor should've been, and the front door was gone.

The slow stomp of heavy work boots descended the stairs, and I recalled the boot I'd felt while groping for matches in the dark. I entered the room that had replaced the parlor, closing the door behind me as quickly as I could. The stomping sped up, then stopped outside the room before heading back in the opposite direction and fading away.

Leaning against the door, I let out a breath and noticed the telltale wheeze of asthma. I hadn't had an attack in years. I didn't even carry an inhaler anymore. I had to calm down to get my breathing under control. If I did that, sometimes the asthma passed. The last thing I needed right now was a full-blown attack. *Music*, I thought. Music helped sometimes.

I put my headphones on and pressed play. The mixtape was at a point where the DJ was talking over the start of a song—normally an annoyance, but right now I welcomed the familiar voice. "'Manic Monday' climbs all the way to number two this week! The song's a hit for The Bangles, but you might be surprised to learn it was written by Prince!"

As he said the last few words, his voice warped as if the Walkman were eating the tape. I pressed stop before my tape was ruined, and moved closer to the window to see if I could fix it.

Then the DJ spoke again. "Je-en...Jennifer... Listen to me, you little bitch! You made the biggest mistake of your worthless little life coming into my house. Now you'll never leave." He started laughing, the pitch growing higher and higher.

Looking down at the Walkman, I saw the tape was still stopped. I yanked the headphones off, and the tape compartment popped open, then vomited tape all over the floor in front of me. I pulled the

Walkman off my waistband and hurled it at the wall where it bounced off, breaking the door off the tape compartment before hitting the floor.

With the headphones off, I could hear sounds around me again. The stomping footsteps were back and drawing closer. My wheezing had only intensified. The stomping stopped just outside the door. I waited for it to open, but it remained closed.

The footsteps started up again, slower now, and *inside* the room. They worked their way around me to the right, and to my horror I saw footprints appearing on the dusty floorboards. I wanted to run more than anything in the world, but my body wouldn't obey. My breathing came ragged and strained and began to speed up along with my heartrate.

Paralyzed, I watched the footprints move slow and steady to where the Walkman lay broken on the floor. They paused there, then turned back toward me, coming closer and closer until they were right in front of me, though I saw no one.

That's when I felt it.

Faint at first like a cool breeze, then an unmistakable, ice-cold weight on my left shoulder. The weight tightened into a painful grip, shaking me out of my frozen state.

This time I did turn, swatting at the empty air to get that invisible hand off me. I ran, forgetting the door was still closed and hit it with the full force of my own momentum. My last thought as I hit the ground was that this thing I couldn't see was still in the room—and then the darkness fell over me.

———

I came to with a pounding headache and no idea how much time had passed. In the sparse light streaming in, I no longer saw footprints in the dust. Raising a hand to my head, I felt a large goose egg but no blood.

I got up slowly, making sure I was steady on my feet before I moved any faster. As I stood, my foot kicked something that rolled across the floor, glinting in the light. An empty, glass bottle with a Jolt label.

I picked it up and saw what looked like Sherry's lipstick on it. But that was impossible. That bottle had smashed, and the label had been torn off and burned.

Looking around, I noticed the candles on the floor, though no longer lit. I was back in the parlor.

A noise pulled me from my thoughts. It sounded like a voice on the other side of the front door, but the words were too faint to make out. I went to the door and tried to pull it open once more, but it still wouldn't budge. I pressed my ear to it to try to hear the voice behind it.

"Hello?"

"Jen? Is that you?"

Andy's voice. I'd never been happier to hear it.

"Yes, it's me! Is that you, Andy? The door's stuck! We can't get out!"

"Stand back. I'm gonna try to kick it open."

I did as he said, then heard a loud pounding followed by a jiggling of the doorknob, then harder thumping as if he were throwing his whole body against the door repeatedly. The door budged a little, and I almost cried. *Just a little more.*

A scream pierced the air, coming from somewhere upstairs. *Sherry.*

"Andy, I hear Sherry! We got separated earlier."

"I think I've almost got this door open," came his faint voice. "Just another second. Wait."

I turned, looking up the darkened staircase, then back at the door. Just beyond it was salvation. I could hear the doorjamb creaking, about to give way. In a few seconds I'd be free of this nightmare.

Sherry screamed again, and I knew I couldn't leave without her, no matter what a jerk she could be sometimes.

"Keep trying the door, Andy. I'm going to get Sherry!"

I ran for the stairs as best I could on my still-sore ankle, following the sound of Sherry's screams. Finally, I reached the room the sound was coming from. As I gripped the doorknob, the image of Sherry with the monstrous grin came to mind.

"That wasn't her," I said, and turned the knob.

"I got it open!" came Andy's voice, louder this time.

I turned toward the sound of his voice, hesitating—wanting to run from my friend's screams, which made it sound like she was being skinned alive on the other side of that door. Freedom was only a quick jog down the stairs.

"Jen, come on!"

I couldn't do it. I opened the door, and just like that the screaming stopped.

Here, enough of the window boards had fallen off that I could see clearly.

There was no one in the room.

I saw a dresser with a lamp on it and a rusty metal bed frame. Above the dresser was a panel that might lead to a crawlspace, but the dust on the dresser itself was undisturbed, so no one had climbed on it to go up there.

There was no sign of Sherry.

"Jen! Hurry!"

This time, I ran back to Andy, taking the stairs two at a time. The front door was already starting to close again as I reached it. Through the narrowing gap, I saw only darkness where I should've seen streetlights and Andy. I hesitated, then reached for the door to stop it, my fingertips just missing the edge before it slammed shut.

I pounded on the door. "Andy!"

No answer.

Tears streamed down my face as I kept pounding and calling his name, but if he'd ever actually been there, he wasn't now. I leaned against the door and slid to the floor, letting the sobs come until I could hardly breathe. The voice from my headphones had been right. I was never leaving this place.

Suddenly, I felt that cold, iron grip again, tightening on my upper arms and pulling me off my feet. I tried to run but my shoes dangled at least five inches from the ground. Then I was flung across the room, slamming hard against the wall where the centerfold had hung—where the names of all those girls still were. I had a second to wonder how they'd managed to make it out of this place before I hit the ground hard.

Before I could even try to get up, I heard footsteps coming toward me at a quick pace. This time, I saw a shadowy form accompanying them. I screamed from a place deep within me.

The shadow came into the light. It was Sherry—and she was holding Morris. "Jen?"

I watched her for a moment, scanning her face for a sign that this was really my friend and not some nightmare version of her.

"It's really you this time, isn't it?" I cried.

"It's me. Is it really you?"

I nodded. She put the cat down and hugged me to her as we both wept.

"I heard you calling me before," she said, "but it wasn't you when I...when I saw—"

"I know," I said. "This house makes you see things."

"I found this cat," she said. "I figured if it got in, it might know how to get out."

"You're right," I agreed. "The cat had to get in somehow, but that doesn't mean it's a space we can fit through. But that reminds me— there was an open attic window when we got here. It's small, but I think we could squeeze through it and climb out onto that big tree outside, then climb down."

"How do we get up there?"

"I thought I saw a crawlspace access earlier when I was looking for you."

"You think you could find it again?" she asked, picking Morris up.

"Assuming the house hasn't changed again...yeah, I think so."

We walked upstairs, moving slowly and cautiously. When we

finally reached the room with the crawlspace access, I couldn't help thinking of Sherry's blood-curdling screams. I wondered if they'd been real or an illusion. I wasn't ready to ask her though and she wasn't volunteering anything she'd gone through while we were separated.

Sherry moved to the window, peering through the gaps between two boards and shaking her head. "Even if we could squeeze out this way, climbing down isn't an option."

I headed for the dresser, used my arm to sweep everything off the surface, then climbed on top.

I touched the access and pushed the cover out of the way, into the crawlspace. Dust rained down and a small spider slowly lowered itself to my eye level. I managed not to scream but couldn't keep from flinching, nearly falling off the dresser in the process.

"Ugh," said Sherry as the spider continued down to where she was able to kill it. "Are you sure there's no other way out of here?"

"I wish."

"Let me go first. I can handle a few spiders."

She handed me Morris, then climbed onto the dresser. I raised the cat up into the crawlspace and he sat there, watching us with a curious tilt of head.

"Boost me up," said Sherry.

I linked my fingers so she could step onto them. She reached up and lifted herself into the crawlspace.

"There's a *ton* of old shit up here."

Sherry turned and reached down to help me up. It took a few tries, but I managed to get high enough to lift myself the rest of the way and squirm into the cramped space.

Enough light came through the small window that I could see most of the space. It was indeed full of old boxes, not to mention a generous number of cobwebs that I wasn't looking forward to crawling through. But if getting out of this place meant crawling through a hundred spider's nests, it was worth it.

"I hear something moving around up here," Sherry said. "I hope it's not rats. I hate rats."

Morris headed for the window.

"Good," I said. "If he leads the way he might take out some of those cobwebs or handle any rodents before we get to them."

Sherry began crawling after Morris and I followed. I could hear her saying "gross" over and over again as she went, but to her credit she kept going. So did I, now and then pulling cobwebs free of my hair, hoping the spiders that had made them weren't in there too.

With Sherry in front, I couldn't see much light anymore so all I could do was keep going, trying to ignore the occasional crawling sensation over my hands. *House spiders are harmless. Cobwebs are just gross. They can't hurt me. Just keep moving, Jen, and this'll all be over soon.*

I'd almost talked myself into believing everything was fine when something big dropped onto my back and began walking on me.

"Oh, God! Sher, there's something big on me, like a rat! Go faster!"

She sped up, but in the cramped space she could only go so fast. I felt the thing on my back take a few more steps, and then it was touching my skin. It had crawled under my shirt.

I couldn't help it—I stopped and tried to reach for whatever was in there. I could feel its legs moving, moving...and then they weren't legs, they were fingers—thick, strong fingers with long, hard nails...digging, digging into my skin.

"Ow! Oh God, Sher! It's him! It's Mr. White!"

I screamed as a nail dug deep and dragged toward my waistband, then what could only be blood dripping down from the burning scratch, tracing a line to my stomach.

Sherry whimpered like a wounded dog and crawled even faster. I could hear her banging into things, but she kept going. I followed as fast as I could, trying to evade the hand—and then two hands— scratching at my back.

"Hurry, Sher!"

We finally reached the window, and here it was brighter. Morris had already slipped out and onto the tree outside. Sherry squeezed through after him. It was a tight fit, and she had to turn awkwardly to get onto the tree, but the branch held, and she soon moved along enough for me to get out, too. By now the unseen fingers were clawing at me all over. I tried to fight them off, but my own hands hit only air.

As I struggled, I caught a glimpse of the sky outside. It was nearly daylight. *We're almost safe.*

I pulled myself out the window, crawling on hands and knees and gripping the tree branch for dear life, even as the clawing hands tore at my skin and pulled on my jeans, trying to keep me inside this Hellish place.

I flipped onto my back as if to kick my attacker—if I could—and then I saw him.

A gaunt, pale face with deep red cuts all over it, like the kind you'd get if an angry father shoved your head through a window. His grin was even more chilling; the same vicious smile I'd seen so many times tonight—jagged teeth glinting in the light, not *like* glass, but *actual* glass shards, stained with blood. His wild, bloodshot eyes stayed locked on me as he snapped that mouthful of glass toward me and he let out a sound—half screech, half roar—that I felt in my bones. He reached for me once more, gripping the leg of my jeans.

That's when the streetlights finally went off.

With dawn in full swing, Mr. White hissed and vanished in a fog.

My leg now free, Sherry pulled me the rest of the way out the window. She sobbed and held me tight. I cried, too.

After a while, I looked down at my torn and bloodied shirt. I lifted it, exposing skin with reddened tracks.

Sherry pulled up my jacket and checked the worst of the scratches on my back. "These cuts look bad. You'll need to clean them soon."

We began our climb to the ground. By the time we reached it, Morris was nowhere in sight.

I couldn't blame him.

"Come on, let's go home."

———

On the walk back, neither of us spoke about what we'd just been through. I wasn't sure we ever would.

We made it to Sherry's house early enough that no one was awake yet. She let herself in and waved as she closed the door.

I didn't have far to walk from her house to mine. It was quiet this early in the day, and the streets were vacant. Even alone, I felt safe for the first time in hours.

Relief washed over me as I reached my house and made my way to the porch. I'd never been happier to see Mom's cheesy garden gnomes or the awful plant hanger she'd made in macrame class.

"Home sweet home."

I reached into the plant pot and grabbed the key to the door. Stepping into our living room, I couldn't help but smile at the familiar sight of our floral couches and brass coffee table. I turned and closed the door, but when I turned back, I was in a darkened room, with candles on the floor next to an old mattress.

To my right sat a cabinet with glass doors. The dust on one of them was smudged where Sherry had wiped it away. On the wall, a name—Mr. White—started to scrawl itself over a new column next to the list of girls' names.

I watched with growing dread as my own name appeared in the column below, then Sherry's.

"No." I turned to the door and pulled frantically, but it wouldn't budge. "No! No! We made it out! We're safe! This isn't real!"

Laughter behind me, then a whisper that began to rise in volume. I couldn't understand most of it except my own name repeated over and over. I turned, pressing my back against the door.

On the stairs before me sat Morris, licking his paw.

He looked up at me, and then his mouth turned into a grin of glass shards, stretching back toward his ears as he laughed that wicked laugh.

ABOUT P.A. CORNELL

P.A. Cornell is a Chilean-Canadian speculative fiction writer who grew up at a time when streetlights told you when to be home and supervision was lax enough that watching R-rated horror movies wasn't a problem. Now fortunate enough to call fiction-writing her full-time job, she's happy to channel some of the energy those old movies had into her work. She writes from her home in Ontario, Canada, with the help of her cats Jax and Rebel, who call her out on any plot holes or grammatical errors. They also insisted she include a cat in this story. A member of SFWA and graduate of the Odyssey Writing Workshop, her short fiction has appeared in several anthologies and genre magazines. A full bibliography and social media links can be found at her website: pacornell.com.

ACKNOWLEDGMENTS

We thank every Kickstarter backer who believed in this book and its writers.

Thank you for making this such an exciting adventure!

A. Arute
Admiral Wren
Andrew C Stackhouse
Angela KG
Ant S Cary
Aric Sundquist
Auralie Blanchette
Aya Smallwood
Boris Veytsman
Brandon Hanks
bsom
BuddyH
Carl Charles
Carmen Maria Marin
Cassi Rae
Cassidy Lucas
Chris DeFilipp
Cody Mower (TDM Shaman)
Craig Page
Dagmar Baumann
Dani

Dante Desmond

David Emmons

David Swisher

Davina Tijani

Dede Sanchez

E Stoppani

Elou Carroll

EMH

Eric Hendrickson

Esteban from Memories of Tomorrow

Evelina Liz

Farley McFluggelhymennachtwurst

Francis The Frog

Frank William Ticknor III and M. Elizabeth Ticknor

Geoff Oki

James Haynes

James Parenti

Jason R Frei

jaymi elford

Jayzar

Jenny Moser Jurling

Jeremy Mahr

Jesse Lawson

Jessica Enfante

Joel La Puma

John O'Hare

John R Holt

Josh Rountree

K. M. Sanders

Kai Alexei "Gabby" M.

Katherine S

Kathryn Dokken

Keats N

Kenny Endlich

Larina Warnock
Lisa Westenbarger
Logan M Porter
M Shedric Simpson
Marcus Young
Mark Harrison
Max Turner
Maxwell Nguyen
Mel McCoy
Merethe Walther
Michael G. O'Connell
Mike Galligan
Miriam Sexton
Mollie Baldus
MrFitz
Mur Lafferty
Nathaniel Clites
Nellie Cole
Nicholas Stephenson
Nigmachangeling
Noarvara
Odessa Johnsen-Dearing
Oliver S
Parker Ragland
Patrick Kelly
Phil J Thomas
Quarter Press
Quinn Flynn
R. Christopher Cornford and Thrilling Suspense Fantasy
R.J.K. Lee
Rachel Unger
Ray Da Silva
Ronan & Freya
Rosio E. Diaz

Sarah Avery

Sarah Fannon

Sarah Russell

Sarah W.

Scott Schiffmacher

Sean Gatcomb

Shae

Shane Hawk

Sky "Voodoo Mafia" Gonzalez

Solomon Forse

Steve Pattee

summervillain

Tamme Schichler

Tea Riffo

The Crawfords

thedrellum

Tim Jordan

Timothy Burkhardt

Tseb

Vulpecula

Wendover Garden Hot Sauce

Wilbert Bishop

William B. Aab

William Crowson

Wuppy

Yurii "Saodhar" Furtat

Z Hambleton

Zoe Kaplan

CONTENT WARNINGS

One of Those Nice Guys

gore, vomit, references to abuse/exploitation, references to child death, the inability to look at truckers (or truck stop diners) the same way ever again

Working the Graveyard Shift

blood, familial estrangement, violence, a feel-good wholesome ending

Just Elaine

attempted coercion, ableism, violence, dying, death, surgery, cannibalism, the sweet feeling of righteous indignation you experience when you see a fictional antagonist get *exactly* what they deserve

Derailed

gore, vomit, dying, death, heart-twisting bittersweet ending that might make you ugly cry

The Neon Knight

light childhood bullying, unnatural child disappearance, nostalgia-triggering arcade awesomeness

Latchkey

child death, deprivation of personal autonomy (metaphorical), a heartwarming ending that will leave you with a smile

Dots and Dashes

isolation, death, a feeling of empowerment that will occur every time you pick up a heavy flashlight

The Day Caroline Bloomed

domestic violence (psychological, physical, and verbal abuse), blood, vomit, self-injurious behavior, chronic illness, sexism, dying, death, a vindicating ending

Designs on Redemption

substance abuse, intoxication, pyromania, child death, stalking, deprivation of and disregard for personal autonomy, gore, fanaticism, and an ending that will make you wonder if *you* hallucinated the whole story

Welcome to Camp Klehani!

body shaming, sexism, light childhood bullying, eating disorders, verbal abuse, blood, gore, violence, dying, child death, a lingering discomfort when hiking through wooded areas

The Angler

domestic violence (psychological, physical, and verbal abuse), child death, and an adventurous ending

Jaws

surgery, intoxication, blood, gore, dying, death, and the kind of ending that feels more like the beginning of something apocalyptic

Brian

ableism, body shaming, extreme childhood bullying, disregard for personal autonomy, physical assault, vomit, dying, child death, and an ending that will make you wonder who the real monster is.

And the Universe Went On

chronic/fatal illness, familial estrangement, dying, death, and a tear-jerker ending that will make you call your parents

Every Day's a Party (With You)

psychological disorientation, blood, gore, dying, death, beautiful imagery, and a revelatory ending

When the Streetlights Go Off

sexual coercion, disregard for personal autonomy, entrapment, verbal abuse, physical assault, spiders, and an ending that might make even the most fanatical cat-lovers think twice about picking up a stray

www.ingramcontent.com/pod-product-compliance
Lightning Source LLC
Chambersburg PA
CBHW021646110726
47902CB00007B/1844